Tradur Gurl

The Sandy Allen trilogy series

P.T. Dawkins

Copyright © 2016 P.T. Dawkins

ISBN: 978-1-63490-893-1

All rights reserved. No part of this publication may be reproduced or transmitted in any form or by any means electronic, including photocopy, recording, or any information storage and retrieval system, without permission in writing from the copyright owner.

Published by BookLocker.com, Inc., Bradenton, Florida, U.S.A.

Printed on acid-free paper.

This is a work of fiction. All characters, incidents, dialogues and some settings are products of the author's imagination and are not to be construed as real. Any resemblance to actual events or persons, living or dead, is entirely coincidental.

BookLocker.com, Inc.
2016

First Edition

DEDICATION

*To my family, as always—
My core*

Also by P.T. Dawkins

The Sandy Allen trilogy series

The Analyst
The Ponzi
Tradur Gurl

ACKNOWLEDGEMENT

With each novel I write, my appreciation grows for the valuable assistance available to authors. *Tradur Gurl* just wouldn't be the book it is without several people's input and guidance. Barbara Kyle, a celebrated author and my former teacher provided critical direction in the early stages regarding my characters and the challenges they'd face. This has been my first opportunity—certainly not the last—to work with Editor Ann Birch. Her insight (and honesty) has added a new dimension to the novel's quality. Of course, I can't thank Anne, Julia, Peter, Christie and Doug enough for their own contributions, each unique in their perspective but consistent in their benefit. Kudos to John, as always, for his help on my website www.ptdawkins.ca.

As this is the last book of the Sandy Allen trilogy, many thanks to the *real* Sandy Allen for the use of your name and your *suggestions* about what my favorite protagonist might get up to next. The trilogy is is, of course, a work of fiction and none of what happens in the three novels could ever, in any way, relate to you… right?

Hmm…

Chapter 1

Police end search for fugitives
Suspects declared legally dead after unconfirmed double suicide

Prisoner No. 3856197, AKA Sandy Allen, laid the newspaper down without reading the story. She knew it by heart. The police, the press, the public… all conned. A double suicide… what garbage.

At five feet, eight inches tall, Sandy maintained a body that, before donning the orange jumpsuit, used to make men stop and stare. Her smooth blonde hair, cut shorter now, would lightly sway, caressing her broad shoulders. Today, even in prison, her eyes remained bright and her posture perfect.

Behind bars, she prompted no gazes other than from a suspicious guard or another inmate with ill intent.

She sat alone on the cold, hard concrete bench, chipped and stained by years of abuse. Her prison attire provided no warmth and her ass was almost numb. She shivered, but she didn't move.

She was fishing.

And Officer Hicks watched her lure.

It was afternoon exercise time in the yard at the Blaine Corrections Center for Women. High chain link fences and concrete walls, topped by spools of razor wire, lined the area. Nearby were the sounds of profanity, racial slurs and the thump and ping of a basketball hitting pavement. Cons sat at the tables playing dominoes, betting cigarettes. Gang members murmured as they completed drug deals. Psychopaths were medicated but still roamed free. It was best to leave them alone. Armed guards in towers high above watched every move.

There! Another nibble.

She looked away, but not as fast as she could have. It was important that she let their connected eyes linger for just the briefest of moments. She stretched, arching her back, jutting out her breasts to the extent the suit would allow. If Officer Hicks' interest was sexual, and it usually was, a little advertising would not hurt. She was careful though. Using intimate suggestion for influence was like trying to hug a shark. Male guards often sexually abused female prisoners in exchange for things like cigarettes and drugs. In response to public outcry, video cameras were everywhere and rules were re-enforced, but in reality, the guards were still in complete control.

She dropped her head, apparently studying the stains in the concrete beneath her feet, as if embarrassed at getting caught looking. No sudden movements. Either the guards or, more likely, the other inmates noticed everything that happened inside a prison.

The officer took the bait, right up the gullet.

He rose slowly, surveying the yard, pretending to search for some form of illicit activity. He meandered along the dusty dirt field, like a sailboat tacking left and right into the wind, but there was no mistaking his intended destination. He would soon stand right in front of her.

She watched him out of the corner of her eye. His shirt pulled at muscles gained from years of weight training. He shaved his head and had no facial hair that could become a liability in a skirmish. Only the towers had guns. The guards received substantial martial arts training because they carried no weapons. In a scuffle, and in the wrong hands, that spelled danger. She had seen one guard intervene to separate two female inmates who were supposedly at each other's throats. In the few seconds it took help to arrive, he had taken a terrible beating to his face. That guard never returned.

Officer Hicks' clothing gave her the idea. Pay was poor and guards had to buy their own uniforms. His frayed shirt cuffs and the thinning fabric between his thighs told her a story. Why hadn't he bought a new uniform? Was money an issue?

Money was always an issue.

Hicks stood over her, feet wide and arms folded. The top of his head glistened in the sun.

"Inmate… you got a problem?"

Pretending indifference, she looked away.

"I ain't got no problem."

On day one, she had adopted the common prison jargon of an under-educated street gang thug. To speak in proper sentences was to stick out like a sore thumb. She wanted to be invisible.

Hicks picked up the newspaper, the one announcing that the search for Michael Franklin and Angela Messina had ended, and laughed.

"Aw yeah, you just like the others—stupid. You think there's some way out of here. Like they was goin' to find those other two and set you free. Well, I guess you're screwed now, aincha? Boohoo."

Sandy looked at the newspaper in his hand.

"I was just readin' the paper. Why you botherin' me, Officer Hicks?"

The guard leaned forward. She did not move.

"I will *do* whatever I *want*, inmate. You've been acting funny—staring at me. I want to know why."

She raised her head, eyes wide in mock surprise, looking from side to side as if to seek help from fellow inmates in defending herself against the outlandish accusation.

"I don't know what you talkin' about. I ain't looking at nuthin'."

He smiled.

"Inmate, don't fuck with me. I've been doing this a long time. Cut out the crap. I asked you a question."

She targeted Hicks because she knew that guarding inmates was a younger man's game. The thrill he must have once felt coming to work, risking his life to do his part to protect society, had likely faded long ago. Unmistakeable crow's feet crept alongside his eyes.

She shrugged. He didn't move.

"If you're looking for drugs, I'm not that kind of guard. Go see your friends over there."

He gestured to the group of gang members on the other side of the yard.

"But watch yourself. They'll rearrange your gut with a shiv if you don't pay."

She looked into the guard's eyes but kept her mouth shut.

"No, huh? Well maybe you're feeling a bit lonely and looking for some lovin'. Can't help you there either. I'm a married man and ain't looking to see the video of you and me on the six o'clock news."

Now, she looked away.

"I'm not botherin' you. Jus' leave me alone."

While the investigation and trial of one of the largest Ponzi schemes in history played out, Sandy assumed she'd be found guilty and become an inmate in the Washington State prison system. So she did her homework. She learned that Hicks, the oldest guard in this facility, was a fifteen-year veteran. He often reminded the inmates that his experience enabled him to smell trouble before it got started. In this interaction with her, Sandy knew he would be certain that he had discovered something early, allowing him to trump Sandy's plan. In his mind, she was a rookie, and against his keen insight, she didn't stand a chance.

He leaned farther forward, his face now inches away from hers.

"Yeah, but those eyes of yours, they keep looking across the yard until they find mine. You got something going on, and I want to know what it is."

She had him now. She just needed to keep pretending to resist until the menacing guard, using his clever probing skills, finally discovered her secret.

"You thinking of doing a hit on me? Don't like the way I run things? Well, go for it. But I warn you. I will snap your neck and the last thing you'll see is me laughing in your face."

She looked at the concrete again, rearranging some pebbles with one of her feet.

"OK fine, inmate. Play it your way. I will watch you double-time now. You can't scratch your ass without me knowing. Sooner or later, you'll talk."

Tradur Gurl

Hicks turned and started slowly walking away. Inmate No. 3856197 played her trump card—speaking softly so the other inmates couldn't hear.

"Besides, you wouldn't understand."

Chapter 2

A repeated car horn shattered the neighborhood's peace. That was Ivan's intention. Everyone, his sister Betty, her man-without-a-pulse husband Charlie, hell, even the neighbors peeking out their windows needed to know that he had arrived.

When they checked to see the cause of the commotion, they would find him: six feet, one inch tall, a fit one hundred and ninety pounds, wavy black hair on the long side, with a neatly trimmed moustache and sideburns that reached a full inch below his earlobes. He called it his Hollywood look. Tonight, he leaned against a bright red BMW convertible, top down, parked on the street in front of the Grays' house. He wore white khaki pants, a pink Lacoste golf shirt and tanned leather boat shoes. His folded reflecting sunglasses hung on the V of his shirt.

Everyone would see that he oozed success.

He knew the Gray family's normal nightly agenda. Charlie watched *Wheel of Fortune* while Betty washed the dishes. If they had dinner any earlier, they could call it lunch.

But he wasn't complaining. It was a free meal.

He smiled as they appeared at the front door: Betty, grinning and wiping her hands on her apron; Charlie, dour face, his newspaper crumpled in one hand, always irritated by anything that disrupted his routine.

"Oh my stars," Betty said, as she ran down the steps to hug her brother, "is this *another* new car?"

Ivan headed towards the covered front porch of their white clapboard Yonkers home, built before World War II. Two spiral metal hand rails with chipped black paint bracketed narrow concrete steps up to the front door porch. There were still a few maple and oak trees lining the street, but over the years their numbers dwindled at the hands of developers, storms and vehicle exhaust. When their mother passed years ago, Betty inherited the modest house and all of its furniture while Ivan received his share in cash. A blue spruce, planted by Betty's grandmother and missing all of its lower branches, leaned slightly on the front yard.

Betty still owned the house. Ivan's cash inheritance was long gone.

Charlie waited on the porch, arms crossed, one hand still holding the newspaper.

"Yeah, maybe," Ivan smiled. "I haven't decided yet. It is kinda fun though, don't you think?"

He thrust his hand out towards Charlie.

"Hey there, Chuckles. How they hangin'?"

Charlie unfolded his arms, moved the newspaper into his left hand and shook hands, perhaps a bit too firmly, Ivan thought.

He chuckled, rescued his hand and slapped Charlie on the shoulder as he walked by him into the house.

"As always, a man of many words."

Betty rushed in after him, leaving Charlie on the porch.

"It's so good to see you, Ivan! Come sit in the den. Can I get you a drink? The hors d'oeuvres are just about ready."

Ivan made a point of sitting in Charlie's chair—a dark brown leather recliner cracked by years of use—just to annoy him. He knew Betty always sat on the frayed, off-white living room couch. Now Charlie had to sit next to her. An antique oval coffee table, with shaped, hand-carved legs and a glass top to protect the wood, was in front of the couch. It rested on a Persian carpet, which hid most of the faded and scratched hard wood floor.

As Ivan talked about the day's business news, he could see Charlie trying to follow the action on the game show out of the corner of his eye.

They took their usual places at the antique dining room table, now warped in the middle. The matching chairs always hurt the small of Ivan's back after a while but it didn't seem to bother them. The aged credenza that held the fancy dishes dominated one wall. A faded wedding picture of Betty and Charlie sat on top of it. Ivan noticed one of the chandelier lights flickering and wondered if the wiring was still safe.

He had asked his sister many times why they did not get a new dining room set but Betty would jump into her story mode and explain that he should know better. She had inherited everything from their mother. The table dated back to the late eighteen hundreds. It was so full of history, it could tell its own stories. She'd point to one burn mark and say, "Oh, I remember *that* one. It was Thanksgiving dinner and Grandmother was absolutely beside herself."

All that effort to preserve history, Ivan thought. Sometimes it was better to let things go.

As Betty ladled the steaming stew into serving bowls, she shifted the conversation from the stock market to Ivan's personal and social life. She was particularly interested in any new girlfriends.

He held up his hand. He needed to divert the discussion to avoid having to answer any awkward questions. The less discussed about him in particular, the better.

"Easy there, sis, it's not that interesting a story. With me day-trading from home—the hours of research and then the execution—I don't have the *time* for all those things. But I'm not complaining. There's an old saying. You have to make hay when the sun shines and the market is very *fertile* right now. I've never seen so many ways to make money. You know what I mean?"

He saw Betty and Charlie nodding their heads in unison, even though he knew they didn't begin to understand or realize he was lying.

"Besides, I want to hear from Charlie."

He turned to face him, a piece of potato poised on his spoon.

"So, big guy, how are things going with the, uh, what do you call it, *claims* business?"

Ivan's thoughts quickly drifted whenever Charlie told a story, but it was better that he had him doing the talking now.

"Well, Ivan, as I've told you before, the insurance claims business is different than yours. We don't have *fertile* periods like the stock market. It's just steady. Except for when there's some sort of disaster, but that's a different department from mine. When you average all of the people across long time periods, the rate of claims doesn't change too much. What we do is to make sure all filings are legitimate and done correctly—in case there is a dispute of some kind later on. That's important. Why, just the other day..."

"Charlie... man, I gotta tell ya. If your job was the last one on earth, I couldn't do it. What you just said sounds like watching paint dry on a rainy day. Just shoot me. Good for you that you found something that fits your style."

The room was silent for a moment. Ivan realized he'd just taken a bit of a shot but he had to entertain himself a little, right?

He was surprised that the usually mild-mannered Charlie didn't let it pass by.

"Ivan... *fits my style*? What does that mean?"

Ivan contorted his face a bit as if sucking a lemon. It was hard, when he was with Charlie, not to inadvertently reveal what he thought of him. But his sister's happiness was the important thing. He brushed one hand in the air as if shooing a mosquito away.

"Nothing, Charlie, nothing at all. I'm just, you know, we all eventually have to find work that suits us."

He could feel he was digging the hole deeper. Charlie put his fork down and wiped his mouth with his napkin.

"... *Find work that suits me*. Ivan, you know what? Every time you come over here for dinner, you ask me about my job and then proceed to tell me how boring it is. It isn't *boring* to me. Fact is, without people like me, doing what I do, you'd pay even more for insurance. I've never said boo about your line of work. Day-trading? I've read the stories. Not everyone thinks it's that honest a profession. It's just for people chasing the almighty dollar. You sit there and play on the stock market. It's a game to you... and then go buy yourself another new BMW. At least my job provides some benefit to society."

It was Ivan's turn to stop eating. His fork made a loud clink on his plate as he looked up. He didn't appreciate taking shots from Tweedledum, but then he realized Charlie had given him the opportunity he was waiting for. The grandfather clock was ticking in the background.

"Sorry, Charlie, what was that you just said? *Your* job benefits people but mine doesn't? I'm not *honest*? Did you say that?"

Betty interrupted as she got up to clear the dishes. Ivan had to stifle his smile.

"Well, it's pretty clear that both of you have interesting jobs and are very successful," she said. "Now, I have some lovely peach cobbler for dessert…"

Ivan leaned back and threw his napkin on the table, glaring at her husband.

"Not for me, Betty, thanks. I need to catch up on work. This has been one hell of a week. I'll show myself out."

Against Betty's protests, Ivan gave her a quick hug and headed for the door. He stopped, turned and pointed his finger at Charlie. He was going to rip him a new one and then paused. He remembered Betty was watching.

"Look… Charlie, I'm going to suggest that you don't know… very much about my job or the stock market. Until you do, you might want to save your sarcasm. Now you question my *honesty?* Where do you get off?"

He wanted to tell his bonehead brother-in-law to shove his criticism up his ass.

It was an earlier end to the evening than Ivan had planned, but that was just as well. He had to get the car back to the dealership.

He did not intend to buy it. He could not have afforded even one of the tires. He'd taken it for an "extended" test drive, and it had served its purpose. It had demonstrated his success beyond doubt. No one, especially Betty, could ever learn the truth about his past, his desperate escape to the east coast and that he was dead-ass broke.

Chapter 3

"*Besides, you wouldn't understand.*"

Officer Hicks stopped, turned and came back to Sandy's bench. Facing her, he spoke in a voice so that the nearby inmates couldn't hear.

"Is that right? I understand a lot of things. Like you been here nine months and," he pointed across the yard, "those walls are looking higher and higher every day. I'm thinking today's newspaper popped your last, flimsy bubble of hope, but I sure as hell don't know why. You did a crime, were convicted, and now you're doing time. The end. I know where your song goes now. Inmate Sandy Allen is an 'innocent girl' who's been hard done by. 'If only someone would just *listen* to her sorry-ass explanation.' Well, look here, princess..."

"I'm guilty, and I belong here."

Hicks, who had been speaking right to her face, stopped. He twisted his head slightly to one side.

"That's not something you hear around this joint very often."

Sandy spoke softly but quickly.

"Officer, I have a 'ting to say to you. Some serious shit, but we gotta talk somewhere else. My story takes a little time."

"Your *story*. I know all about your story. You *almost* went to jail in New York for insider trading but threw some crazy Russian CEO under the bus to buy your freedom. But oops, you were barred for life from ever trading stocks again. That musta stung, huh? Since you shit your bed on the east coast, you had to find a new place to play. You color your hair, change your name and move here. Jennifer Salem. Nice ring to it. But it didn't take you long to step in it again. *This* time you didn't get away with it and now you're my problem."

"Officer Hicks, there's more, much more that you don't know. But the other cons are already looking at us for jawin` as long as we have."

He glanced sideways, and saw she was right, then grabbed Sandy by the hair and pulled her up to a standing position, yelling now for all in the yard to hear.

"You will *not* speak to me like that, inmate. I've a mind to slap some respect into you. You get *out* of my face or you're headed to the doctor!"

The shock of the sudden yank on her hair shot pain through Sandy's body. She screamed.

"Ow! Fuck me, what the hell?!"

Officer Hicks, still holding her hair, leaned closer, their faces almost touching. Whispering, he hissed his final warning.

"Meet me in the back of the library in fifteen."

He threw Sandy's hair aside, causing another yelp. Glaring, she waited for him to move out of sight. She could hear whistles and cat calls from the basketball court.

Sandy hadn't spent much time in the library. When she first arrived at the prison, she walked up and down the stacks that resembled an old man with yellowed, missing teeth. The books that weren't stolen were in bad shape, often with missing pages, expletives penned in the margins or "you didn't want to know how that got there" stains. The most in-depth novels were written for readers at a high-school level. Prison rules prohibited those with interesting sex and/or violence scenes.

The daily newspaper was Sandy's only contact with the printed word. The guards usually made it available two to three days late, if at all. They justified their subtle abuse by saying the "inside" was the inmates' new world, and time stood still. What happened outside was no longer of any importance.

Sandy never wanted to lose touch with that world, because she knew she would return to it…someday.

She found a table on the far side, out of the librarian's line of sight, and sat with her back facing the wall. The guard arrived shortly after, turned a chair around and straddled it.

"All right, Allen, you've got fifteen minutes before you have to go back in your cell for head count. Spill."

Sandy inhaled deeply, and blew out her air like cigarette smoke.

"This... is going to take more than fifteen minutes but it will have to do for now. Like I said in the yard, I'm guilty… to an extent."

Sandy dropped the prison twang. She needed to sound intelligent to earn his trust. Ultimately she would lay out a sophisticated strategy, crafted by someone she hoped he would believe was a knowledgeable, talented individual. Officer Hicks must have confidence in in both the plan and her ability to carry it out.

"You say you know my story. Then you know there were two other people deeply involved in the Ponzi scheme who supposedly committed a double suicide. That's how they got away. They are alive and well."

The guard scratched the back of his neck and smiled.

"I don't know if dying is a good way to beat a rap."

Sandy folded her hands in front of her, as if in prayer.

"They're not dead, Officer Hicks. The two of them are lying on a beach somewhere, sipping drinks with little umbrellas in them. He, Michael Franklin, set me up. His whore of a girlfriend, Angela Messina killed her husband and collected his insurance money. I'm in here, and they aren't. Does that make any sense to you?"

The guard shook his head.

"Yeah, that's what I thought. Why didn't you just say this in the yard and save us both some time?"

He started to get up. Sandy grabbed his arm. His eyes were like a laser aimed at the felonious gesture.

"Inmate, remove your hand from my arm."

Sandy quickly put both hands in her lap.

"*Please*, Officer, hear me out. Just once."

Hicks stood over her, arms folded.

"You know how many times I get to hear this story? *Oh Officer, I've been framed. The true villains are running free.* Just can it, Allen. Even if what you're saying is true, and it isn't, you're the one that's in here. You were convicted for stealing, what was it, one hundred million? Now that's big time. I forget how many consecutive life terms you got. It doesn't matter. You're going to die in here. That's all there is to it. Better for you to just accept your fate and drive on."

He chuckled.

"You get busted only to find out your boyfriend both gave you up *and* cheated on you. Nasty stuff. You're right, the cops suspected the other girl had her husband killed. The two of them were like rats in a trap. There was only one choice. Not the first time we've seen that. So you got nothing to say to me. I already know everything."

"Officer Hicks, I'm telling you they aren't dead. I will prove it."

"There was a search for the bodies in the harbor, but the sharks ate 'em first. Just to make sure what you're suggesting *didn't* happen, there was a big man-hunt for the girl too. How is it, inmate, that all those policemen and all that time and money came up with zeroes? How could you *possibly* know something they don't?"

Sandy could feel moisture in her armpits.

"Look. It isn't important how I know. It shouldn't matter to you anyway. But the cops, once they got me, they didn't look so hard for anyone else. They made it sound like they did, but if they had—like I want to—they'd have found them. They'd already spent a lot of time and money, like you said. But they figured, 'hey, we already got someone in jail. The public is satisfied. We got lots of other open files. No point wasting any more resources on this one.'"

The guard looked at his watch.

"Hey, you know what, Allen? That's how it goes sometimes. You're gonna say 'that's not fair' and you're probably right. But guess what? Life's a bitch and then you die. I'm going to give you some friendly advice. The prison shrink would call what you're going through as 'denial'. Hard as it is, you just got to accept the fact that this is your life from now on."

He started to turn away. Sandy played her next card. There wasn't much time.

"Officer Hicks, can I ask you something... a little personal?"

He stopped.

"I already told you, little girl. I'm not looking for love."

"No, not that, I was just wondering. A woman notices these things. When was the last time you bought a new uniform?"

His face flushed.

"I'm pretty sure that's no goddamn business of yours! Now get back to your cell for head count."

Sandy looked him up and down.

"No, listen. I know how much you make. I did my homework. It isn't very much, given that you risk your life here every day, amongst a bunch of killers and psychopaths. Help me and I will help you. I have money, a lot of it, on the outside."

The sides of the guard's mouth dropped and his eyes narrowed.

"Today's your lucky day, girl. Attempting to bribe a federal corrections officer is a very serious offence. I'm going to pretend I didn't hear what you just said."

He started walking away, stopped and turned.

"Wait two minutes, so we aren't seen coming out together. Then get your ass back in your cell."

As he disappeared around the corner, Sandy pursed her lips. She had planted the seed. She had money and was ready to spend it. *Everyone* knew there were guards that were quite willing to supplement their incomes in creative ways. You just had to identify them.

She could only wait. It was his move.

Chapter 4

The taxi dropped Ivan off in front of a convenience store. While he wondered if the driver would find the route—from a BMW dealership to here—curious, he imagined that in this town, the man had probably seen much stranger things.

Ivan paid him and stood on the street. A bus must have just left; the exhaust fumes were still thick and his eyes watered. He looked through the wired front store window at the placards advertising milk and *cold* beer. The neon lottery ticket poster was the most prominent. Below it was a faded sign boasting, "This store sold a $10,000 winning ticket!" He could see a large woman inside, wearing a dark-brown paisley dress. She was watching a mini black-and-white TV behind the counter. Her thick black eyebrows matched her arm hair. She and her husband were his landlords. They spoke to each other in a language with sharp consonants that Ivan didn't understand. He paid his rent in cash at the beginning of every month, no questions, no receipts.

He went inside the store to check his ticket. Not a winner. Never a winner.

Back outside, with the street lamps as a guide, he found the lock in the door beside the caged window—his front door. The sounds of the city—cars, buses and sirens—serenaded him. With all three deadbolts secure, he walked up the narrow, dark, steep steps, sure that the hand rail, with just one good tug, would completely tear away. At the top of the twenty-nine steps, he turned right into his apartment directly above the store. There were two rooms, one towards the back for sleeping and one in the front for everything else. There was a hot plate on the counter, but the fuse had blown six months ago. A small, noisy mini-fridge sat on the floor. A ceiling light, one bulb burned out, highlighted the cracks in the plaster. Across the street was the unisex hair salon that specialized in brightly colored Mohawk haircuts and body piercing. It was full, as usual, with young people. They reminded him of a zombie movie; they only came out at night.

The only sink was in the bathroom separating the two rooms. The tub/shower was cracked and stained. Hot water was irregular—

like the tenants. The toilet didn't flush well and the plastic seat was loose.

The bedroom was quieter, being farther away from the street, but the windows to the back opened up to a flat roof. During the day, he jokingly thought of it as his patio. But night crawlers would sometimes climb the fire ladder. Although thick, brown curtains covered the windows, Ivan could hear drunken or drug-induced people trying to see what was inside. He kept a baseball bat by his night stand.

He sat on the end of his bed, listening to the sounds of the city. He wasn't even thirty. How could a man sit on top of the world one day, and sink to this? He thought about growing up in Los Angeles. He had dreamed, as nearly everyone in LA did, of becoming an actor, certain that his outgoing, aggressive behavior was just what movie producers were looking for. After scraping through UCLA as a drama major who was more interested in partying than attending classes, he had started a job as a waiter at Sammy's Oyster Bed, a popular bar frequented by successful stockbrokers. One night he peppered one of the regulars with questions about how to get into the business and how you could learn about the markets. The guy thought it was amusing that a waiter would ask such questions and gave him his card.

In the interview, it turned out that desire and salesmanship were all they really wanted and he had plenty of both. A regional firm in the Pacific Northwest called Milne, Ohara, Grady Investments—nicknamed MOGI—was opening a new branch in Seattle and, if Ivan was willing to move, they had a desk for him. They trained him on how to build his client list, but all he needed was a telephone and business cards. He quickly succeeded in the midst of a raging bull market where everyone seemed to make money. It was all good for a while, like a dream come true. Cash, cars and companions seemed to effortlessly flow his way.

His dream turned into a nightmare after the takeover by Fifty States Investments, a big, blue-blood Wall Street firm with ambitious growth objectives. During the process of integrating the two businesses, the local Seattle papers were bemoaning the inevitable back-office firings following such a merger. Ivan didn't care about that; he knew that revenue-producers were always safe in any corporate combination. He didn't realize, however, that he also now worked for a company with a far more disciplined compliance department. Without anyone's knowledge, they carefully reviewed the trading records of every newly acquired MOGI broker.

Ivan's list of violations, any one of which was cause for termination, grew like crabgrass and they soon fired him.

But something far more sinister drove him out of town.

When he showed up at Betty and Charlie's house the first time, unannounced, he said he had moved east because all it did was rain in Seattle, and he missed his family. In confidence—while Charlie was at work—he told Betty the big lie. He laid out to his sister the heart-rending story of Ivan against the big evil Wall Street machine called Fifty States Investments. He said he hated the new regime and decided he would branch out on his own to start a private money-management firm. The company got wind of his plans. All his former accounts—and their money—were somehow frozen. It was nothing short of *theft*, he said. To make sure none of the clients or their money would go to his new firm, they created rumours—that they couldn't prove—but which completely tarnished his reputation. He had no choice but to resign. Betty bought the whole nine yards and was horrified. What terrible people.

She lent him seventy-five thousand dollars, what was left of her inheritance from their mother's estate.

Her retirement savings.

Ivan encouraged her, given Charlie's attitude, never to tell him. She agreed that was probably for the best.

He looked around his room and noticed a new spider web. He used to have three platinum cards. The cost of clothing was not an issue because in order to *achieve* success, you had to *look* successful. Now the cards were gone and he was down to one suit. Faded, like his spirit, it too was about to give out.

He turned off his light and lay on his bed, clothes on. Tomorrow was Saturday. He would complete some research and try to find a winning stock to trade on Monday.

He desperately needed a winning trade.

Chapter 5

This time Hicks refused to return Sandy's stare.

She'd heard if you stare at a person long enough, eventually he'd look back, but that was shit. She'd been sitting on her concrete spot all week, following the guard's every move. She was sure her shot about clothes had hit the bull's eye. The man *was* hurting for money. Judging by the rush of blood to his face, she'd embarrassed him.

She heard his bit about regulations but everyone had a price.

Still, he refused to acknowledge her. Was he too honest or just afraid? She thought about the cartoon of the person, faced with a difficult choice, the devil on one shoulder, an angel on the other. Most people, at times like this, took the easy way out. They did nothing.

Doing nothing did not fit in with her plan.

She thought about how men behave and how a woman would react differently to her proposal.

Then it hit her. She knew how to attract a man. Every woman did.

Make him *jealous*.

She had made it too easy for him. Suppose she moved out of his immediate sight. Where might she be? Would Officer Hicks think she might bribe another guard? Would he miss his financial opportunity?

It was worth a try. Her present telepathic efforts didn't seem to work anyway.

She stood up and made an exaggerated stretch, arms spread as wide out as they would go. Although Hicks would provide no clues of noticing, Sandy knew that he would. That was, after all, what they paid the guards to do—watch the prisoners.

She found her spot in the library, sat down and waited. She grabbed a book from the stack, called <u>Prison and the Law</u>, opened it and laid it on the table in front of her, in case anyone came by.

Her thoughts drifted. The law. What was it about the law to her that was like a red flag to a bull? She didn't think it was the money.

She could have easily earned a living the honest way. It wasn't a lack of respect for authority either. She didn't think so anyway. She'd read somewhere that your parents greatly influenced the core of the person you were today.

When she thought about her parents, the same sensation would always come back. Drowning. That was her nightmare. The bad dreams stopped, mostly, once she left home. She remembered that feeling, the sensation of not being able to breathe. There was no way for her to escape the fighting, but listening to it, living with it, would kill her. She was sure that, one morning, she just wouldn't wake up.

It was that haunting feeling of helplessness. She broke the law because it was her reaffirmation to others, and more importantly to herself, that she *could*—whenever she wanted, whatever the transgression, the bigger the crime, the greater the sense of security. Until the day she died, she would crave that feeling of empowerment.

They said bad times made you strong. They made her invincible.

But then how the hell had she ended up in *prison*?

The trick that Michael Franklin and Angela Messina pulled on her was a constant ache in her gut. That's what really pissed her off. She'd been outsmarted. For someone to outwit her was stark evidence that she was *not* in control. The desire to take that very thing back would not go away, ever. And this particular game was far from over.

She didn't hear Officer Hicks enter her area. Like before, the man with the shaved head straddled a chair and leaned forward towards her. He kept his voice low.

"Inmate, I noticed you left the yard. I wanted to check to make sure you were OK, that you weren't... ah... contemplating a misguided course of action."

To Sandy, he might as well have held up a huge sign. He was worried that someone else would get his meal ticket. He wanted to make sure that Sandy avoided the "mistake" of entering into a lucrative financial arrangement with another guard before he'd had a chance to consider it. The seeds of greed, indeed, had taken root.

"Thanks, Officer. I've been hoping to tell you what I have in mind. I don't think it will waste your time or mine. You didn't let me explain it before. Can I now... please?"

This time Hicks nodded his head.

"OK. To start, last time we spoke you referred to my plan as some sort of 'bribe'. It's nothing of the sort. What I have in mind is a business transaction. It is legal and will hurt no one, inside or outside of this prison, except for two people that are supposedly dead. I think you'd agree that my capabilities are quite restricted in my present circumstances. However, my desire to employ people to carry out my wishes is not. I am entirely within my rights as a citizen to hire a private investigator to gather facts to support my claim that I have been wronged."

"You twist words well. You should've been a lawyer. But whatever. We got phones in here. Go ahead, use one and hire your P.I. You don't need me for that."

"Officer Hicks, you know someone listens to every word we say on those phones. The other inmates listen, too. Imagine what would happen if they heard me saying 'I've got money,' which I'm not supposed to have, that I'm going to use to get myself out of here."

He smiled.

"Yeah, you'd be a popular girl all of a sudden."

She spoke deliberately now.

"That's where you come in, Officer Hicks. I need access to a cell phone. I won't use it to talk. It's too easy for others to hear. I just need to send emails and get on the Internet to transfer money."

The guard now sat straight up and shook his head.

"Come on, Allen, you know it's against the rules for prisoners to own a cell phone."

"Yes, of course it is. I don't want to *own* one. I want to use yours: the one that I am going to buy for you and pay the monthly costs. I just want to use it for one hour, probably daily at the start, but less often later on. After my hour, I will return it to you. At the end of my transactions, the phone belongs to you."

Hicks just stared at her.

"Maybe I didn't say it right. It is against prison policy for inmates to use *any* communications devices other than the bank of handset phones we offer. If I became involved in what you're suggesting, they'd fire me on the spot and end my career as a corrections officer. I might end up in a cell just like yours."

Sandy wanted to say something like, "Go look in the mirror. How's that *career* working out for you?" But she refrained.

"I didn't say my idea wouldn't 'test the edges' a bit. I recognize what I am asking is somewhat out of the ordinary. In any business transaction, where there is risk involved, the *price* increases. So I am prepared to pay you a monthly retainer fee for procuring and looking after the phone."

The guard should have immediately stood and walked away. Sandy was thrilled that he didn't.

"I believe your annual salary is around forty thousand. That probably works out to about twenty-five hundred per month, after taxes. In today's world, that's not a lot of money. In return for your services, I will deposit an additional twenty-five hundred every month into your bank account. My math says that would double your pay. And by the way, Officer, when I am successful at finding the fugitives, your career could sky-rocket as being the person who understood and supported my plan."

Double his salary. She watched him consider this.

"How could you possibly have that kind of money? The Feds would have cleaned you out before they put you in here."

"They're called Bitcoins. Look it up. They're real and I have some—a lot of them. Even the Feds can't find them."

Hicks stared at her, processing the information, then quickly rose and left the area.

He didn't say no.

Chapter 6

Charlie smiled and waved as the front door closed.

"See you later, Ivan. Come back real soon. Now, Betty, what's that I heard about peach cobbler?"

Charlie's night wasn't ruined after all. He got his chair back and he could probably catch the rest of the Yankees game. As he sat back down, he noticed Betty still standing in the kitchen, arms folded.

"What? Why are you looking at me? What did I do?"

"You... sometimes you are such a... Ivan is my brother. We invited him over for dinner and you were so... rude! You made him feel like he wasn't welcome at all. I am completely ashamed and embarrassed... for you!"

Charlie watched and listened. They'd had this conversation before.

"Embarrassed for me? Your brother has, once again, ruined my night. You and he are so *close*. How about looking at things from *my* side for once? He thinks I'm a joke. He criticizes my job and me for having it. Well, last I checked it pays the bills around here. And *we* didn't invite him, *you* did. If you ask me, the guy's just a free-loader looking for a meal."

Her eyes narrowed.

"My God. You're jealous of Ivan and you just want to tear him down."

"Betty, he personally insulted me. He does it every time he comes over. It doesn't seem to bother you any, but it does me—a lot! And you know what? I'm not going to take that from him anymore. I'm surprised you didn't say something yourself—in my defense."

She lifted her head up, her expression now a deep frown.

"Are you serious? Your rudeness is my fault? That's your problem, Charlie. It has been all along. You blame others when you should just go look in the mirror. Here's my brother, a very successful businessman, happy as a clam, and that bothers you. Then he comes over for a purely social event and you spoil it. He ribs you a bit about your job. So? He's just teasing. People joke around all the time but not you. You get all huffy and there we are—another dinner ruined. I don't think I'm going to invite him over again—not that he would come anyway—until you change your attitude."

Charlie remained silent. Where was she going with this?

"Frankly, you *should* call him right now and apologize. Offer to go buy him a coffee tomorrow and settle this. A cloud is hanging over this room. You brought it on. Now it's your job to make it go away."

Charlie just continued to stare. He knew it was making her uncomfortable.

"And that's all I have to say on the subject."

In the past, Charlie might have gotten up, run his fingers through his hair and said something conciliatory. Not tonight.

"Until *I* change *my* attitude?"

Charlie stood up and moved towards her.

"That's right. Nothing is going to improve until then."

She wasn't backing down, not a bit. He could feel it. He was going to start yelling. It didn't happen very often, but when it did, he always regretted it afterwards.

Instead, he turned and walked towards the basement door.

"No, oh Charlie, don't go down there again. Stay up here and we'll talk this through. Maybe you're right. Maybe I should have a chat with Ivan."

But Charlie was halfway through the door and was closing it behind him. He didn't hear the rest of Betty's sentence.

The pounding in his head came from the fact that Ivan was bang on. He was incredibly bored with his job and he'd done nothing about it—for far too long.

He sighed. If Betty, and even Ivan for that matter, only knew the truth.

Chapter 7

Sandy was back, seated in her usual spot, watching the guard—and waiting.

Since the bars to her cell first closed on her she'd been waiting… waiting for end of the so-called investigation. She knew a P.I. wouldn't get involved until the cops were done.

Now they were.

Michael Franklin and Angela Messina were *not* dead. She had to admit, it was a fantastic deception. But it was infuriating that *she* was the mark.

It didn't matter. She would find them, earn her freedom and exact her revenge. With the police now out of the way, her chances improved greatly, but there was no time to waste. An already cold trail was getting colder.

She was still waiting.

A less-experienced person would have missed the signal entirely. For Sandy, the subtle jerk of the guard's head in the direction of the library might well have been a cannon going off.

Behind the stacks, Officer Hicks started the conversation this time.

"Look, Allen. I still have a problem with your plan. No matter how you sugar-coat it with words, you're asking me to violate prison rules in exchange for money. Where I come from, that's a bribe. I should report you just for making the offer to me."

All of Sandy's ploys played out like journeys that came to a crossroad. A choice was required, from which there was no return. But she was a master planner, the Bobby Fisher of cons. She'd already identified her potential vulnerabilities, like if Officer Hicks got cold feet or had a sudden bout of ethics. It was as if her own thought process "matured" as her schemes progressed. A few days ago she'd considered him critical to the success of the arrangement. Now, she realized that replacing him might actually save time.

"You know, Hicks, I see your point. I don't want to make you uncomfortable. Besides, you must trust me. It could take a year or more to find my outlaws. I'm going to have to use every trick in my book. I could use that phone every day, and I most certainly won't report back to you about my communications."

She wondered if the guard had noticed that she'd failed to address him by the proper title. He did not seem to. Was it a sign?

"Why don't we stop talking as if I *could* go ahead with my plan? The fact is that I *am,* with your help or not. There are other guards in here that might have less of a problem with violating policy than you. You said it yourself to me before. If I wanted drugs, go talk to the gang, right out in the open in the yard. How do you suppose the drugs they sell get in here? At least what I'm doing is for a good cause. If I'm right, two felons including a murderer end up behind bars where they belong. If I'm wrong, I just blew my last penny. No harm. No foul."

Sandy started to rise, signaling an end to the conversation.

"Somebody's going to get their salary doubled. I thought, why not you?"

Hicks didn't blink. He grabbed her wrist.

"Sit down, Allen. You're playing a risky game of poker here, but I'm holding the aces. The difference between you and me is, while the extra money would help a lot, I'm used to living with what I got. My uniform may look shabby, but I'm OK with that. You, on the other hand, are not used to the idea of spending the rest of your days in here with society's garbage. You think you got a way to get yourself out? Well, you're a crazy fool. But if you want to piss away this money you supposedly hid somewhere, then you go ahead and piss all over me."

He adjusted his tie.

"Five thousand per month or forget it. Final offer."

Sandy's mouth dropped and she started to protest as the officer, looking left and right, put up his hand as if stopping traffic. She had scheduled the finances carefully, along with everything else, and that much going to the officer wasn't in her plan. With one problem solved, a new, more threatening one reared its head. She closed her eyes. The greedy pig!

"I guess it's true that everyone has their price."

Hicks nodded, then turned and walked away.

The phone arrived in a week. It had everything she needed including an oversized glass screen, a keyboard and, most importantly, internet and e-mail access.

Chapter 8

Sandy prayed he was still working the New York City market.

Why would he ever leave? With the sheer number of marital affairs and deadbeat parents reneging on alimony, it was fertile ground for his line of work for many years to come.

Mr. Silas Marker, private investigator. Retired head of NYPD drug squad. Served and protected the public for thirty years. Now, instead of three a.m. takedowns wearing bullet-proof vests and carrying serious heat, he often rested at his desk with a coffee—she knew the man liked coffee at his desk—and searched the Internet. People didn't realize the amount of their personal information that was available, if you knew how and where to look.

When she lived in New York City—before the Feds made her leave town—she met him in a bar one night. Just a random thing. His badge was gone by then. They started talking. She was a single white female, but he didn't immediately move in for the kill, which pleased her. He said he never married because he couldn't live with the thought of the cartels going after his family too. He said, in his line of law enforcement, you were married to the badge and your working partner was *always* your best friend. Someone you trusted with your life. That was as close to a wife as he ever got.

It sounded reasonable enough. She figured him for a guy that never learned to sacrifice for a deep relationship, so his were a bit superficial. That was fine. For her own reasons, she wasn't so different. They'd had a couple of close encounters over the years, when it suited her mood. He never asked her too many questions, nor she him. The perfect relationship. After a couple of drinks he used to brag about how stupid people were. It seemed the harder they were trying to hide, the easier it was to find them.

She was relieved to see he still had his website, with his smiling face saying he would personally return all messages within twenty-four hours.

Her fingers sped across the phone's keypad.

OK then, Silas, how about one for old time's sake?

"How long is this going to take? You hired your P.I. yet?"

She had double checked that her strategic place in the library was as close to a protected corner as she could, and out of the librarian's and security camera's line of sight. She didn't want any surprises or to let someone see the phone. Yet, because of her intense focus when writing her message to Silas, the guard surprised her. She'd have to remember that. Type a bit then look.

Hicks waited for a reply and she rolled her eyes. She probably expected too much for him to just leave her alone. Why should he trust her? She was a con with an illegal phone, thanks to him. Imagine all the trouble she could create. He could go from hero to zero in a heartbeat.

He agreed she could have it one hour a day, for now, but he was cutting into her time. Every second was precious. She spoke with narrowed eyes and a clenched jaw, as loudly as she could without anyone hearing.

"I *told* you this was going to take time—and that you were *not* to watch me."

"Yeah, well, don't tell *me* shit. It doesn't take that long to hire a guy. You look him up, tell your story and as soon as he believes you will pay him you're done. I will not approve of any other activity using that thing."

Sandy rubbed her forehead.

"This isn't that easy. To begin with, I have to convince the *guy* why he should reopen a case when the cops have given up. Good P.I.s won't take a dead end, even for the money. So, if you must know, I'm gathering some evidence to convince him about my theory."

"*Theory*? You said you *knew* they were still alive."

"Officer, you've stolen five minutes of my time. Why don't you just go away and let me work?"

He didn't move.

"There's your first lie. I'm not surprised. I'm sure you will tell more. But there's another problem. You have your phone, how nice for you. I go look at my bank balance and what do I *not* see? I don't see any deposits. All I do see is that I'm out the six hundred bucks it cost to buy that gadget. Do we have a problem here—with your bat coins?"

Sandy tried to hide the pained look on her face. She was hoping to delay making any payments to the guard until she found out what Silas would charge. Money was already tight.

"They're called Bitcoins and no, there is no problem. I was going to make my first transfer in thirty days, you know, like a normal business deal."

The guard grabbed the phone away from her.

"This ain't normal business. This is monkey business. Here's how it's going to go. Your time is up today. After I give you the phone tomorrow, you transfer the cost of it, plus not one but two month's payments. As soon as I see the money in my account, you get to use *my* phone again. Are we clear?"

Sandy just glared.

"And if you don't, if this is all one big scam like I always thought, that's OK too. It's like what you said; *somebody* is going to use this shiny new phone. *I just thought why not you?*"

After hiding the phone inside his pants, the guard appeared to snicker as he walked away. He seemed quite pleased with himself that he had used her words against her.

Chapter 9

Charlie left his house for the bus that morning with a flushed face. His normally pleasant wife would only grunt in reply to his comments.

He didn't like that—at all. He walked quickly to the bus station, down the city street lined with parked cars and the few remaining trees. He didn't acknowledge his neighbor taking out her garbage can. On the bus, he jostled past a few people to reach the back and wondered why they always seemed to need to crowd the front. He found an empty seat, metal frame covered by a blue vinyl cushion, next to the window. If someone sat next to him, he could ignore them, in total concentration, staring out at the world passing by. His stomach growled and he realized he'd forgotten to eat.

His mind raced, but he reminded himself to slow down and sort things out. Identify the true source of his angst. He went through his mental checklist. He wasn't upset at Betty for being mad at him, but it bothered him that such a usually pleasant person was so disturbed. It wasn't Ivan's repeated condescending shots at dinner about his work and, by extension, him as a person either. While Ivan was rude, cocky and irritating, if Charlie was honest with himself, his brother-in-law had a point. Why else would his own wife take his side, even going so far as to accuse Charlie of tearing Ivan down because he was jealous?

Those confrontations were disturbing, but Charlie knew they were symptoms, not a cause. He also realized whatever it was that was eating him had been for a long time.

When the bus pulled into the depot, all passengers had to depart. During his meditations on the ride, and, as he walked towards the office, Charlie Gray came to the full realization of what was bothering him.

It was his conscience.

Charlie had lived in his office cubicle for sixteen years. There were forty of them on this floor, identical, in four rows of ten. New employees sat in sections the farthest away from the windows;

Charlie's was on the row closest. A fabric the color of vomit covered the outside of each pod. Each desktop was white vinyl. There was a bulletin board-like partition between pods to post important information. Although the dividers were supposed to provide some privacy, if Charlie strained his neck upwards, he could see the tops of heads down the entire row. On the front of each pod, attached by Velcro to make changing easy and cost efficient, was a rectangular white plastic name tag bearing each employee's first initial and last name. Charlie's read "C. Gray."

See Gray. For the first few years, the play on words made him smile. Not any longer.

It was a quarter after eleven and, as usual, Charlie just finished his first batch of claims. In a *normal* office, he'd have the authority to head downstairs for a coffee because the next batch almost never came until after lunch. But if Mr. A saw that you were missing, you'd face a thorough period of questions, after which he'd find a way to pile on more work.

Charlie called up his chess program. He was in the middle of a good game against the computer and he was winning. But he had to keep an eye out for the boss.

They all called him Mr. A, short for Abernathy. Secretly though, in the lunchroom and outside, they said the "A" stood for asshole. His approach to leadership included walking amongst the cubicles doing *bed check*, making sure that people were working. He monitored what was on their computers and listened to their phone conversations. He would yell at people for their mistakes—in front of others—and rarely, if ever, pass on even a token compliment. But no one ever called him out or complained. So he didn't stop.

Charlie knew Mr. A's abusive behavior paled in comparison to a bigger, much more serious problem.

He heard the familiar footsteps and was just able to minimize his screen. He smiled as the boss went by. Unacknowledged.

He decided to go back and check his morning's work, even though he knew it was perfect. He looked at one form. A man, thirty-two years of age, had tried to claim his dropped and broken cell phone as part of his insurance. Obviously Charlie denied the request for coverage. He wondered how people thought such filings were appropriate.

When he first started, they told him it was his responsibility to do his part to preserve the integrity of the insurance claims business. That sounded good to him, because if there was one thing he valued highly, it was honesty. Charlie's was a tireless, never-ending task because questionable claims happened all the time. Ripping off insurance companies was like a sport to some but, no matter how they might justify it, it was stealing. Every time Ivan teased him about his job, Charlie had always drawn comfort from the fact that at least he was doing his part to keep the system clean.

In one quick heated conversation, his comfort disappeared. The clash with Ivan at the dinner table, where Charlie questioned the integrity of his brother-in-law's profession, brought something to the surface that he'd been denying—fooling himself—for a long time.

He wasn't *doing his part to keep the system clean*. He was a complete hypocrite.

Without warning, Mr. A entered his cubicle, frowning with his arms folded. He spoke in a hushed tone so that only Charlie could hear. Normally he barked orders from his office door.

Charlie knew what was coming.

"Please join me in my office, Mr. Gray."

No one knew much about Mr. A. They thought he was from somewhere out west, Omaha maybe. His computer dominated his brown fake mahogany desk, facing towards him and away from his staff. It was not unlike him to start typing and peering at his screen while an employee was in mid-sentence. He'd say, without looking at them, "Keep talking. I'm just looking something up." Charlie wondered if the others found the practice as unsettling as he did. Behind Mr. A's chair was a credenza with a picture of a smiling wife and two kids—boy and girl—but no one had ever met them or knew their names. Mr. A didn't attend the Christmas parties. He told all employees to address him as "Mister Abernathy." Charlie wondered, in today's world, why the formality?

Mr. A was waiting behind his desk, pointing to a small swivel chair.

"Sit."

As Charlie did, they both noticed the door wasn't fully closed.

"How about we close the door, too?"

Charlie rose, closed the door and then sat down again. His face burned.

The boss now adjusted his black reading glasses, looked up at his employee and pulled out a manila folder from his desk drawer.

"I'd like to go over your work from last week. There were a few claims you denied that, frankly, have me scratching my head."

Mr. A opened the file.

"Alright then, let's see what we have here. You denied this claim made by a dentist on behalf of his patient for an emergency root canal."

Working in the department required training in deceit detection, to look out for claims where the patient was not directly involved. Services that were never rendered were sometimes added to inflate a bill for a standard procedure. The patient thus became part of the fraud without even knowing it.

"And here's another one you turned down where a G.P. ordered a series of blood tests for a patient complaining of headaches. Could you explain, please?"

Charlie sighed. This type of discussion happened all too often. Mr. A questioned and then overturned one or two claims at a time. Charlie figured he kept the frequency down to avoid detection. But if the claims were, in fact, fraudulent, Mr. A would have to know. Over time, Charlie concluded he was likely receiving compensation of some kind for turning a blind eye. An example, Charlie wondered, was why he had never seen a dental claim from Mr. A go across his desk. The family picture in his office showed both children wore braces.

"I didn't *deny* either claim, Mr. Abernathy. I simply suggested that these two were suspicious and might warrant further review. That is, after all, what you pay me to do."

Mr. A's eyes widened and he frowned. He removed his glasses and twisted them in one hand.

"Suspicious... why?"

Charlie imagined that any other boss would quickly agree and send both claims to Investigations.

"Well, sir, to begin with…"

Shattered by the telephone ring. Mr. A held up his hand towards Charlie's face.

"Abernathy here... Hello, dear... Yes….No… Now Henrietta, I don't have time for that sort of thing and I'm not interested in the arts anyway. You go off with your girlfriends if you like. Well, you should've checked with me before you promised that, so that really isn't my problem, is it? Now look, dear, I'm in a very important meeting so we'll have to discuss this later. I don't care about my ticket. Now look, I never agreed to that! I have to go."

He banged down the phone and, shaking his head, turned his attention back to the file on his desk. He picked up his pen.

"Now, where were we?"

The back of Charlie's neck burned.

"Mr. Abernathy, these two claims, how can someone require an *emergency* root canal? Proper dental procedures provide ample warning about when these are required and a quick check of the records would verify that happened. Ordering blood tests for a headache? Why in the world would a doctor choose that? I can see an MRI maybe or…"

Mr. A flipped the pen on the desk, quickly followed by his glasses. His eyes were closed and he was pinch-massaging the bridge of his nose.

"This is what eventually happens. One of my responsibilities is to prevent wild goose chases caused by an overzealous employee who has likely read too many crime novels. You and others like you will, if left unchecked, flood the system with unnecessary work and waste expensive human capital resources. Charlie, no one is interested in your opinions about why doctors and dentists, who spent many more years at school than you to earn their professional designations, recommend certain procedures for their patients. You work for an insurance company. Your armchair quarterbacking has to stop. I'm going to reverse your recommendation and approve both claims."

Then came the worst part.

Mr. A turned the two forms around, held his pen out towards Charlie and pointed where he was to sign, approving the reversal of his original recommendation.

Today, for the first time, Charlie didn't move.

Mr. Abernathy leaned back.

"Charlie, is there a problem? You recommended that we review these two claims. We just did."

It had happened so many times, the charade Mr. A forced on him, pretending that the truth wasn't staring them both in the face. Did he only do it to Charlie? Had other employees faced the same moral dilemma and, like Charlie, done nothing about it?

"That's not what I meant, and you know it, Mr. Abernathy. Why are you always overturning my decisions? Do you do that to the others in here?"

Mr. A chuckled.

"Charlie, I don't overturn *all* of your decisions—just the bad ones."

"But if I repeatedly make mistakes, after sixteen years at this, I must be a pretty bad employee. Why haven't you fired me—a long time ago?"

Charlie had dreamt of that scenario many times. Termination meant escape from a terrible situation… and severance money to move on to something better.

"Fire you? I'm sure you'd like that, but it isn't going to happen. You're a perfectly useful employee. Besides, as I'm sure you've figured, if I fired you I'd have to pay you a severance. There'd be far too many questions, which might not be in either one of our best interests."

It was at this point, normally, that Charlie would sign, get up quietly and leave the office.

"Yeah, maybe."

Mr. A leaned forward over the desk. His eyes had narrowed to slits.

"I'm not sure I like the tone of your voice, Charlie. Where exactly is this conversation going?"

He'd come this far. He couldn't turn back. After all these years, he knew it was a choice he now had to make.

"Mr. Abernathy, I'm thinking of sending copies of my past 'recommended review' claims that you overturned directly to the Investigations group, just to make sure that everything is above board. I've copied all my original reports, every single one."

Mr. A leaned back smiling, holding his hands together as if in prayer and touching his lips.

"Oh, I see what's happening. Charlie Gray has decided he's going to play the role of whistle-blower. He'll show that darn boss, go right over his head, right to the president's office if he has to. Very interesting. I didn't think you had something like that in you. Regardless, before you slit your own throat, let me remind you that you personally *signed* all the forms where we *discussed* reversing your suggestion, meaning you were in full agreement. I didn't reverse them, *we* did. If, by some completely unlikely chance, the review group did find something amiss, where would that put you? Let me help you. People that commit, aide or abet insurance fraud go to prison."

Charlie had thought about this many times.

"I could just say you coerced me to sign, threatened to fire me if I didn't. It would be your word against mine."

"Your word? Sure, Charlie, let's talk about the power of your word against mine."

He reached into another desk drawer and pulled out a different colored file that Charlie had never seen. Mr. A had referred to something, some other kind of review history before but never revealed it. Charlie had wondered if it was a bluff.

The boss opened it.

"This is my *special* file on you, Charlie. The Human Resources department doesn't know it exists and you should thank your lucky stars they don't."

He picked up the top sheet and turned it to face Charlie.

"Look familiar, Mr. Gray? It's a bit old now—actually sixteen years. Time goes by so fast when you're having fun, don't you think? It's the form you signed on your very first day, pledging allegiance to follow the company's code of conduct to the letter and acknowledging that the penalty for *not* doing so is immediate termination."

Charlie remained quiet while Mr. A picked up the next sheet that appeared to contain a list of some sort.

"This, Charlie, is a list of the number of times you have used the company computers to access unauthorized websites. Our people in the technology group haven't updated it for me recently, but it does go back several years. Clearly the amount of time you spend playing games at work has negatively affected the quality of your judgment on claims. That's why I have had to spend more time watching you. It explains why you and I have to have our little meetings. The techies have strongly encouraged me to expose this and fire you on the spot. But I am a gracious man. I don't know, for example, what other things are going on in your life. Maybe this games addiction represents some form of release for you. I have thus used my management authority to protect you. Thank me later because, if this were to ever get out, it would kill your reputation. In this business that relies so much on *integrity,* you would be unemployable."

Mr. A closed the file.

"And I imagine you'd have to explain a few things to your wife."

Charlie knew he should get up, now, and get back to his pod before it was too late. But he hadn't slept much since dinner with Ivan. Images of the insults flooded his mind. Betty always took her brother's side. He didn't think about his monthly bills, that Betty had been complaining that their ten-year-old car was always in the shop or that the house badly needed a new roof. And he knew all too well why he was a *valuable* employee. Mr. A was doing it to him again. Bend over, Charlie, that's a good boy.

There was no one to stick up for Charlie.

Until now.

"Mr. A, did you know that all your employees made up that nickname for you? It stands for asshole—pretty appropriate, if you ask me. I'm tired of this pussy-footing around. You're getting kickbacks. I don't know where or how, but I'm sure of it. All I need is the review group involved and your goose is cooked."

Mr. A doodled on a yellow pad of paper as he spoke.

"My, oh my, Charlie, those are some very strong words you just used. So, today is the day, is it? After all this time. Are you a gambling man? I guess, in poker, they'd call what you just said as going all-in. On the one hand, we have an employee that repeatedly breaks company policy and has defrauded the firm by accepting pay while he was playing games when he should have been working. On the other hand, his compassionate boss kept the issue under wraps because he knows the employee is in the late stages of his career and, if terminated, would likely have a difficult time finding other employment—at least in this industry. This employee of questionable ethics is making some very serious, but unfounded, accusations against his boss. This boss is a three-time winner of the Manager of the Year award, a devoted family man, a coach of his children's soccer teams, and a past chairman of the company's United Way campaign."

Mr. A frowned and looked Charlie directly in the eye.

"Are you sure you want to bet everything with a hand like yours against one like mine, Charlie?"

Charlie closed his eyes and rubbed his forehead. Mr. A put the file back in his desk and closed the drawer with a bang.

"Actually, the hell with it. It doesn't matter what you think. This conversation and your bald-faced accusations have crossed a line that we haven't before. You have now out-lived your usefulness to me and to the organization. I am more than angry. But I am a reasonable man. I'm going to give you a choice. On the one hand, I'm going to yield to the repeated requests from our technology manager to fire your ass for complete misuse of company resources and a violation of about ten company policies. Under that scenario I would have you immediately escorted out by security. And I would make certain that the grape-vine hears exactly what you were doing on your computer when you should have been working. I might say something like 'we were thinking there were *other issues*, but we decided to just part ways rather than spend the time and resources investigating.' You'd likely have to find employment in an industry where honesty doesn't matter. How does sanitation engineer sound?"

He smiled.

"Or, your other option is you go back to your pod and draft your letter of resignation, effective today."

He folded his glasses, put them in his shirt pocket and pointed towards the office door. Smiling, he said, "Your choice. Now get out."

Chapter 10

Ivan emerged from the Internet café that rented computers, shuffling his feet, hands in his pockets, looking down at the pavement. People rushed by in both directions skillfully avoiding the slowing moving figure.

Another losing trade. He had five thousand dollars left. The number zero loomed.

The sun tried to break through the city smog. A woman came over to buy a newspaper from the sidewalk vending machine, and he rushed to grab the door before it snapped closed. She looked at him for an awkwardly long time, but he did not care. She had no idea. He had to read the news to come up with something, anything. Only a successful trade could save him.

He found an empty park bench under an old oak tree across the street. A squirrel chattered its teeth at the intrusion. Formed concrete ends held the hard wooden slats for the back and the seat in place. Layers of dark green paint covered years of carved initials and other graffiti. Ivan tried to find a more comfortable position as he unfolded the paper. He kept reminding himself not to focus on his failures. He had a system, a philosophy, a plan. Find bad news stories, calamities or disasters of any kind that would knock the stuffing out of a company's stock price—the worse the better. He was a *contrarian* investor.

An unshaven man with black curly hair on the back of calloused hands sat down next to him on the bench. Ivan wanted to say, "Dude, there are empty benches all over the place. Why pick mine?" But he refrained. In New York, you sometimes could not be sure what you were dealing with.

The man was looking at him.

"Nice day dere, hey, friend?"

Ivan had opened the paper and glanced around the side at the unwelcome intrusion. He quickly moved back behind his shelter. Now he understood. The guy was a wanderer, looking for cash. He could have slept on this very bench last night.

"Ya gots to be hot in dat suit on a nice warm day like dis. New Yawkers, they complain about dere wedder, but it's a hell of a lot better than where I's from. Fuckin' rains all da time, ya know wadda mean?"

This time Ivan didn't even look around the paper. Hopefully, the man would soon take the obvious hint. But he kept talking.

"Ya may have heard of it, my city, I mean."

The man paused. What the hell was his point?

"I's from *Seattle*."

Ivan caught his breath and his face burned. He pulled the paper higher and remained quiet.

"What was dat ya said dere, friend? I dint catch it... *Ivan*."

Hearing his name, after all these weeks, Ivan Diversky closed his eyes. His posture sagged forward.

"Like, if ya dint know no better, ya'd say a guy holding his newspaper up like dat was tryin' to *hide* somethin'."

Ivan now slowly lowered the paper and turned to face the intruder.

"Ah, dat's better now, Ivan. Ya see? It's a small world out dere deez days. Don't matter how hard ya try, ain't nobody can hide from nuthin'."

The corners of the newspaper trembled.

"Normally, Mr. Ivan, I'd introduce myself. But *who* I am ain't important to ya. It's *what* I am dat ya should be thinkin' about. My boss in Seattle, he says ya left in a hurry—middle of the night—without paying ya bill. I's sure ya just forgot, right? But we're in the money business and we always remember. So he sent me to ask ya a question. When ya going to pay back the loan? It was for twenty-five large, in case ya forgot, plus ten in interest expense. Ya owes us thirty-five grand."

Ivan looked at the ground.

"I don't have your money right now."

The dark-haired man sat up straighter and rubbed the stubble on his chin.

"Ya don't say? Well, dat's confusin' to us. I've been followin' ya all over Manhattan. Even saw ya driving a red BMW the udder night. No money? Ya sure ain't act like a man with no money."

Ivan's head sank even lower.

"So look, Ivan my friend, I'll make dis short. If ya want to blow all ya money on fancy cars, dat's ya business. Ya owe us thirty-five big ones and collecting dat is *my* business. I's goin' to give ya one week to come up with it—or else."

He leaned over and put his massive, scarred hand on Ivan's forearm. His voice was quieter and deeper.

"And Ivan, we's watchin' ya now. Ya can't fart without me knowin'. If ya try to run again, dere won't be no more 'friendly chats in the park.' Ya get what I's sayin' to ya?"

Ivan nodded his head.

The intruder got up slowly and appeared to admire the scenery. Whistling, he walked away.

Ivan's stomach reminded him that he hadn't eaten yet.

He wasn't sure if he had slept or was just in a daze, but he noticed the sun was now high in the sky and people were pouring out of buildings for lunch.

He was still on his bench. It didn't matter. There was no better place for him to go. They'd been watching him. They probably were now. That bothered Ivan the most.

But... what did he expect? He knew these weren't nice people when he took their cash. What did he think was going to happen when he'd skipped town? That they'd just forget about it?

Where was he going to come up with thirty-five thousand dollars? He sighed. He only had one chance. He must continue to believe. He *was* a good day-trader. He was an *expert* on investing and researching stocks. The world was full of stories about fortunes made by just sitting behind a computer. And he'd had some beautiful wins.

Unfortunately, the losses were uglier.

Ivan considered jumping in front of a car, but yellow cabs and smoke-belching buses clogged the street. Traffic was moving too slowly to have the desired effect.

He couldn't lose faith. He would figure out a way. What other choice did he have?

Chapter 11

Sandy had a text message!

The following morning, hidden in her corner behind the library stacks, Hicks gave her the phone. She pretended not to notice the icon on the screen, clearly mail from Silas, but the guard hadn't opened it. Either he was respecting her privacy—not likely—or he wasn't in tune with all the phone's features. Either case was good. She had lots to write and none of it was for the guard's eyes.

She asked him to wait while she accessed one of her two Bitcoin accounts and transferred two months of their deal, ten thousand dollars, to him. She wanted to impress him with the ease by which she moved money around. He had threatened her and she had responded. That should keep him quiet for a while. Now back to the matter at hand.

Silas was still in business. She'd found him!

What is it, April Fools already? Who is this? It sure as hell isn't Sandy Allen. The Sandy Allen I know is locked up and there ain't no email where she is. What's your game, man?

She wondered when he sent this.

Silas, it IS me, Sandy. You want proof? New Year's Eve. The Chrysler building—in the stairwell. Ring any bells? How would I know about that if it wasn't me? Yes, I have a phone with email in prison. Don't ask me how. Look, I'm very short on time so I'll get right to the point. I have a job for you, a big one, the biggest of your life and mine.

She was about to close the phone, hoping he would read her message and reply by tomorrow at least, but then it vibrated. She bit her fist. He was online—now. They were live!

Well, holy shipyard. New Year's Eve. Took two weeks for the bruises to go away. It IS you. What the hell kind of job could you want me to do? You're in jail sweetie. Did you not get the memo? Or I THINK you're still in jail.

Silas, I only have a phone for a few minutes so I have to make this short. You're the expert in finding people who skipped town and are in hiding. I've got two people I want you to find, Michael Franklin and Angela Messina. Remember them?

Pause. The phone showed Silas was writing a reply. This one was taking longer.

OK then, this really is Sandy because that's some crazy shit and she's the most whacked out chick I know. Thanks for the compliment, but I'm not good at finding DEAD people!

Sandy's typed as fast as she could onto the small keyboard. The guard could appear any minute and want the phone.

Silas, listen to me. They're not dead. They faked their suicides and the cops didn't bother to investigate fully because they had me. The public was happy, so case closed. But there are way too many unanswered questions. If Michael and Angela were supposedly on the boat, how did they get there? They must have rented a car since the cops came up empty on the taxis. Why rent a car to your own funeral? Why did Michael Franklin's face show on the marina security cameras but not Angela's? I doubt she could get on board without being in the video. When the Coast Guard found the boat, the throttle had been set to low and the steering wheel tied so it would run in slow circles. If you're going to kill yourself, why would you care what happened to the boat? They wanted it found to make sure the FBI 'discovered' Michael's so-called confession that fingered me. But don't you see? That also took the spotlight completely off them. More things don't make sense, but Silas, the point is they're alive. I know it. You're going to find them and, when you do, it's my ticket out of here. In exchange for my freedom, the cops will get the real mastermind of the Ponzi scheme and the woman who killed her husband to cash in on the insurance. Nice trade, I'd say.

Another pause. Sandy could hear the guard's heavy footsteps. Come on, Silas, respond!

You're serious about this, aren't you?

The guard was about to turn the corner.

YES! Gotta go. Be on your phone. Same time tomorrow. PLEASE.

She flipped the folding phone closed as the guard approached.
"That's enough for today, Allen. What are you doing with this thing anyway, ordering pizza?"
"Yeah, Officer Hicks. Thirty minutes or it's free. Hope you like pepperoni."

Chapter 12

Next day, things were apparently going according to Sandy's plan. Hicks seemed happy that the money was in his account. Silas was online with his phone when he said he would be. Sandy looked up from her library hiding place to make sure no one watched her.

Hi, Silas. Can we get started? I've got some ideas of where you'll find clues of how they got away.

Hold on, Sandy. There's one little item we got to sort out first. I'm sure the cops took every penny of your hard-earned illegal money, so what were you planning on paying me with? Sex in a stairwell ain't going to cut it. And you're not available even if it did.

Silas, I'm not stupid. I've got money or I wouldn't have bothered you. I transferred it into Bitcoin accounts. No one knows they exist but me and now you.

Bitcoins? I heard about them, but never knew anyone who used them. Now I do. Do they actually work?

Yeah Silas, they're awesome. They're hard to explain. I guess they are like a form of money that lives on the internet, but you can't put them in your pocket. A "coin" is a bunch of numbers and letters, but you can buy and sell things just like real money. The best part for me is they are completely secret. But look Silas, how much? Be gentle. I'm just a little girl in prison with no means of support, right?

Yeah… gentle. Innocent little girl. Right. But it's no matter. I've had worse clients than you. Long as you pay me. But Sandy, I've thought about this case. Not easy—not easy at all.

SILAS. How f'in much?

It's fifty grand, twenty-five up front and twenty-five when I either find them (which I won't) or when I prove they're actually dead. Pretty sure I'll never see the second payment in that case.

WHAT? That's WAY too much. You know that!

Sandy, I don't WANT this job. But I'll take it because it's you. I pretty much got to shut my business down for this one. Plus, I'm not even sure how many illegal things are going on here. If they catch you, the jet engines will suck me in, too, and leave a shredded reputation, not to mention fines.

Silas, please?

Plus expenses. I might have to travel all over the world trying to find these dopes. This could end up costing you 100 yards. You want it that bad? Your call. Take it or leave it. When I see $25,000 in my account, I'll get to work. If not, good luck to you.

One hundred thousand dollars. The guard would cost another sixty thousand if the search took all year. She had one hundred thousand in each of her two Bitcoin accounts, so if the whole thing cost one hundred and sixty, she'd have forty thousand left to start her new life when she got out. Not as much as she was planning on, but she had done lots with much less than that.
Her freedom was worth every penny. She would check her accounts and transfer the twenty-five thousand to Silas tomorrow.
The guard arrived, took the phone and asked what was so funny.
She had not realized she was smiling.
Thank God for Bitcoins.

Chapter 13

Charlie got up, put on his suit, tie, and had breakfast, just like any other weekday morning.

He tried not to look Betty directly in the eye so she wouldn't notice the red; he'd hardly slept all night. At least she was speaking to him again. He knew she was still unhappy, but this woman blessed him. She never held a grudge.

He wondered how she'd handle the latest news.

He couldn't go to work even if he wanted to because, when he left for the last time, it was without his picture ID card and the electronic pass to get through the secured door. He was sure they'd already removed and discarded his Velcro name tag. Mr. A had probably relocated another pod-dweller to his preferred space. That person would consider the transfer a form of promotion, recognition of time in the department. But Charlie knew Mr. A would think nothing of the sort. The closest pod allowed for the quietest conversations. The new person likely was the boss' next target.

Charlie found a coffee shop where he could sit quietly and think. There were so many things running through his mind. He was ashamed that he was keeping something as important as this from his wife. But he could never tell anyone the truth. Mr. A made the consequences of that clear, saying he wouldn't hesitate to personally sue Charlie for libel. But he also hadn't yet come up with a plausible explanation of why he suddenly quit a job he'd held for sixteen years. Betty would fuss anyway, but if his explanation was garbled and incoherent, it would make matters worse.

He was also afraid. Nothing like this had ever happened to him before.

In another way, though, it felt glorious. He had *hated* his job and the man he'd reported to for longer than he could remember. He was finally free.

But his elation gave way to shame. He didn't just hate his job. Mr. A had forced him, repeatedly, to do something illegal. At the very least, he could have walked away. He never found the courage to do anything about it. In the end, the very man he detested did it for him.

His mind drifted back to when he was young. His parents had sent him to summer camp. A group of boys found a small cliff that fed into a pond. They were taunting him to jump. It might have been six feet, but it looked like a mile to him. His stomach still tightened when he thought about it. They pushed him. He had screamed...

And, he reminded himself, come to the surface. He was all right. In the end he had realized that the jump, and the pond, all of it was exhilarating.

But now he had to decide. Which way did he swim?

Ideas had commandeered his dreams all night. He could quietly go find a similar job at another insurance company. Potential employers should value his years of claims experience. However, he knew that path was the easy way out, moving from one pod to another. It was safe and disheartening. But at least he would not have to report to a criminal.

Unless the next firm had their own version of Mr. A.

Another idea came to him at some point during the night. The solution was right in front of him. Much as his brother-in-law's arrogance and flamboyant attitude annoyed him, Ivan's continued success was undeniable. As Betty kept repeating, her brother was happy and confident.

Charlie deserved happiness and confidence, too.

He was worried about having been so rude at dinner. Would Ivan hold a grudge? Charlie would explain that stress at work caused his behavior. He'd been thinking of resigning for some time. He'd heap a lot of blame on his boss. His day at work before Ivan came over was just another one of belittlement and sarcasm at the hands of Mr. Abernathy, which had gone on for years.

Charlie would apologize profusely. Ivan had been right all along. His job *was* boring, incredibly so. He would explain to his brother-in-law that yesterday the tyrant had crossed the line. For some reason—it didn't matter why—Charlie had reached the end of his rope. He wasn't going to take it anymore.

"Ivan. It's Charlie. Thank goodness I reached you! I have something important to talk to you about. Can we meet... for lunch... today?"

At first, Ivan just looked at his phone, afraid it was the man with hairy hands harassing him again. How would they have gotten his cell number? Was there was no escape from these people? But then he saw the name of the caller.

It was his sister's loser of a husband.

"Uh, hi there, Charlie, I'm pretty busy. What's this about?"

Ivan couldn't imagine anyone he'd rather not talk to and certainly not now. He went to his sister's for dinner only because he needed to make sure her perception of his success was intact. So now her deadbeat husband wanted to go have a chummy lunch. Not likely.

"Well, Ivan, I'm sure you *are* busy. You must put in many hours, but I'm willing to make that commitment, whatever it takes to achieve success."

Ivan felt like he had walked into the middle of a movie scene. He had no idea what was going on. Charlie was babbling.

"I haven't talked about it with Betty yet, but she is your biggest fan. I would have a lot to learn, but there's nothing wrong with that. Can we meet? I want to pick your brain."

Ivan could think of nothing to say. He'd never heard Charlie talk like this.

"I'm going to become a 'day-trader,' just like you."

Chapter 14

In real life, there was no such thing as a "get out of jail free" card.

Silas was sitting at the linoleum dinette counter soaking up egg yolk from his plate with his toast. The waitress, wearing a baby blue apron, her black hair tied in a bun, leaned over and refilled his cup with steaming black coffee. The place was filing up. Service would be slower. But Silas was a twenty year veteran at two eggs over easy. His cup never went without and they knew he tipped well for that. He could be related to some of the staff, he'd known them for so long.

He'd been sure Sandy would choke on his price, but she didn't and now he had to plan. She seemed to believe her improbable fantasy. Maybe he should have asked for more.

And he wondered, was the world not better off with her exactly where she was?

But he didn't need to have a philosophical debate with himself because she wasn't going anywhere. While he had learned over the years to never say never, this little hunting trip had a snowball's chance in hell of succeeding. If Franklin and Messina *had* faked their deaths, it was to ensure neither would ever see the wrong side of jail cell bars. Wherever they now lived, they'd keep the lowest of low profiles, likely considered by their neighbors—if they had any—as the quiet couple that kept to themselves. No Facebook or Twitter. No address, phone number or registered auto. They'd take cabs everywhere and only when they had to expose themselves. They would rent, not own their home. They'd have no driver's license, health cards or credit cards. They would bank through a numbered offshore trust, paying everything in cash. They would be invisible people, virtually impossible to find.

Still, though, another part of him was intrigued. Solving the impossible. Showing up the cops. It had a nice ring to it.

Where to start? His many years of training trying to find and convict murder suspects had taught him to always follow a trail, even if there wasn't an obvious one. Everyone left a footprint of some kind somewhere. The trick was to find the start of the trail and track its path. Even though the cops likely picked this stream of evidence clean, as Sandy said, they appeared to give up investigating when they seized her. A fresh set of eyes might find some hidden gems.

He decided to start at Angela Messina's last residence before she disappeared. Silas did a quick search of the real estate records and learned that not long after her husband suffered his fatal car *accident,* she sold their home. Obviously priced low, it went in only one week and closed in a very fast thirty days. A quick sale would be appropriate behavior for a bereaved widow wanting to escape memories. Silas knew, though, it would also make sense for someone wanting to disappear forever—and needing as much cash as possible. Sandy either wasn't aware or hadn't considered this in her rationalization for Angela's fake demise. But it fueled Silas' interest.

After selling her home, Angela moved into an apartment at the edge of town. It was an older, two-story building. Faded yellow paint chips from the stuccoed walls salted the shallow, weedy garden and one of the full-length gray shutters on either side of the front door was missing slats. A plastic sign yellowed by years of sun read "ABSOLUTELY NO SOLICITING" and, just below it, a twisted red neon tube said "NO VACANCY." The manager was unreachable.

So Silas waited.

He could see a reflection of the elevator through the front glass and, when the ground-floor light came on, he started his routine, frantically looking through his jacket and pant pockets. Where was that key? He was muttering to himself, still actively involved in the self-frisk, when the young woman emerged. He grabbed the door before it had a chance to close.

"Oh, my God. Thank you so much. I am such an idiot. I'd lose my head if it wasn't attached to me."

The woman smiled and walked on. How trusting people were. But he still wasn't *in*. He was just in the foyer. He pushed the button with the faded word "Superintendent" on it. There was no answer. He waited two minutes and rang again.

"ENOUGH BELL! What you want?"

It was a female voice, older, Asian accent of some sort. Not friendly.

"Good morning, ma'am, my name is Silas Marker and I am a private investigator."

He held up his official-looking P.I. badge to the camera, even though there was nothing legitimate about it.

"I was hoping you could spare me a couple minutes. I just want to ask you a few questions about a former tenant of yours."

"The sign say NO SOLICITING. How you get inside? Get out, now, or I call cops."

"No, really, ma'am, this won't take long, I promise. I just want to ask you about Angela Messina."

He held up her picture to the camera.

Silence.

"She dead. You get out now or you be too."

Then he held up a hundred dollar bill in front of the camera.

"I very busy woman. You have five minit."

The door buzzed, releasing the electronic lock.

Chapter 15

Ivan stared at nothing across the park as he listened to his brother-in-law on the phone.

Charlie wanted to meet right away—to talk about becoming a day-trader. What a joke. He started to hang up on him, but thought, if he cut him off, his brother-in-law might go back and whine to his sister. He didn't know. Had Charlie and Betty discussed it? Maybe it was her idea? He had gone out of his way to show her how successful he was. Maybe her dopey husband was waking up.

He didn't want to create any friction with his sister. He knew that she loved this guy—he could not imagine why. He also preferred to avoid any discussion about how her "investments" were doing.

So he agreed. Any port in a storm. Besides, maybe a lunch with Charlie would take his mind off his other problem.

Ivan arrived twenty minutes early in order to get a table in the back of the restaurant. While he waited, he wondered how Charlie ever imagined himself as a day-trader.

Looking around, he smiled. This was exactly the kind of place Charlie would pick. Waitresses wiped the clear-plastic laminated menus with a wet cloth for the next customers. He sat down in a booth and inspected the sugar packet holder. It was all white. The sweet and low always ran out first. A busboy with a water pitcher offered him some. It was not quite noon, but he ordered a scotch. His nerves were already shot.

When the waitress arrived with his drink, he started to look around for Charlie. He saw a figure coming through the front door and started to wave, at least until the man came into the light. A black suit walking with clenched fists. Ivan quickly turned his face away, but was too late. Hairy Hands slid into the other side of the booth facing him. When the smiling waitress asked him if he would like something, he frowned at her. She closed her order pad and walked away.

"Ivan," the man glared at him, "my *associates* want to know whacha plans is. We jus' spoke, if ya remember, on the park bench. When will ya pay us?"

The man's voice was even, as if he was reading Ivan a story.

"What? That was, like, a few hours ago. You can't expect me to get your…"

The man grimaced and his eyes darted to the floor leading to the booth. He held out one hand over the table. Ivan stared at it. He recognized the scars he'd noticed at their first meeting.

"Ivan," the man said quietly, "we're in a public place here. Raisin' ya voice at me probably ain't gonna help eider one of us."

Ivan wiped his forehead with his napkin. He was breathing heavily now.

"That's a good boy," the man said. "Now, I ask again. I know ya ain't got our money yet. Ya sat on that bench all morning so ya must have a plan. We'd like to know what it is. Going out to lunch and drinking scotch don't seem like much of a plan to me."

Words escaped him. He knew he couldn't lie. The man continued.

"And I remind ya, just ta make sure ya understan, trying to skip town again would not be ya smartest move. It would be ya last move."

"Well, I am, uh, having a *meeting*. Right now. He should arrive any minute. This person might have money. He might give me a loan, which I'd give to you, right away."

The words were out before he had time to think.

The man in black leaned forward.

"He *might have* money? How much?"

Ivan was recovering. There was the slightest sliver of hope. This story might buy him some time. All he needed was time.

"Well, I don't know. That's why we're having the meeting. You asked me to get your money and I'm *trying*. But it takes time. You have to give me more time."

The man smiled.

"Ivan, we don't have to give ya shit. Ya took money from us and left town. That's called *stealin'*. Very bad. We want our money back and soon or ya going to be one sorry motherfucker."

He paused, playing with Ivan's tumbler of scotch.

"Tink about ya sista. It would be a shame if sometin' happened to her because ya spend ya money like a drunken sailor."

Ivan's lips parted. They hadn't mentioned his sister before. The man—seeing that his arrow had hit its mark—smiled again.

"OK, Ivan. I just wanted to let ya know that we're still here. We'll always be here. And time is runnin' out. We'll be very interested to hear how ya *meetin'* goes."

As he started to get up, he picked up Ivan's glass and finished it in one gulp.

"Tanks for da drink."

Chapter 16

A dingy, unmarked door in a narrow, weakly lit hallway creaked open. A small Chinese woman with lines down her cheeks and jet black hair tied into a bun appeared, wearing a Mandarin dress. Also called qipao, the style was created in the 1920s in Shanghai. It was body-hugging and one-piece, but, Silas noted, it might as well be on an ironing board. She held the door and motioned Silas into a small room with a plain, scratched desk and an old, wooden chair for visitors. He could see the steam from a cup of tea—it smelled herbal—sitting on her desk. As she took her position on the other side, she held out her opened hand and said, "Messina woman dead."

Silas gave her a crisp bill that quickly vanished into a drawer.

"Right. You're obviously a busy woman so I'll get to the point. Someone who believes very strongly that Ms. Messina and her friend Mr. Franklin are not dead has hired me to find them. This apartment was the last place Ms. Messina was seen alive. I'm here to ask you a few questions."

The woman nodded.

"The police already ask me question. You get same answer. Then get out."

"OK. Tell me about what she was doing the last few days before she disappeared. Everything you remember. Don't leave anything out."

The landlord looked at the ceiling and made a noise in her throat that sounded like spit.

"If *woman* alive, *owe* me. Six month rent! *Ugght.*"

Over the years, Silas learned to listen for people's hot buttons. Sometimes, they would give them up freely without even realizing.

"Yes, ma'am, I'm sure she does. But listen, I know it's a long time ago now, but can you think of anything you didn't tell the police that you might have overlooked, or maybe something that occurred to you later?"

The woman stared at him. Motionless.

"You know, if you help me and I am able to find Ms. Messina alive, I would be willing to help you recover your lost rent money from her."

He had no legal way to accomplish anything of the sort, nor was there any reason for this woman to believe he could. But people often heard what they wanted to hear. He needed information. It wasn't the worst lie he ever told.

It was small, almost imperceptible, but one of her eyes twitched.

"And I will pay you more right now if you provide me with anything of value."

"Five hundred dollar."

Silas controlled the urge to snicker. He'd seen this so many times. Somehow the sight of Benjamin Franklin's picture on a one hundred dollar bill resulted in amazing recollections.

As he started to reach into his wallet, he repeated, "Well, yes, I said anything of val…"

The woman opened another desk drawer, reached down and produced a small laptop computer. Silas' eyes widened.

"Did that belong to…? Why didn't the police…?"

"I hide. Keep to bargain. But she never come back."

After the woman had collected her second round of cash, she added, "Computer worthless. Hard drive wiped. You take."

Silas was trying hard to conceal his grin. It was a possible gold mine. The small woman leaned over the desk, this time staring at him.

"Tell no one. I have friends. Can hurt you. Understood?"

Silas rose and put out his hand, which she accepted and vigorously shook.

"You have my word, lady. This is our secret. I won't reveal it to a soul."

He handed her one of his cards. She turned it over several times and threw it into the drawer.

"If you think of anything else, please…"

"You go now."

Chapter 17

Hairy Hands almost knocked Charlie over as he pounded through the door, but Ivan's brother-in-law didn't notice; he seemed to be on a mission. He approached the table grinning.

"Ivan! Thank you, thank you so much for coming. You'll never know how important this is to me."

Ivan nodded. His pulse was just starting to ease. He had perspired clear through the back of his shirt.

"Hello, Charlie."

Charlie stopped in his tracks.

"Oh no, that's what I was afraid of. You're still mad at me for the other night. Look, I'm *really* sorry. The stuff I said, the way I acted was way out of line. After you left, Betty let me have it, both barrels. But you have to let me explain. Something's happened and I really need your help."

Ivan sighed. He didn't care about Charlie's dilemma because he had the mother of all problems himself. While he hated sitting here, listening to Charlie's nonsense, doom was waiting for him somewhere outside. He'd told the mob that, because of this meeting, he'd have their money. He did not want to think of what would happen when they found out he didn't.

The waitress broke the ice. As she was reading the specials from the back of her order pad, Ivan realized that being here was a dangerous waste of time. He needed solitude to form a plan.

He wondered if there was a window in the bathroom.

He didn't hear a word she said, but he realized she was gone and Charlie was looking at him.

"Look, I am very busy. Let's make this quick. I have to go across town. Whatever you have to say to me, go ahead and say it."

Charlie's eyes opened wide. Ivan read his concern, but he did not care. His life was on the line.

"Ivan, I *know* how busy you are or at least I think I do. But right now, you're the only person I trust. I couldn't begin to tell Betty, at least not yet. And I don't want to upset her. That wouldn't be fair."

Ivan closed his eyes and slowly shook his head. Charlie and Betty had been married forever. Their partnership, in today's world where commitment was as strong as wet paper, was the most wonderful thing he knew of. He dreamed of having their life of stability and companionship.

"Aw, Charlie, really? *That's* why you brought me here? You and Betty? I had no idea you were having problems. I'm very sorry to hear that."

Charlie frowned while he apparently tried to decipher what Ivan was saying. Then he smiled.

"Oh! Oh, gosh no, Ivan." He laughed and shook his head. "I guess that didn't come out right. Betty and I are fine... at least we will be until she hears what I have done."

Ivan relaxed a bit. The woman brought their sandwiches and while she offered ketchup, the second part of Charlie's sentence registered.

"OK, that's good. But then... what have you done that's going to upset her?"

Charlie looked left and right and then back to Ivan.

"Guess what I did yesterday, Ivan. I told my boss that I'd had enough and I quit. Betty thinks I'm at work right now, but I am one hundred percent unemployed."

Ivan stared at him.

"Wait... what? What did you just say?"

As Charlie repeated, Ivan whistled. This was incredible, or maybe ridiculous. Ivan wondered if Charlie had ever before done anything so bold.

"Seriously? Man, you're like Steady Eddie over there. I figured you for the retirement party followed by a fat pension. What the hell is going on?"

It seemed to Ivan that Charlie was having trouble controlling his breathing.

"Yes, you're right. I probably thought of myself that way, too. But Mr. Abernathy, my boss, well, my *former* boss, he's the meanest, rudest man I've ever met. And he's a bully. Yesterday was the worst day ever. I decided right then that was it. That tyrant has seen his last chance to kick around *this* Charlie Gray. It'll never happen again."

Charlie then told some anecdotes describing Mr. A's treatment of his employees.

"I see what you mean. What a dick. But Charlie, you know what? Work's hard on everybody. That doesn't mean you just up and quit because you had a bad day."

"No, Ivan, there's more. I actually have to thank you. The other night, when you came over for dinner, I was so rude! I kept asking myself *why* I behaved that way because I'm not usually like that. Betty said it aloud and if I'm being honest with myself, I have to agree that she's right. I'm *jealous,* Ivan. Not because you make a lot of money. I mean, that would be great, but that's not it. It's because you've figured out your life. You know who you are and what you want to do."

Ivan thought about what Charlie said. If he only knew the truth...

"But Charlie, man, you can't just quit your job without having another one. No one does that."

"Betty said that's what you did when you left Seattle and came here, right?"

Ivan shrugged. It was just another reminder that he was living a life of lies. Leaving his job in Seattle certainly hadn't been his choice.

"But Ivan, look, that doesn't matter. This is about me and my life. You said it yourself. My job was awful and boring. You were right, but I wouldn't admit it. It was *safe*. It seems like all my life I've just wanted safety. Well, not anymore."

Charlie continued to talk, but Ivan's mind was drifting back to the scene with Hairy Hands. He was losing interest in hearing about Charlie and his climactic event because his own crisis loomed. He needed money, and soon.

"Yeah, well look, Charlie. That's a tough story, but it doesn't involve me."

Charlie sat up straighter. He looked apologetic.

"The funny thing is, the answer to my problem was right in front of me all this time and I ignored it. Not anymore. I've thought about it a lot. There's no reason why I can't succeed like you and a lot of other people."

Ivan slowly shook his head.

"I'm going to become a day-trader, Ivan. When you read about people's stories, oh my goodness, they're amazing. But Ivan, I need you to teach me. I've never asked you for anything before. I will work very, very hard."

Ivan wanted to protest. Charlie thinking he could just become a day-trader—with no experience—was ignorant. In no way would he even think of taking him under his wing. Extra baggage at a time when he needed speed and decisiveness could literally cost him his life.

He had to bring this meeting to a finish. The mob was waiting and he didn't have a sniff of a plan.

"Whoa, Charlie, wait a minute, you don't know… are you serious? I can't…"

Charlie grabbed Ivan's hands.

"I've never been more serious about anything in my life, Ivan. I've got *money*."

Ivan caught his breath. Charlie had said the magic word.

"So… you're… serious about this, Charlie. You quit your job and now you want to be a day-trader, just like that. Have you really thought this through? It's not that easy, you know. Not everyone makes money at it. Most people don't."

Thoughts flooded his head. He'd blown whatever cash he started with, the meager severance he got when he was fired, his sister's seventy-five thousand dollar retirement savings and the twenty-five thousand dollars he borrowed from the Seattle mob.

He was broke or dangerously close to it. The mob had found him and their threats had never been more real.

Really, what choice did he have?

Charlie had money.

His sister seemed to believe his mirage of success so she likely wouldn't object to the new partnership. In her eyes, her brother was a star. Betty said it every time he came over.

Charlie continued.

"Yes, Ivan, I am very serious. I think... no, I *know* what I'm doing. If you're willing, I'd have the greatest mentor ever on my side and you'd have one heck of a student."

It was ridiculous but Ivan kept reminding himself. Charlie had money.

"God, Charlie, I just don't know. You as a day-trader? Whew!"

Charlie leaned closer, whispering.

"Ivan, this could be the most important day of my life. I'm begging you."

As Charlie continued to plead, Ivan sighed and rubbed his chin. He had to make sure that Charlie perceived this as a terribly difficult decision that could go either way. Then he could ask for anything.

"Well look, Charlie. *If* I did agree to take you on—and I mean *if*—you need some serious coin to day-trade. The regulators require you to post a certain amount of capital to make sure you're for real. If you can't honor your trades, then the whole thing collapses. Do you understand what I'm saying? You'd need at least fifty thousand for capital and another twenty-five thousand to trade with."

Ivan knew the actual amount required by the Financial Industry Regulatory Authority was twenty-five thousand, but that only applied to people who traded several times per day. He wanted to keep his option open to do that at some point because the regulators stopped all trading if an account's equity value fell below that level. Ivan did the math. If Charlie came up with only fifty thousand and Ivan gave the mob twenty-five thousand, they would immediately be down to the minimum and their choices of how often to trade, restricted. He had to get the extra cash now or the entire discussion was pointless. He also had to ensure that Charlie understood there was no easy or fast way out of the agreement.

Charlie was silent for a moment.

"I don't have that much, but... I'm sure I can get it. I would have to go talk to the bank, though."

Ivan knew that "talk to the bank" meant take out a loan. Day-trading using borrowed money was the riskiest kind.

"The bank! Charlie, you'd have to borrow?"

Charlie nodded.

Ivan leaned back in his chair and frowned. Charlie did not actually have the money, he just had access to it, or so he thought. That was another reason for Ivan to walk away right now and try to find another solution. There was also his conscience, as much as he tried to ignore it. Charlie did not begin to understand the risks of what he was planning, but Ivan did and he had the power to stop him.

Besides, he had already lost Betty's entire loan. How much money did this couple have?

But he had no choice. He had to ignore his scruples, if he had any. Charlie's money would be the game changer. He could focus. He'd gone through a string of bad trades that didn't work out, that's all. This would work and it would buy him the one thing he needed to get himself out of this mess—time. He could trade the way he knew he could, pay off his debts finally and make everyone happy.

He was only using their money, not stealing it. That's what he told himself.

Besides, he was facing potential death. Desperate times called for desperate measures.

"Well, I'll take you on under one condition, Charlie. You have to give me all of your money and trust that I know what I'm doing. You will learn by watching. As soon as you start second-guessing me—one word—then I'm out."

A beaming Charlie made a motion of zipping his lips. His sandwich was half-eaten, but he got up, throwing three twenties on the table.

"Ivan, I promise, you won't regret this. I'm going to go talk to the bank right now."

He paused.

"I, uh, might ask for your help in explaining all this to Betty. It's quite a bit of change to throw at her all at once."

After Charlie left, Ivan asked for the bill, which was forty-two dollars, including his scotch. Maybe without realizing it, Charlie had left an eighteen dollar tip. That was far too much. Ivan pulled a five dollar bill out of his wallet, replaced it with one of Charlie's twenties and left.

Chapter 18

A "wiped" hard drive did not exist in Silas' world. He sat in his "office"—his kitchen—surrounded by stacks of papers, old magazines and numerous partially disassembled computers. Years of intercepting intelligence linked to pending drug deals had turned Silas into somewhat of an expert on the machines. People casually discarded computers with hard-drives intact thinking they'd erased all information. But with some skill, luck and the right software, some information could be restored. While he could have done the work himself, it was a time-consuming process. He farmed it out to one of the techie kids he knew.

He needed time to think and that he did—most of the night. He tried to mentally list every what-if, if-then, and if not this-that scenario. By four-thirty a.m., he capitulated, made a cup of black coffee and assumed his usual spot at the patterned white linoleum table with aluminium legs.

His apartment was small, a studio in fact, but clean. He bought it new four years ago and still had not hung any pictures, painted or papered. When the developer was pre-selling units, he chose one with the worst view and on the second floor. It was cheaper and besides, he knew from experience, standing at your open window admiring the vista meant that someone could concurrently appreciate the view of you. He himself had done it many times. Some might call it voyeurism. He called it private detective work.

It was still dark outside as he carefully sipped his cup and pulled a white, unlined note pad out of his faded and torn satchel. He then sharpened three new yellow pencils. He started by drawing diagrams and timelines. He always began a case this way. It was how it was done. To succeed, a P.I. had to create a plausible scenario and then find the facts necessary to support it. If the evidence did not materialize, he created a new, possible story-line. As he walked through his mental maze, whenever he hit a dead end, he changed direction. Creativity was essential.

He answered the knock on his door at noon. The kid was standing there, laptop in hand, looking like an unmade bed. Silas wondered if he'd slept either.

"OK, the recovery platform is done. Ran all night. I think it got something, but you never know with these things. You'll have to go through it and see what you find."

Silas knew the process was like trying to restore a window from tiny pieces of shattered glass, grain by grain.

As the kid handed the laptop back, he said, "It's all set to go. Just open it up. It will run automatically. All you'll need is the password."

"And what is that?"

"That is five hundred dollars," said the kid.

Silas shook his head. He was handing out money like candy. But that was usually how it went with these things.

After the kid took his money and left, Silas set the laptop on the table and opened it up. The software ran through its initiation and he caught his breath. The computer showed eighteen "recovered" files. He knew that wasn't a guarantee of success. Once the program pieced together over half of a file's data, it called it a recovery. Silas knew, though, that over eighty percent was necessary for usable information. He clicked to open the first file, arbitrarily named RF-001.

FILE CORRUPT - INSUFFICIENT DATA

He clicked on it again, and an unintelligible stream of letters and numbers started to flow across the page. He hit the ESC button.

He tried RF-002 through RF-010 and shook his head. There was a way to wipe a hard drive truly clean, but it took some expertise. Could this Angela woman have figured it out?

File RF-011 was the first to open. It was a computer spreadsheet with names, dates and dollar amounts. Silas assumed from the beginning that the Messina woman was in on the Ponzi scheme with Michael Franklin in some fashion. This likely was a record of cash received from the victims. Even though all of the stolen money was deposited into a single off-shore account— Michael Franklin had provided the banking information in his suicide note—it would have been important for the scam operators to keep track of each individual's transactions to provide the appearance of legitimacy when they issued fictitious statements.

While this spreadsheet was worthless because the investigation had already recovered a pile of phony documents, it did provide a greater sense of hope that he might recover something of value from the computer. But his hopes diminished when he reviewed files RF-012 through RF-017. They were almost identical to RF-011, only with different client names and cash flow amounts.

Had Silas wasted his money? Was this his first dead end? He could not use seventeen of eighteen files. He held his breath as he clicked on File RF-018. Last chance. He was trying to think of his Plan B, but the truth was he did not have one. Then he noticed the familiar icon of a word processor program opening. That hadn't happened before. The last file was different from the rest. Not everything was intelligible; most of it was gibberish, so he tried to pick out words in the middle of a long stream of letters and numbers. As he did, he wrote them down on his pad of paper.

He leaned closer to the screen. Someone, he assumed it was Angela, had kept some sort of diary or checklist. He could make out:

* Patriotic rental car. Confirmed late pick up. Drop at Sea-Tac airport RCA13998 42

* Passports!!!

* Wipe laptop

The rest of the lines were unrecognizable.

Silas pushed the laptop away and closed his eyes. Sitting back, he started his reasoning process.

He had access to the police evidence since the case was officially closed. There were the marina videos of Michael getting on the yacht called "For Love of Money." Angela's face never appeared on any of them. Her fingerprints were never found on the boat either. Logic prevailed that she never set foot on that boat, so the double-suicide idea had holes.

From the laptop data, it appeared that Angela had at least *intended* to rent a car, drop it at the airport and fly somewhere. Why would she go to all that trouble if she was getting ready to kill herself? Rationally, she would have just taken her own car, which was found—

cold—at her apartment. Was she trying to create a distraction for the police? Then why go to the trouble of wiping data from her computer? If it was a false lead, she would have wanted to make it easier, not harder for the police to find. That was further evidence that she didn't commit suicide.

And the transportation wasn't just for her. The word "passports" was plural. She expected a travelling companion. Michael Franklin was likely that other person, but not necessarily. Was there a lovers' quarrel of some sort? Money could certainly cause that. What was it, one hundred million stolen from clients? People had certainly killed for far less.

Why, why, why?

It was better than Silas might have hoped for because it allowed him to create a possible scenario. Angela Messina and Michael Franklin faked their deaths to escape going to jail—him for co-running a Ponzi scheme and her, according to the newspaper reports, for arranging the murder of her husband.

There was nothing in the evidence so far to argue that his story was wrong. So, he would continue down this path until a dead-end forced him to change course.

Next stop, the rental car agency.

Chapter 19

Something was up. Betty knew it. Charlie wouldn't look at her.

She had made him his toast and put the plate in front of him. Instead of talking about the usual things like the weather, how he slept or his prospective day at work, he just started into an obviously rehearsed dialogue. She watched, almost in fascination as he spoke, not seeming to acknowledge the highly unlikely message he delivered. He just sat there, casually as you please, seeming more interested in buttering his toast.

"That's right, Betty, I *want* to invite Ivan over. I apologized like you said I should. Now I want to make up for the dinner I ruined."

His toast now apparently ready for eating, he carefully placed the butter knife on a plate.

"And there's something else we want to discuss with you."

She started to ask him a question, but he stopped her… interrupted, really. That wasn't like Charlie either.

"Look, when I made up with Ivan, we spent quite a bit of time… talking. In fact, we renewed our friendship and spoke about the future, how we might help each other going forward. But please, wait for Ivan to arrive so we can explain together."

She was about to ask him how a friendship that never existed in the first place could be *renewed*, but decided to wait. There was more information coming, for sure.

That evening, Betty handed Ivan and Charlie their plates of pasta and started talking before she sat down. She knew that was bordering on rudeness; normally she would have prompted the dinner conversation with some pleasantries, news about the neighborhood, that sort of thing. Tonight, however, was different. She needed to get to the bottom of this.

"Ivan, Charlie says you have something to tell me."

Charlie adjusted his position in his chair and cleared his throat. Ivan looked up quickly and then over to Charlie, who nodded his head. They reminded Betty of young boys at their first dance.

"Betty," Charlie said, "Ivan and I have a bit of a, uh, long story to tell you, but the first part relates only to me. I should warn you. What I have to say might seem like bad news at first, but, please hear us out and you'll see that it's anything but that."

Betty slowly turned her head from Ivan to Charlie and folded her arms. Speaking softly, she said,

"Whatever it is Charlie, I'm sure it will be fine. Just go ahead and tell me your news."

Charlie inhaled deeply.

"I quit my job this week."

She put both her hands to her mouth. Her face and neck reddened.

"Charlie, what? How could you…? What in the world… happened?"

Charlie told her the entire story he'd told Ivan about the years of mistreatment by his bully of a boss. As he spoke, Betty kept shaking her head. She started to speak, but her throat was too dry. She reached for her glass of water and drank half of it.

"Charlie. For goodness sake, I had no idea that was going on. Why didn't you tell me?"

He put his fork down and wiped his mouth. Betty noticed he still wouldn't look right at her.

"Well, I didn't want to worry you. I kept hoping things would get better, and now, finally they will—just not like how I thought they would. You know what's funny, Betty? I have you to thank for planting the idea in my head. I kept thinking about what you said. You were so right. I *was* jealous of Ivan and his success. Then it dawned on me. If you can't beat 'em, join 'em."

Betty listened, looked at Ivan and then back to Charlie. This was making no sense.

"Once Ivan and I met, he was as excited about my idea as I am. It was clear what the next step would be. You should have seen the look on that tyrant's face when I quit. It was one of the most satisfying days of my life."

He paused.

"I'm becoming a day-trader, just like Ivan!"

She put her hand to her chest and paused. She had to let this sink in. Blinking, she said one of the first things that came to her mind.

"But Charlie, you can't just quit your job. How will we pay our bills?"

She watched him look at Ivan, who, now, leaned forward to speak. They had *practiced* this!

"Betty, relax, don't worry. You guys will be fine. It's a different way to earn a living, but you'll get used to it."

He winked at her.

"You might have you noticed that I seem to be doing OK, right?"

That comment made her pause. When Ivan first came into town, he borrowed a lot of money from her—what remained, other than the house, of her mother's inheritance. At the time, he had explained to her why he needed to borrow so much. She didn't understand all the stock market rules he laid out, but he was her brother and she trusted him. She told him to pay it back when he could; there was no hurry. Since then she watched the way he seemed to carry himself, his apparent free-spending ways including his repertoire of potential new cars. She would never, of course, say anything to him, but she wondered. Could he not have paid just a little of her money back by now?

"I don't know, Ivan. Relax? Everything is moving so fast. In the pace of five minutes I learn that my husband has quit his perfectly good job that he's had for sixteen years and then I discover he's going to work in the stock market like you. Don't you think that's enough to unsettle anyone?"

Ivan nodded his head.

"Yeah, Betty, I suppose. I have to admit, when Charlie first approached me, I was a little surprised, too. But then I thought about my own path and it dawned on me. Someone just doesn't *decide* to become a day-trader. It's in their blood. While it's not easy to do well, once you recognize that you are meant to trade, you can't imagine any other career. Charlie has had an epiphany and I get that."

Betty couldn't hide her frown. This discussion was getting more ridiculous by the minute. Epiphany?

"No, Betty, hear me out. I said it wasn't easy. Nothing of any value is easy. Charlie is definitely a hard worker and committed. Look at how many years he slaved at that one job. From what I see, he has all the makings to be *very* successful at this. With me as his teacher, it's pretty much a sure thing. Think about the positives. In addition to potentially enormous profits, day-trading will give Charlie freedom. You just heard that horrible story he told about his awful problems at work. As a self-employed professional, he is his own boss and answerable to no one. Wait 'till you see the smile on his face when he makes his first big score, all thanks to his own efforts. And when the neighbors find out that he is now an independent businessman, living by his own rules and doing it his own way, well, they will look at him differently."

Betty could see out of the corner of her eye, one of Charlie's feet pumping as Ivan spoke. The two of them had obviously discussed this at great length, putting her at a disadvantage. She needed to slow things down.

The room was quiet. For effect, she put both palms to her face, closed her eyes and sighed. She looked directly at Ivan when she opened them, sat up straighter and wiped her hands on her lap, as if brushing away crumbs.

"You know, Ivan, thank you for your insight and your willingness to become Charlie's mentor. However, you two have given me quite a bit to think about and that will take time. Charlie and I must discuss another issue, which doesn't involve you, as well. I'm sure you understand. Let's change the subject."

She forced the conversation to shift to other matters. She had to deal with Charlie one on one.

"For example, there is a matter far more important than business. When, my dear brother, are you going to enrich some young woman's life and settle down?"

Betty forced a smile as she led him through their often repeated routine; put Ivan on the hot seat and let him gave his predictable responses. Soon after he finished though, she rose from the table—no offer of dessert or coffee—and showed her brother to the door.

After Ivan left, Betty placed the dirty dishes in the sink.

"Charlie, why don't we go into the living room?"

As she sat in his chair, she pointed to the couch.

"You sit right there."

The only sound was the ticking of the antique grandfather clock. She could tell he was watching as her eyes roamed around the room.

"You know, Charlie honey, this is a pretty nice life we have built for ourselves. We live in a lovely house in a nice quiet neighborhood. It's taken us a long time to build this. I thought you appreciated our blessings as much as I do. Then, out of nowhere you want to turn everything on its head, just like that. I would never in a million years have imagined… What's worse, you haven't given me much time at all to think about your *idea*. I'm feeling that you should have a much greater consideration for my point of view at a time like this, but you apparently don't. To start with, you quitting your job was a very big decision. We've been married for almost twenty years. Don't you think that would have been something we should have discussed first?"

"Well, Betty, we *are* discussing it—right now, but the decision to quit was something I had to make on my own. I wasn't planning on doing what I did—or at least in the way that I did it—but Mr. Abernathy, this time Betty I'm telling you he went too far. I can't take it anymore and, you know what the good thing is? I don't have to. I've got Ivan and my new career now."

She watched him. It wasn't like him to do anything as drastic as this. She wondered. Is this what a mid-life crisis was like? She'd heard it could happen to men Charlie's age.

"But, Charlie that was your *job*. It's what puts food on the table and keeps the lights on. To leave like that was—there's no other way to say it—irresponsible."

The story about how Charlie's boss treated him, at face value, disturbed her. But had Charlie and Ivan dressed it up to make it sound worse than it really was? The more she thought about it, she knew Charlie, acting alone, would never do anything like this. Ivan must have put him up to it.

But why?

Charlie's continued out-of-character behavior interrupted her thoughts. His voice was a bit louder, somewhat more aggressive with a deeper tone. It wasn't normal at all.

"All right, fine, Betty. I should have told you sooner about my frustration. This might seem sudden to you, but I have thought about it. I didn't tell you until I was sure. To discuss this idea with you if I wasn't convinced myself would have been *very* irresponsible. And of course I had to have Ivan on side or there'd have been nothing to discuss anyway."

"But Charlie, the *stock market* as a career? That's not a very stable thing, don't you think?"

"I don't know, Betty. It seems good enough for your brother. You always make such a big deal out of him, every time he comes over in his new cars. So, what's wrong with me doing it? I'll make a lot of money and we'll both be happier."

"Ivan is not my *husband*, Charlie. He has his life and we have ours."

She had been looking directly at him up to this point, but now she looked down at her hands in her lap.

"Frankly, Charlie, day-trader or not, walking out on a job that has provided well for us for many years is nothing short of reckless. You are married, mister, so you should consult me about decisions that affect me."

She looked up at him again briefly and then back at her lap.

"But never mind about that. I'll get over it. The immediate issue is I have a husband who has made several impetuous and irrational choices, clearly while under duress. I think if you take a bit more time to consider working with Ivan in the stock market as a career, you might reconsider. You know what they say, *'Act in haste, repent in leisure.'* I have an idea, Charlie—call it sober second thought just to make sure you aren't making a mistake that you will forever regret."

She looked up into Charlie's eyes.

"I want you to speak with Mr. Abernathy first thing tomorrow. The shock of what you did will likely have subsided some by now. You were a good, solid employee of his. Charlie... I want you to ask him to give you your job back."

Charlie bolted off the couch.

"Christ Betty! Are you insane? How could you say that? After everything I've told you. How that man treated your own husband like a piece of dirt. Why aren't YOU mad... for ME? You're just sitting there thinking about yourself. What about MY HAPPINESS?"

Neither of them expected it. That look of anger... and he was *yelling* at her. Tears streamed down her face. He reached for her hands, but she pulled them away.

"I'm sorry Betty. I, uh, I didn't mean to upset you."

He started pacing. Neither of them looked at the other. But neither could leave the room. This was important. Betty wiped both eyes with the dinner napkin.

"Charlie, I... didn't know... you... never said..."

"Betty, stop. Maybe I should have told you about my work. Maybe I didn't even realize how unhappy I was. Maybe, maybe, maybe. It doesn't matter anymore. I am forty-six years old. I'm bored. I've hated my job for years and I'm not going to live like that any longer. Starting today, I am a day-trader. Ivan, who, let me remind you, you *fawn* over every time he is here, has agreed to teach me what I need to know. I am a hard worker and I will not fail. Yes, we might not have a steady paycheck for a little while like before, but we will be fine."

It didn't seem real to her. She was losing the most important argument they'd ever had. She tried to hold it together, but she felt like she couldn't breathe.

"Charlie, Ivan is my brother and I love him, and yes I'm very proud of him. But he's always been such a 'free spirit.' He moves back and forth across the country. He doesn't own a house. He doesn't have a *stable* life like you and I do. Maybe this day-trader business is right for him—but not us. What's so bad about getting a regular paycheck anyway?"

Charlie walked across the room and sat on one arm of his chair. He put his hands on top of hers.

"Betty, the horse has left the barn. I couldn't get my old job back if I wanted to. Do you remember what your mother used to say? *You can't change the past, only the future.* Well, that's what I've done. I am going to change my future! Maybe there is some risk… and change is never easy. But I've thought about it for a long time. I'm doing it and it's done. I want your support but…"

He stopped and chuckled.

"There I am using the 'B' word. There are no buts, Betty. I'm going ahead and you just watch. I'm going to be the best day-trader there ever was."

Betty sighed and looked at the floor.

After his dinner with Charlie and Betty, Ivan was both relieved and worried. He was pleased because neither of them noticed that he had taken a cab to their house. With the mob watching him so closely, taking a fancy car for a test drive was not an option. But he was anxious, too. His sister wasn't fully buying her husband's new career choice. He knew she was going to try to talk him out of it. She usually prevailed.

Ivan *had* to have Charlie's money.

As he undid the three locks of his street-level apartment door, he felt like someone would jump up and startle him at any moment. They were everywhere, probably watching him now.

He breathed a sigh of relief, reminding himself that they would leave him alone once he paid them. Good riddance. He would *never* make the same mistake again. Thanks to Charlie's money, this nightmare would soon be over. It was just a matter of time.

He almost tripped over the newspaper, carefully placed on the first step of the stairs up to his apartment. How did it get there? Leaning forward, he could see it was the *Seattle Times*, dated about eighteen months earlier.

Tradur Gurl

The headline read:

LOCAL BUSINESSMAN FOUND DEAD IN TRUNK OF BMW
Police suspect mob-related slaying

Chapter 20

The car rental terminated at the Seattle-Tacoma Airport. As Silas drove towards the Patriotic Car Rental office just next to the main terminal, he realized there could be a wealth of information contained in that simple statement. He followed the logic.

Finding Angela's personal car at the airport would have raised too many questions. It made no sense to drive your car to the airport when your real destination was a marina fifteen miles away.

They probably figured—correctly—that the police would never look for a rental car in their search for evidence. They would assume the bereaved couple took a taxi to the marina. After all, it did not matter *how* they got there, ultimately all the focus would shift to the abandoned boat—the rigged boat that would only go in circles—making it easier to find. The vessel, in effect, became a diversion. Clearly, that could have been part of their plan.

Since someone meant to drop the rental car at the airport, it strongly implied that at least Angela was taking a flight somewhere, but that was an easily changeable plan. Still, at least she had gone far enough to receive what looked like a reservation number.

Of course, they both could have gotten on the plane.

Rental car agreements at airport lots often asked for relevant flight information to help coordinate things. If Silas could only get his hands on it… but the rental would have been over a year ago now. Did they keep records that far back?

He walked up to the counter at Patriotic Car Rental, at the end of the row of car-for-hire kiosks, distinguished by different signature colors. He showed the attendant his fancy-looking-but-of-no-consequence ID and asked to see the manager. He had called earlier, relayed his story with as much compassion and sincerity as he could, and the voice at the other end agreed to try to help. Now a man calling himself Mr. Fawnstock came out from the back, shook Silas' hand and ushered him past the counter into his office. It was barely big enough to fit the aluminum desk and chair. An award for "Most Favored

Sponsor" from the Sassafras County Little League, with a picture of a group of what Silas imagined were ten year olds in baseball uniforms, hung on the wall behind him.

"Mr. Fawnstock, thank you so much for seeing me. I have to admit, I haven't worked on many cases stranger than this one. I'm trying to locate a woman. All I know is that she rented a car from you about a year ago and returned it here at this location. I've been hired by the executor of an estate. The parents forbade their daughter from marrying her boyfriend. See, it was a very wealthy family and they didn't like his breeding much, thought he was just a sponge. There was apparently a big fight and she ran away with the man. She left a note saying she and her lover had eloped and were never coming back. She'd told them that she had created a false identity so they shouldn't look for them. The parents apparently tried for a while, but to no avail. If they were mad at her, they didn't show it because they never changed their wills. Maybe they felt a sense of guilt. I guess we'll never know because both parents died recently in a tragic car accident. You might have heard about it… over there on Route 427. Got mixed up with a tractor trailer, fire, oh dear Lord, what a mess."

Silas had scanned the local papers for something, and that accident fit the bill. He knew he was skating on thin ice—looking for a missing person when he didn't even know her name. Any sense of familiarity he could create with the manager could go a long way. He saw the recognition in the man's eyes. He had heard about the accident.

"Anyway, this woman, whatever her fake name is, has inherited a considerable sum of money. I need to find her."

Mr. Fawnstock listened, looking at his desk while slowly nodding his head.

"Yes, well, Mr. Marker, as I said on the phone, I will try to help. But how can you find someone when you don't even know their name?"

He was questioning Silas on the facts rather than just dismissing him. The fairy tale was holding together.

"Amen to that! But here's the thing. I think I have a lead, a thin one for sure, but it is something. After the daughter left, the parents had to go clean out her apartment and they just threw all her personal papers into a box. The person helping to value their estate was going through their house, found the box and turned it over to the executor. He went through it, realized it was the missing daughter's stuff and found a sheet of notepaper with the name of your company and it looks like a reservation number. I'm praying your records go back that far because if we find it, it might contain some incredibly useful information."

Silas shook his head, but continued.

"How sad is that, huh? The parents could've had the missing clue to their daughter's whereabouts right under their noses and never realized it."

Mr. Fawnstock sat up straighter, took off his glasses and massaged his temples.

"The IRS requires that our records go back seven years and they are impeccable. The rental car business has always been a concern to the authorities. You just never know the real identity of your clients or the purpose of the rental. The story you just told is a good case in point. But this represents a highly confidential and time-consuming search that is only appropriate for a properly authorized person, in this case, me."

Silas recognized the negotiation had started.

"I understand, sir. I am sure you are a very busy man. I am authorized to compensate you for your time."

Silas started to pull an envelope out of his jacket pocket.

Mr. Fawnstock held up his hand.

"Would you close my office door, please?"

Ten crisp hundred dollar bills later, the man moved over to his computer and said, "Now, slowly please, read me that reservation number."

Silas wanted to ask him about the "highly time-consuming" part of the search and whether the man would like a receipt for the IRS, but he just did as he was told.

Mr. Fawnstock's fingers moved quickly across his keyboard. After each flurry, he would pause, lean towards his screen and adjust his glasses, sometimes muttering "hmmm" under his breath, other times turning his head slightly as if a modified sight line would provide different clues. Then he would punch the keys again.

Silas felt like he was in a doctor's office waiting for a diagnosis. He rubbed his hands on his pant legs.

Without warning, the rental car manager pushed back from the computer screen. He was shaking his head.

"That just isn't right. I really have to admit that I don't understand."

Silas' head dropped as he deeply inhaled and released. The man had seemed so... sure of himself. But these were the rules of his game. When you hit a roadblock, you just had to choose another path. Kiss a grand goodbye. He started to get up.

"Well, Mr. Fawnstock, I appreciate you trying. I knew it was a long shot, but hey, if you don't ask you don't get, right?"

The manager looked at the now-standing man, a puzzled frown on his face, and then he seemed to realize what was going on.

"Oh no, Mr. Marker, please sit down. I found the information you were looking for. What I was referring to was the fact that our program is not operating properly. We changed all of our transaction codes last year, but the system is supposed to adjust for that. To retrieve your information, I had to, what you might call 'go through the back door'—totally unacceptable."

Silas sat down.

"So you...?"

"Of course, I told you our records are impeccable. The contract is printing."

Silas hadn't noticed the soft hum of a printer hidden somewhere behind the desk. Like a magician, Mr. Fawnstock reached down and produced the three-page agreement.

"As you know, this is highly confidential information. You certainly can't take these sheets with you without proper authorization, which is, under the circumstances, probably not available."

He laid the sheets on the desk, facing Silas.

"But I am willing to let you read them, under my supervision, of course."

Silas tried not to grab. His hands shook as he read. At the top were the first nuggets. The woman's fake name was Capulet and her fake address matched that on her driver's license. Silas smiled. The fictitious name came from the Shakespearian play *Romeo and Juliet* about the ill-fated couple who killed themselves because they could never be together. Nice touch. Car rental rules required two pieces of ID. Attached to the sheet was a scan of her fake driver's license. The picture matched that of Angela Messina perfectly. In the right-hand margin was a series of numbers and letters that clearly came from a passport. While Angela probably wasn't happy about giving up this information, she had no choice. Silas pulled out his note pad and started writing quickly. You never knew when the manager might want to cut the session short.

On page two, he wanted to reach over and embrace Mr. Fawnstock. The car return date was the day after she and Michael Franklin supposedly committed suicide.

"Mr. Fawnstock, just to be clear, it appears the car was returned on time."

He leaned over, turned the contract to face him, and read quickly.

"Yes, that's correct. You can see the time stamp. There were no additional charges."

He turned the document back around to face Silas.

There was more.

Expected return time: Early morning.
Return location: Seattle-Tacoma International Airport
Airline and final destination: United Airlines. BZE

BZE? He did not recognize the airport code, but he would soon.

Silas was feeling lightheaded, but it was important now to downplay it. He sighed again.

"Well, Mr. Fawnstock, I guess that helps. I'm not sure what information I thought I was going to get, but boy, talk about a needle in a haystack."

He stood, slowly, sad.

"But look, you lived up to your end of the bargain and I have to thank you for that. I'll just keep grinding away. Hopefully these people are out there in the world somewhere."

He shook the manager's hand with both of his.

"No problem, Mr. Marker, always happy to help. Oh and…"

He looked at his desk drawer where he had deposited the cash.

Silas frowned and shook his head. Mr. Fawnstock nodded.

Silas nearly ran to his car where he had his portable computer. Where the hell was BZE?

Chapter 21

The lights flickered, as Ivan seemed to jump down his apartment stairs.

His landlord would have something to say to him about the noise, but he didn't care. Charlie had just called. He said Betty was "thrilled" with their new partnership. Ivan doubted very much that was true, but it did not matter. Charlie said he only needed to visit the bank. An action as simple as picking up the mail would save Ivan's life.

He had Charlie's money.

When he undid his three deadbolts and emerged onto the sidewalk, it was a bright sunny morning, the city air was unusually clean and he thought he could actually hear birds singing!

Hairy Hands was leaning against the brick wall, waiting for him. He moved over, put his arm around Ivan's shoulder, and diverted his direction towards a quiet alley, away from the traffic.

"Let's take a walk."

When they got into the alley, the man stopped and faced Ivan. He hadn't shaved in days and the darkness of the alleyway highlighted the yellow stains on his teeth.

"How did the meetin' go? Don't lie to me, numb nuts, or I'll kill ya right here."

Ivan leaned up for support against one of the grimy walls decorated in gang insignia.

"Oh, it went well. He…"

"How much, fuck face?"

"Ah, twenty-five thousand. He said he'd lend me twenty-five thousand to help me out of my jam."

Hairy Hand's eyes narrowed.

"That's it? He can't give ya more? Did ya ask him for thirty-five? How much money does he got?"

Ivan felt like he might fall over. He seemed only to have the strength to whisper.

"No, yes, oh, I don't know. Please, I will get more. I just need time."

His adversary stood up, reached into his pocket and pulled out a stained piece of paper.

"Transfer da money into dat account. Ya got three days. Miss the deadline and ya're a headline."

Charlie waited in front of the bank manager and tried, without being obvious, to take measured breaths.

He was in a "meeting room" created by modest drywall supported by thin metal frames. He sat in a chair covered in black vinyl material. The manager, who had put on his tan suit jacket for the consultation, offered him coffee or water. Charlie looked at the man's fresh face and smile. His voice and handshake were modest, Charlie thought. It made him seem young, certainly younger than him.

"My goodness, Charles, how long has it been? It's wonderful to see you again. How is Elizabeth keeping?"

Charlie thought the last time he'd entered the branch was when he and Betty opened up their checking accounts. He knew he had never met this manager before and, judging by his use of the names "Charles" and "Elizabeth," he, them. He must have just looked at their records.

The manager leaned forward over the desk.

"Now then, what can we do for you today?"

Charlie cleared his throat before speaking.

"I need… I'd like a loan, please."

"Yes sir, of course we can certainly help you with that."

He reached into a drawer and pulled out a pre-printed form. Pen poised, he said, "I just need a bit of information and you'll be on your way in no time. Now, what were you thinking? A line of credit for paying down monthly credit card balances perhaps. They're very popular these days because of those high interest rates the credit card companies charge. Five thousand is a common amount, but, if your credit situation is solid, I could probably get ten thousand easily approved."

Charlie shifted in his seat, cleared his throat again and took a sip of water.

"I need seventy-five thousand."

The manager's eyes widened a bit and he sat up.

"Oh... I see. That is a different type of loan. The line of credit is unsecured, backed only by your promise to repay. For the amount you just mentioned, an asset, likely your home would have to secure the loan. In effect, you'd be taking out a mortgage. Just guessing about property values in your area, and assuming your home does not currently have any encumbrances on it, I think you'd be fine."

Charlie said, "I had a real estate agent ask me once if we wanted to sell. She said it was worth two hundred thousand."

"That's valuable input, Charles." As the manager spoke, he removed the initial form and replaced it with another. "In either case, we need some information. Let's start with the intended use of the loan. Theoretically, if you ask my opinion, we shouldn't have to ask that, but you know the banks these days. I would guess, for that amount of money, you've decided on some home renovations. That's very wise. Many clients are doing that."

He paused and Charlie realized he was waiting for an answer.

"Oh, yes, right, home renovation, that's what the loan is for."

After several more questions, Charlie could feel the tension in his neck start to ease. He was going to get the money and the process was easier than he thought it would be.

The manager continued. He had pulled a desk-top calculator from another drawer.

"It is a great time to borrow money with interest rates so low. The computer will confirm this, but by my calculations a seventy-five thousand dollar mortgage amortized over twenty-five years with a fixed five-year rate of four-point-eight percent would only cost four hundred and twenty-five dollars per month."

Charlie started to say that he certainly wouldn't need the loan for twenty-five years; he hoped to pay it all back within twelve months. Then he realized that a loan for a *renovation* would, in fact, likely be outstanding much longer than that. He didn't want to explain.

After a few more entries, the manger turned the form around for Charlie to sign.

"All right, Charles, we're almost good to go. All we need is for Elizabeth to come in and co-sign the loan application."

Charlie caught his breath.

"Betty?"

The manager chuckled.

"Yes, of course. I am assuming the house is in both your names."

Charlie forced a smile.

"Oh, yes, of course."

"Right. And then we just need a letter confirming your current occupation and salary from your present employer and you can bring on the hammers!"

Chapter 22

Ivan now had another reason to hurry over to Charlie's. He wanted to set the wheels in motion before either his new partner lost his nerve or Betty found more of hers. In addition, he had only three days—seventy two hours—to make a twenty-five thousand dollar deposit.

The newspaper inside Ivan's apartment had made two things clear. Hairy Hands was a murderer, and he had access to his apartment. After his "discussion" with the thug, Ivan went back upstairs and packed as many clothes into a single suitcase as he could. He imagined someone was still watching him, but he didn't care. He had to get out. His home was no longer safe. They could easily kill him in his sleep if they wanted to. Walking at an angle away from the front of the convenience store window, so his landlords would not see him, he hailed a cab. On his way to Betty and Charlie's house, he replayed his story in his mind. He would phone Betty on the way, saying he had a terrible sleep because construction had started right next to his apartment. Could he stay with them for a few weeks in the basement bedroom? Just until they were done with the jackhammers? He and Charlie would be working closely together now anyway.

It wasn't the reception he hoped for. Betty was waiting at the front door, frowning, with her arms crossed. She started to fire up the conversation Ivan wanted to avoid. She didn't even appear to notice his bag. He ducked in quickly behind her towards the basement door. Charlie had told him he had set up for his new job down there.

"Don't worry, Betty. Everything will go great, you'll see. Just trust me."

Charlie was already sitting at his workstation staring into the screen. He'd set up an old folding rectangular table against a wall made of unfinished drywall. He'd positioned his computer screen on top of two old telephone books with the keyboard and mouse in front and a printer off to the right. He'd placed the computer case on the floor and pushed it to the side—as far as the wires would allow—for leg room. He found an extending table lamp and screwed it onto the table's side. He tried to stuff as many of the wires in behind the screen as he could.

Ivan sat in the chair next to him, amused by the equipment set up and surprised that Charlie wasn't smiling. Perhaps his new partner was nervous. He rubbed his hands together.

"OK, Charlie. This is awesome. Let's get right to it. The first thing is to set up your own online account. I just need to pull up the required forms and you can enter all your information. Then we're good to go."

Charlie's lips moved quietly.

"The bank wouldn't give me the loan."

Ivan felt slightly dizzy, as if he might faint. He whispered, "What? Why? What happened?"

"I told them we were renovating. I didn't think they'd give me the money if I said 'day-trading'. They said we'd need a mortgage on our house and that Betty had to sign for it, too. Ivan, I haven't told her that I'm borrowing money to do this. She's already upset enough. Also, the manager said I'd have to get a letter from my current employer."

Both men now stared hopelessly into the computer screen. Ivan hadn't realized Charlie would have to mortgage his house. That put the risk of their venture into the stratosphere. Ivan could live with the idea that he and Charlie could—temporarily—lose money. But with a mortgage that required regular monthly payments, they could end up forfeiting their home.

"Ivan, I still really want to do this. I saw something on TV, an advertisement for a company that will lend you money 'if the bank turns you down.' I pulled up their website. The interest rate is like ten percent minimum and they want a five percent fee up front, but they said they reject no one. They automatically deduct the required monthly payment so, to start, I could just leave some of the seventy-five thousand in the account until we started making regular money. Then I wouldn't have to worry about missing any payments. What do you think of that?"

Ivan knew the ultimate cost of these loans could be triple or more what a bank would charge, particularly when Charlie couldn't produce a letter of employment. It was a terrible avenue, reserved usually for people with the worst credit. Although they would not call it a mortgage, with the personal guarantee Charlie would have to give, he could still be forced to sell his house. Ivan knew catastrophe often resulted when people used borrowed money to make required payments on borrowed money.

It was a terrible decision, but Ivan would not stop him. He reminded himself; after all, whatever loan Charlie secured would be transitory, minimizing the actual cost of the higher interest rates. It was certainly a better option than borrowing from the mob as he had.

Besides, he was out of choices—and time.

"Under the circumstances, Charlie, I think that's an excellent idea."

Later that day, the money now secure, they sat by the same computer as Charlie carefully read each line of the application form. Ivan wanted to say something sarcastic like "this is how the dinosaurs became extinct," but Charlie was his man now. He made sure his new partner registered the account in his own name, with no mention of Ivan. Ivan wasn't sure about the mob's technological ability, but once they realized he had left his apartment, they would search for him. If they could infiltrate the firewalls of online trading platforms, their search would miss someone with the last name Gray.

Besides, there was the odd trade that Ivan would make using inside information—when the gift sometimes came to him. Insider trading was a felony offense. For safety's sake, better the account in Charlie's name.

Charlie pulled his hands away from the keyboard.

"Ivan, just a minute. They want a lot of very personal information—my birth date, where I was born, my social security number, *Betty's* social security number, my passport information, my income, and my assets. I don't want to tell them all of that."

Ivan raised his shoulders to his ears and opened his hands to face the ceiling.

"Hey, Charlie, ever since 9/11 and the 2008 market meltdown, the government has put in all kinds of rules. They just want to make sure you're not planning to fund some terrorist activity or commit a felony. There's all kind of ways bad people try to use the stock market."

Laughing, he added, "You weren't planning any big-ass crimes now, were you, Charlie?"

Charlie wasn't smiling.

"I'm sorry, Ivan, I am not comfortable giving out that information and I know Betty wouldn't be, either."

Ivan stared. This couldn't fall through, not now. He lowered his voice.

"Charlie, this is the world we live in today. If you want a credit card or a car loan, you got to give them what they ask for."

Charlie stared at the screen.

"Well, maybe that's why I don't have either of those things."

He turned his head to face Ivan.

"Oh yeah, that reminds me. You said I had to give the government something, what was it called, capital? Why is that again? And how much is it anyway?"

"You're not *giving* them anything. The exchange just wants to make sure it's dealing with fiscally capable people. It's fifty thousand dollars, remember?"

Charlie pushed his chair away from the table.

"*What*! Oh my God, you didn't tell me that. That's a lot of money, Ivan. I had no idea. Now I'm not so sure I want to go ahead with this."

It was a crossroad. Ivan sat quietly for a moment to consider the best approach. Honesty was out of the question. In situations like this, you had to size up your adversary quickly. Charlie, Charlie, Charlie. Not a big fan of change. Basically boring. Married to the same woman forever. He worked at a job he hated for years, but didn't have the nerve to quit. He avoided confrontation.

He chose to be intimidated.

Ivan got up to pace around the room, pushing his chair away in mock frustration.

"You know what, Charlie? You're starting to make me mad. Aren't you the guy who *begged* me to help him? You assured me you knew what you were getting yourself into and now you say 'I had no idea.' Is this a joke to you, Charlie? Some sort of game? Well it isn't to me. This is my *profession.* Yeah, these forms are new… to you. But you've never had a brokerage account before either. This is the way it's done. You went on and on about me teaching you all you need to know. Well, that actually *is* a joke. You don't even trust me. And yes I *did* tell you that you'd have to lodge capital. I also told you you'd get it back when you were done, which by the looks of things is going to happen sooner rather than later."

Charlie's face was white.

"I don't have time for this garbage. You got two choices. Maybe you should do what you told me Betty said. Go back to kissing your boss' ass, *after* you apologize. You think he treated you bad before? He's going to stand on his desk as he pisses all over you now. Or why don't you get back to filling out the fucking form, which is a legal *requirement* if you want to trade stocks. If not, I'm done."

Charlie closed his eyes.

Chapter 23

Belize! The day after they "died," Angela Messina and Michael Franklin appeared to have taken a flight from Sea-Tac Airport, under assumed names and using fake passports, and travelled to the Philip S. W. Goldson Airport—code BZE—near Belize City. It was a beautiful, remote country known for its isolated beaches and favorable tax laws. It was a fantastic hiding place.

It was also famous for illegal immigration. Silas spent hours researching the country and its history, focusing on how a US expatriate could come to live there with the least fuss and exposure possible. Even the country's immigration minister was quoted as saying that, though the majority of his people were honest, a fifteen thousand dollar cash payment to secure a residency permit "could tempt some."

All the evidence was lining up with Silas' theory. That's what the couple must have done. They probably immigrated using a second set of fake ID's just to cloud the trail further. That's if they were forced to use any ID at all. Therefore, there was little point in Silas trying to influence a government official. They likely couldn't trace the couple if they wanted to.

This might take some time. The country was eighty-eight hundred square miles and had over three hundred and twenty-five thousand citizens. However, now with the additional supporting evidence, Silas could refine his thinking, based on the facts, and narrow down his search area.

Fact 1: The couple absolutely wanted as much seclusion from people as possible. They were, after all, supposedly dead. Identification was their Achilles heel. This eliminated the largest cities from the search list, which was a benefit in itself. In effect, their desire for isolation made them easier to find. Silas also assumed that the couple would choose to live on a secluded beach rather than next to the rain forest and its howler monkeys and various species of carnivorous cats. Silas Googled *Best beaches in Belize.*

Three came back: Ambergris Caye, Placencia and, touted as the smallest choice, Caye Caulker. The last community was only five miles long with thirteen hundred residents. There were no cars and people moved around on foot or by water. The headline read, "If you thought Ambergris Caye was laid back, Caye Caulker is completely asleep."

Silas noted the number of the local real-estate agency. How else would the secretive couple find a place to live? Apparently, there was only one in this area.

Fact 2: As a result of Fact 1, the couple would never apply for a driver's license, own a car, boat or home or open a bank account. Cash-only defined their lives. They would rent and perhaps hire a staff for security and maintenance, cleaning, and shopping for food. Taxi would be their only means of travel.

A truly cash-only existence… Cash! Even though they likely had their money safely stored in an off-shore account, they would still need to go to the bank to initiate wire transfers and get cash to pay for their living expenses.

He'd start by showing their pictures along with the inheritance story to the real-estate agency. The banks would not offer information freely because clearly one of the major attractions was for people to hide themselves and their money. But eventually the couple would have to physically enter a bank building to get cash. How many banks could there be?

It wasn't much to go on, but it was a start. If he had to sit in front of a bank under the shade of a palm tree for a while, well, he had had worse stakeouts.

First things first. If the local officials were used to an "entry fee" of fifteen thousand dollars, it was likely that many others were on the take, too. He was going to need a lot more money to buy expensive information.

He emailed Sandy to give her the good news.

Chapter 24

Ivan realized he might have gone too far. Charlie still stared at the partially completed form that he didn't want to finish on the computer screen.

"Hey, Charlie, you know what? That wasn't called for. I've... been under a lot of pressure lately. When you run your own show, you gotta be chief cook and bottle washer, right?"

He pulled up closer, speaking to the side of his partner's face.

"I apologize. I guess I've forgotten what it felt like to bare your soul to these guys, it was so long ago. It is unnerving the first time you fill out the forms, but anyone who has ever traded on the market knows it's the law. You have to trust me, brother. I wouldn't ask you otherwise. But look, if you don't want to go ahead, I understand. No problem."

Ivan prayed the image of Charlie's boss standing on his desk pissing on him had sunk in.

Charlie continued to stare at the screen as he spoke.

"That's all right, Ivan. I guess change is hard on anybody and you're right, I did say all those things to you. I certainly don't think that you or your job is a joke."

"Look at it this way, Charlie. By making people provide all that information—and the capital—the exchanges are trying to keep criminal or unprofessional behaviour out. That is good for the people who trade."

Ivan thought to himself... unless you use another person as your front.

After Charlie had completed the form, Ivan took control of the keyboard.

"It'll take them a day or two to program you in, but let's go ahead and set up your online trading account. We can get all the money in place now. I will look after lodging the necessary capital with the regulators."

Right in front of Charlie's eyes, Ivan transferred twenty-five thousand dollars to the account number Hairy Hands had given him. Ivan knew, and Charlie didn't, that there was no requirement by the exchange to transfer any money anywhere. They simply required a minimum twenty-five thousand balance in the account.

"There, that's done. But we don't need to just sit idly by while some civil servant bides their time. Let's start your training right now. I've been thinking about the best way for this to work. You definitely have a lot to learn. But rather than sit here for a month while I teach you, why not just start right in trading? At first, I'll explain everything to you as I go along. Over time, you'll start to understand and I'll hand you the wheel. That's how they teach kids to drive a car, right?"

Charlie was grinning again.

"Excellent, Ivan. That sounds excellent."

"OK, here goes. Using my research technique, I have already identified my, uh our, first trade. It's a junior drug research company called Integrated Pharma Development Corporation. They are into Phase III trials for a drug that will *cure* MS! Apparently, the investing public thinks that the final announcement of full FDA approval for the drug is overdue. The stock is down twenty percent from the all-time high. I went back, did my homework, and found out that the Phase I and II trials went great. That's why the stock was doing so well. Now, just because there is some delay in government paperwork, everyone gets nervous. That's when I smell money! This one falls right into line with my investment philosophy."

Charlie scratched the back of his neck.

"Investment philosophy? What's that?"

Ivan didn't want to slow down, but he realized it wouldn't take much to scare Charlie again. The account needed approval before they could trade anyway.

"Great question. It is how you pick a stock. Your investment philosophy is something you develop over time. As we go on, you will learn about yourself and discover what you are comfortable with. Some guys want to find the hot stories and just climb aboard the train. Technical types look for stocks that have broken out. Then there are the quant guys that just pour numbers into a computer and it tells them what to buy. There's no shortage of ways to do it. Each one is sort of like a religion, if you think about it. You just have to find the one that works for you."

Ivan watched, as Charlie seemed to hang on every word. He'd intentionally used as many clichés as he could to increase the chance that Charlie would latch onto one that sounded good. But his protégé's eyes seemed to glaze over when he said, "Climb aboard the train."

"OK, I understand, I guess. Which philosophy is ours?"

Ivan smiled.

"Not *our* philosophy, Charlie, yours. For now, you'll watch me using mine. Eventually, you will decide if you are comfortable with it. Maybe you'll adopt it as your own."

Charlie was waiting.

"I am a *contrarian*. I start every day looking at the 'new lows' list. I like to find *stories* that people are afraid of; the worse the news the better."

Charlie put the palm of his hand over his chin.

"Remember I said your investment philosophy was something you believed in. I have a famous quote always rattling in my head. Baron Rothschild said it in the seventeen hundreds, I think. You've heard of the Rothschild family, right? *Serious* coin. He said, 'The time to buy is when there's blood in the streets.' Apparently he made a fortune buying everything he could during the panic that followed the Battle of Waterloo. *That's* how I invest."

The actual quote finished with the words 'especially when the blood is your own,' but Ivan chose to omit that.

Blood in the streets. Charlie couldn't get the image out of his mind. Ivan's investment philosophy aligned with capitalizing on terror and chaos. This day-trading stuff really was serious and Ivan was totally committed to it. That's why he became upset about filling out the silly forms. This was no joke and he realized now what a huge act of generosity it was for Ivan to take him under his wing.

"The next thing you need to learn, Charlie, is options. It's a bit complicated, so I'll just give you the basics. Let's say you go to a furniture store, see something you like, but you don't want to buy it now. Maybe you're too busy, or don't have the money, whatever. A smart salesman says 'No problem. I will give you the *option* to buy this item at the price you see today for three months. Even if the actual price in the store rises, you can buy it for today's price.' After three months, your option expires worthless. If you decide to use your option, it's called *exercising*."

Charlie nodded his head. He understood that. The furniture companies advertised that sort of thing on TV all the time.

"Options are common in the stock market. They give you the right to buy a stock at a set price for a set period of time. But in the stock market, no one gives them to you; you have to pay for them. And, once you buy them, you can sell them. Still with me?"

"I think so, but... that's allowed?"

Ivan laughed.

"Absolutely. We're going to use options on this trade! Let me show you a calculation and you'll understand why. The drug company stock we're thinking about is currently trading at twenty dollars per share. The chat lines are saying that when the FDA approves the drug, the stock could easily go to thirty dollars or higher. If we bought the stock at twenty and sold it for thirty, what is our gain?"

"Well, you'd make ten dollars on your twenty dollar investment. That would total fifty percent, right?"

Ivan nodded his head.

"Yep. If we bought ten thousand dollars worth of stock, we would make five thousand in profit. Not too shabby."

Charlie smiled. He was pleased with himself that he came up with the right answer. And that return wasn't too shabby at all.

"But instead of buying the stock at twenty dollars per share, you could purchase an *option* that gave you the *right* to buy the stock at twenty dollars per share for three weeks. I won't try to explain option pricing, but just trust me that today you could buy that option for two dollars per share."

Charlie still nodded his head. Ivan hoped he was still with him.

"We just talked about buying the stock at twenty and having it rise to thirty for a fifty percent gain, right? Let's see how the same scenario works using options. Let's say we paid two dollars for the right to buy the stock at twenty dollars for three weeks, and before the option expired, the stock rose to thirty dollars. Calculate what would happen to the price of the option."

Charlie couldn't.

"Remember I said that the option itself had a value of two dollars. Since this thing gives me the right to buy the stock at twenty dollars, and if the market price of the stock rose by ten dollars, the value of the option would go up in lock step, also by ten dollars. The option we paid two dollars for would now be worth twelve dollars. Calculate the percentage return on that."

Charlie shook his head. "I can't."

Ivan was beaming.

"Think of it like this, then. If we made the same ten thousand investment using options instead of stock, buying five thousand options at two dollars each, our options value would now total sixty thousand. That is, five thousand options that would trade for twelve dollars. Our *profit* is fifty thousand dollars!"

Charlie's eyes bulged as he mouthed the words *fifty thousand dollars.*

"On the street, it's called a five-bagger."

Chapter 25

Sandy read Silas' email with the good and bad news.

He led off with the positive. The police never had access to Angela's computer, but he did. She smiled at his comment that maybe they should use Benjamin Franklin's picture—on a one-hundred dollar bill—when they investigated. There was just a single piece of evidence that mattered on the hard drive, he said, but it was huge. He had followed it to the next lead, and that too appeared solid. He said the odds of getting two solid leads in a row—the police had spent months with no luck—were like a baseball team hitting two grand-slam home runs in the same inning. Not impossible, but highly unlikely.

Silas told her he was beginning to accept her "wacky" scenario. There were still many ways the trail could turn cold but, on the other hand, he'd run into nothing yet that refuted her plausible speculation that Angela and Michael were alive and well.

So, he said, he would continue down the yellow brick road in search of Oz.

Then he delivered the bad news. He told her that the couple *might* have flown to a remote country. He didn't mention which one or even the geographic region. She speculated that their possible whereabouts was his bargaining chip. When he'd given her his original estimate, he had never expected the search to go this far. To find two people, hiding in every way they could in a remote country, would be a far more expensive prospect.

Sandy had to fight back her tears of joy. She'd always believed they were still alive, but having an independent source partially verify that was more comforting than she had realized. There still was a shadow of doubt, but light was infiltrating its cloud.

But there was a potential new storm on the horizon. When she had formed her plan, she had plenty of money. Silas would want more. She decided to use the rest of her phone time to log in to her accounts.

She knew how much she had by heart, but she just wanted to make sure.

Before the Feds busted her for her involvement in the Ponzi scheme, Sandy had made a regular practice of changing her real money into digital Bitcoins through one of the many currency exchange services that had mushroomed around the world. She could easily change these—online using her phone—into good old-fashioned American dollars which people like Officer Hicks, Silas or other sources would require.

She had decided to create two digital "wallets" to hold her Bitcoins, and house the electronic files inside one of the largest Bitcoin marketplaces. With the high volume of Bitcoin transactions in that arena, liquidity and transaction speed were virtually assured.

She called up the host website to access her wallets and make sure everything was in order.

An unusual message appeared on the first page:

Important note to clients. While the exchange makes every effort to ensure security without sacrificing anonymity, periodically hackers attempt to access secure wallets or otherwise interfere with Bitcoin transactions. We believe that the security of our site may have been recently compromised through the identification of an obscure anomaly in the software protocol. We are making every effort to confirm this, and, if so, identify the offending parties and recover any missing Bitcoins. We apologize for any inconvenience and will provide updates as they become available.

Sandy's fingers raced. She knew Bitcoins were not completely safe. Without a central bank supporting the currency, the desire for total anonymity came with increased risk. But what choice did a convict living in prison, hiding two hundred thousand dollars of stolen money, have? She had heard about one theft a while ago for about one hundred million, but no one was sure if it was actually a theft or just a series of transactions because everything was always stealthy. Her two wallets were at only one hundred thousand each, small by Bitcoin standards. Scammers were far more likely to go after the big money. That greatly reduced her own risk.

At least that's what she thought.

She called up her first wallet and sighed when she saw that her coins were intact. There were just the two recent transactions, the exchange for US dollars she had transferred to the guard and Silas.

She called up the second account and dropped the phone.

The balance was zero.

She picked up the phone and re-entered the account access codes.

Zero. There had been one transaction one week ago transferring all of her coins in this wallet, one hundred thousand dollars' worth, to another account. There was a series of numbers and letters. She tried to open that account.

Access denied. Incorrect login information.

"Mother fu—"

The guard appeared around the corner. She hadn't heard him coming.

"That's all for today then, Allen. Hey, you OK? You look like something crawled up your ass and died."

Her hands shaking, Sandy handed him the phone.

Chapter 26

Ivan wasted no time.

Fifteen minutes after receiving the email approving Charlie's online account, Ivan entered the order to buy five thousand options on the Integrated Pharma Development Corporation at two dollars each, strike price twenty dollars, expiry three weeks. The looming expiration date did not concern him at all because the company's announcement was imminent. The option price would fly. He could taste it.

With this one trade, he would pay off the mob for good. He was days, if not hours, away from freedom. Maybe he would buy that BMW after all. He could visualize the vanity license plates—OPTNS.

Charlie seemed good with it all, which was a bonus, but Ivan knew why. He clearly did not appreciate the risk. But he did worry about the size of the investment.

"Ivan, I trust you, but ten thousand dollars is more than ten percent of the money I borrowed to invest. What if something goes wrong?"

Ivan wanted to respond that, since he'd already given the mob their chunk, that percentage was much higher. But the point his partner was making was valid, and he had to acknowledge that. Investors shouldn't put all their eggs in one basket. All day-traders knew the universal rule of thumb to never risk more than one percent of your capital on a single trade. Their next trade should have been for five hundred dollars, not ten thousand.

But this one... sometimes you just had to step up to the plate.

"Normally, Charlie I'd agree with you. But you don't see slam dunks like this very often. I'll tell you what. I wanted you to have all the benefit of the first big win, but to help you sleep better I'll cover you for half. So you and I both have five thousand at risk. Does that make it better?"

He lied. Charlie's money was virtually all they had, but hopefully his partner would never know.

Charlie and Betty let Ivan live in their basement, accepting the story about construction around his apartment. Ivan knew the mob followed him here, but he hoped with the additional witnesses around, he would have the time he needed. He couldn't show his face outside again until he had the rest of their money. Since he hadn't been around his apartment for a few days—his landlords wouldn't hear him walking on the floor above—they might wonder if he was skipping out on this month's rent. He envisioned them tossing his remaining clothes into the Goodwill bin.

Please God, let this trade free me.

At dinner, Betty asked about their new stock market business and Ivan suggested that Charlie explain the merits of their first trade. He butchered the part about options, but Ivan didn't expect Betty to get it anyway. He knew most people were intimidated by the market, and would rather just listen than risk looking stupid. That was working in his favor.

The one thing Betty did understand was the ten thousand dollars.

"You know, Ivan, I hardly understood a word of what Charlie just said. Listening to him talk, I'm not sure he did either. This is all moving pretty quickly. But ten thousand dollars? That is an awful lot of money. I know you're an expert and everything, but did you need to spend that much?"

Ivan smiled.

"Betty, thank you for that. I don't like to toot my own horn, but I am *very* experienced at this. I will treat Charlie's money like my own, and we're in this fifty/fifty. Besides, we've *invested* the money, not *spent* it, like you said."

There was no corporate news release by Friday. Ivan thought the company obviously wanted to get as much publicity as possible by making its announcement at the beginning of the trading week. He was right. Monday at nine thirty-five a.m. the "blockbuster" news hit the tape.

…Integrated Pharma Development Corporation announces that the FDA has denied its patent application for a new MS drug based on Phase III clinical trial results, citing dangerous side effects.

…Several trial participants reportedly suffered strokes.

Ivan started slamming keys, but it was no use. The exchange had halted trading in the stock and the options for ninety minutes to ensure all investors were armed with the same information.

Charlie had been looking over his shoulder.

"That's our stock, isn't it, Ivan? The big drug they were working on wasn't approved? What? You were so sure. Now what happens? Will they reapply or something?"

Ivan knew the company would scrutinize the results and check the potential to alter the drug's properties. They had likely spent hundreds of millions so far, so they wouldn't just walk away until they'd tried everything. But that scenario could take years to play out.

The options expired in two weeks.

Ninety minutes later, the first trade on the shares was for fifteen dollars, down five dollars from the last price. Ivan hadn't described what happened to option prices when the stock went *down*. In a matter of seconds, their ten thousand dollar investment was worth two hundred and fifty dollars.

"That's not very good news, is it? Maybe we should sell our options."

Ivan wouldn't look Charlie's way.

"Charlie, if we sold now, the proceeds wouldn't even cover the commission. I'm sorry, partner."

"But wait a minute, Ivan. Three days ago this was worth ten thousand dollars. It's got to be—"

"Zero, Charlie. Gone. It's all gone."

Ivan heard what sounded like the beginning of a sob. He turned to see Charlie, eyes closed, holding his head in his hands.

"Don't tell Betty," he whispered.

Chapter 27

Like a punch to Sandy's throat.

Hard! She grabbed the chair. The room spun.

Her foundation had just collapsed into a sinkhole. She had committed to making payments of as much as one hundred thousand dollars to Silas and the guard could be another sixty thousand. Now she no longer had the money. When the payments to the guard stopped, the phone would disappear and Silas would wave goodbye.

Then she truly would spend the rest of her life behind bars.

Deep, slow breaths, finding her base. Logic, structure. She was still in the game. She had a plan. It just needed some *adjustments.*

She sat in the chair and stared into her palms. She could make the money back trading— she was sure of that—but there was no way to open a brokerage account from inside. The hacker was a complication she hadn't seen coming. If a person sitting in front of a computer could so easily drain funds out of her one Bitcoin wallet, what was to keep them from coming after the other? These things weren't as safe as she thought, but the idea of converting everything back into dollars and opening a bank account was out of the question. Both a brokerage and a bank account would require her social security number, which belonged to a convicted felon. Even if they did give her an account, they would eventually figure it out and seize her assets.

Nothing sounded good. She looked around her as if to find an answer. Her eyes settled on a tattered paperback in the stacks.

Using Your Contacts for Personal Gain

What a stupid book to have in a prison. It was meant for people on the outside. The only contact that mattered here was your lawyer and there was no "personal gain," other than surviving. In jail, you were cut off from the world and existed in a cruel imitation of real life.

The title made her think, though. She needed to trade to raise money. She couldn't open a brokerage account from inside. She hated the thought of relying on someone else because, over the years, every time she did, she regretted it. Her new *associate* would need naïveté or poor moral standards and her list of potentials was short. Hicks, a former cop, didn't qualify because the only sure way she knew to beat the market was illegal. Besides, he might ask *why* she needed this new outside account and she didn't want to go near that question. Silas represented the same problem. If he learned she wanted market access, his natural level of suspicion would soar. He might assume she'd lied about her cash resources and ask for more money, faster—that she no longer had.

There was that crazy Russian CEO and his insider trading plan from several years ago, but he was reckless and almost got them both busted. Besides, he'd been deported somewhere. She scratched him off the list. There was Blackie, the old head trader she worked with. He had, unsuccessfully hit on her before. Maybe if she held out the possibility, he could more than fulfill her needs. But he was probably too honest and definitely no one's fool. There was that David Heart guy, the wet-behind-the-ears research analyst, but he apparently had gone over to the dark side and now worked in compliance. He was far too respectable for her needs. Michael Franklin's father died so he was of no use either. That was a shame. She'd slept with him. She could have used that against him.

She grimaced as the head count call came over the PA system. There was that stock broker Michael Franklin used to work with at MOGI Investments. She remembered meeting him at some corporate function. His greasy hair stuck in her mind. He flat-out told Sandy that he would eventually take over Michael's book of business that he had inherited from his father, whether he liked it or not. He said he was only thinking about the clients' well-being. Right. Bullshit. Then he suggested they "get together" some time, perhaps when Michael was out of town, even though he and everyone else thought she and Michael were a couple. He was a ballsy, unethical man who didn't care about "rules."

He could be the perfect candidate, if she could only remember his fucking name! She had to hurry now, back to her cell. It was some weird handle that began with a vowel. It was not "U." Oliver? No. Allen? Yes! No, but it was close. Evan... ?

IVAN!

The guard looked at her funny as the cell door closed. Most people didn't grin when they got locked up.

The next day, when Sandy got the phone in her corner, she waited until she was sure no one could hear. She called Fifty States Investments in Seattle where Ivan last worked and learned that he'd *left the firm*. She knew that likely meant he was toasted. Based on the Ivan she remembered, if true, that was no surprise. The person on the line said she wasn't sure, but thought he had relocated to New York City. In Sandy's mind, Ivan got fired and couldn't find a local job so he moved across the country. Greener pastures and a fresh face—and fewer people would know of his past.

It was, after all, what she did, just in the other direction.

She had no way of knowing whether this scenario was even close to the truth, but she could hope.

Hope was now an important part of her plan.

The Internet provided numerous ways to find a person. Sandy thought one website that Ivan likely enrolled in was LinkedIn, the online E-commerce application. In her search description, she included as many words she could think of that Ivan might have put on his resume. She even put in the phrase "Investment Manager" because, even though he was nowhere close to having the qualifications, he probably used the title anyway. She knew there was little chance of success, trying to find a single person in the world, but she also knew she didn't have a better idea.

Sandy hit the "search" key, and, within seconds, almost laughed aloud. She looked at the words on her screen as if they were a foreign language.

She found Ivan's online resume!

Her face was now inches away from the screen. According to the website, Ivan was self-employed, listing "day-trading" as a skill. That would not immediately impress anyone who understood the markets. It was a losing proposition for most people. It looked easy but…

If Ivan had trouble finding work, and potentially lost money day-trading from home, he would likely at least consider her plan. He was becoming an increasingly attractive option.

There was no address, just *New York metropolitan area,* and no phone number or email contact. Wasn't that the point of LinkedIn? She would have thought that someone like Ivan, trying to find work, would have listed as many connection points as possible. Instead there was only a "Contact me through LinkedIn" tab. It was as if Ivan wanted to screen who could associate with him. Interesting. He could be hiding behind a hyperspace protective wall.

From what or whom? She would find out. She typed in her message.

Oh, hey there, Ivan. It's a voice from your past! Sandy Allen ... or, as you first met me, Jennifer Salem. I've been trying to reach out to you. All I see is that you have listed day-trading as a skill and you don't appear to work anywhere else, which is an amazing coincidence, because that's what I do... or did.

She didn't know how much time she had before the guard came back, so she got right to the point. There was no way to ease into this discussion.

Ivan, I'm sure you know my story, and where I am now. There's a lot more to it than most people realize. Maybe we'll get into that someday. I will say, though, that in prison, you have a lot of time to reflect on your mistakes and I've certainly made my share. One of them, I realize, was with you. I was interested in getting to know you better after the first time we spoke, but then my hands were kind of tied, right? With Michael Franklin having killed himself, obviously that is no longer a problem.

I know this is way out from left field, but I've been thinking about this—and you. Why am I contacting you now, after all this time? Well, some things have happened that have given me a real wake-up call. This morning, I just told myself, life is short so why not reach for it all? Besides, I've been afraid—afraid that you wouldn't respond given who and what I am now. I really hope you will, though. It would hurt me if you didn't. This place is full of weird people, both the good guys and the bad. I'm desperate to communicate with a real man.

Then she signed off, *XOXO, Sandy*.

She hoped that using the words "desperate" and "man" in the same sentence would make him think, "hey, why not?" Sexting had grown in popularity in the digital age. She hit the "send" button and gently placed the phone down on the table.

Now she could only wait.

Chapter 28

Ivan pretended losing money like that was part of the day-trading process.

And maybe it was, but not for those that *succeeded* at it.

He told Charlie that, in day-trading, the wins were often as unpredictable as the losses. His partner responded with a weak smile.

"I guess we didn't lose *all* my money. We'll get the next one, right?"

Ivan agreed and then quickly shifted gears, telling Charlie he had to go out, but his lesson for today was to research their next stock. Charlie's shoulders seemed to sag, but then he straightened up a bit. That was a good sign. Ivan knew it was critical not to let him focus on their adversity because he might get scared and bail. That truly would end everything.

When he reached the top of the basement stairs, Ivan didn't accept Betty's offer for lunch. He was sure she would quiz him relentlessly and he needed air. Charlie's seventy-five thousand was disappearing fast. Twenty-five went to the mob, they needed to keep their minimum account balance at twenty-five, and they lost ten grand on their first trade. The mob said he still owed another ten thousand dollars and they wouldn't give him the time to make the money gradually. He and Charlie were, in effect down to their last fifteen thousand and he was out of time. He'd have to make another big trade. He knew what that meant—all or none. If that didn't work, it was all over. Telling Charlie that he'd lost and given away about half the value of his house would represent the least of his worries.

The mob would kill him. He wondered how. Would they just sneak up behind him and shoot him in the head? That would hurt the least. No, they were mad at him for skipping town and making them chase him across the country. They would make sure that pain was an integral part of his final scene.

He found his way to the park and his bench. He didn't care if they were watching him. He needed to clear his head. He still had one more trade. He pulled out his phone and started searching the web.

How many times, when he felt most alone, had he surfed the many websites and chat rooms filled with day-traders lamenting their latest loss or bragging about their wins? You could never tell how much of it was true. It was just a mass of people, lonely and intimidated by their quests to beat the market, wanting to share their stories and redeem some solace in the fact that others, many others, had suffered similar fates.

This morning the chat rooms were full of discussion about the FDA not approving the new wonder drug that would cure MS. One trader said he had lost his house. Another said someone should call the police. This was clearly a swindle. A third told both writers to suck it up or get out. This was day-trading.

Ivan was about to close his cell when he noticed the red icon off in the corner of the screen. It was an invitation to connect from a member of LinkedIn. Under the circumstances, it was amusing. Someone out there actually thought he had value as a business associate. He called up the site and, sure enough, his page was still there as if life was a bowl of cherries. He had spruced up an old resume, highlighted the few accomplishments in his life, and added his new employee picture that Fifty States Investments took before they decided to fire him.

His life had been hell since that day. The Seattle press had been right in saying, that when the big Wall Street investment dealers like Fifty States took over small regional firms like Milne, Ohara, Grady Investments, they ripped out their hearts, all to feed investors' insatiable desire for earnings growth.

From Ivan's way of thinking, they had systematically destroyed him as well, all over trumped-up compliance violations. His records revealed unnecessary and unauthorized transactions to increase commissions. He explained that his clients thought of him as their money manager rather than just their broker, and had given him complete discretion to trade in their accounts at will. He could not, however, produce supporting documentation and several client interviews revealed the arrangement was news to them, too. They also found kick-backs from badly underperforming mutual funds that, by all rights, should have been jettisoned. These funds inexplicably remained in client accounts. If they'd kept digging, they would have found more. Rather than tie up valuable resources in a lawsuit, Fifty States negotiated a termination agreement with a modest severance package which, under the circumstances, was not a legal requirement. They wanted to clean out the trash as they moved forward with their new, combined firm.

After they fired him, Fifty States management spread the word all over town that, while they would not incur the time and expense of a legal proceeding, Ivan was bad, like spoiled milk. Avoid him at all costs. That was all it took. Every employment-seeking call in the Seattle area went unreturned. On the street, when you lost your integrity, you lost everything.

Day-trading was all he had left. He started in Seattle, but quickly ran through his severance money. Sitting at a bar one night, sharing his woes, he learned of *a guy* who could help with a loan. He went through that too.

They wanted their money back and he didn't have it. As the demands for repayment became personally threatening, he knew he had to leave. He picked the middle of night and took the Amtrak to New York City.

When Ivan showed up in Yonkers, New York, he stayed in his sister's basement for a couple of months while he searched for "just the right place" to live. He tried to land a job with local firms, but they all wanted a reference from his former employer, which he said he'd provide, but never did. One actually checked the SEC records and saw the language *terminated for cause*, which led to a series of awkward questions. He remembered walking out of that interview.

He was hiding. When her husband Charlie was at work, he had told Betty the big lie about him starting up his own business and resigning. While he felt a bit bad about that, he felt worse about the fact that he had day-traded away her retirement money. She thought it was "invested."

As he started to read Sandy's email, his eyes grew increasingly wide. She explained that she was contacting him after all this time due to some big life event. She used phrases like "a real wake-up call" and "life is so short." It was all coming back to him. Sandy Allen. She was in jail or supposed to be. He didn't think they had computer chat rooms in there. So how had she sent him this message?

It didn't matter. He remembered her conviction for her role in a Ponzi scheme—with that guy Michael Franklin. He ended up killing himself, apparently out of guilt. It was too bad, Ivan thought. If they didn't fire him, he could have picked up Michael's old accounts.

He kept reading. Sandy said she was afraid Ivan wouldn't respond to her because of her reputation. That made him laugh.

Ivan stared into space for a minute and then back to the phone. His finger paused over the delete key. Adding a convict into his life sure wasn't going to make things better. On the other hand, she was a criminal and so was he. He could talk to her, honestly before his final curtain. There was no reason not to respond.

It was the last line that helped him decide.

I'm desperate to communicate with a real man.

He remembered she was hot. So maybe they could talk about sex. That would, at least take his mind off his other problems.

Hi there, Sandy. Long time and all that. Sure, let's chat or whatever you want. I have to tell you though; I'm in a bit of a fix right now. Actually, a hell of a lot more than a bit. So, if all of the sudden I stop replying to your messages, I hope you'll understand. It means someone turned out my lights.

Chapter 29

Ivan, thank God you're there! You're my last hope. I need your help and I don't have much time.

Ivan looked at the phone and shook his head. Whatever.

Yeah, OK, what's your problem?

I need to hire a private investigator, right away, it's urgent.

Why is that Sweetie? You know that saying "day late-dollar short." Did you forget you're in jail?

From Ivan's perspective, this conversation was a waste of time, but at least, for a brief moment, it diverted his attention.

Well, Ivan, you might not believe this—many people don't—but I'm innocent... and I will prove it. I won't get into the details now, but I've tried to convince the warden and he just laughs at me. He will have to listen when I hand him the hard evidence.

Ivan had seen enough prisoner movies to know all cons, at some point, try to play the "I'm innocent" card once they finally face the reality of their future. But he'd go along with it.

Sure, Sandy. Let's say I believe you. How does that involve me?

Thank you, Ivan, you have no idea how important those words are. In order to hire a P.I., I have to raise money... that I don't have right now.

Ivan sighed. *She* wanted money from *him*. That's why she contacted him. This conversation was over.

Sandy, you're talking to the wrong guy. I'm virtually broke. Good luck with your little mission. I gotta go.

No, Ivan, wait, please. I'm not asking for any money from you. I just need someone on the outside to help me.

Ivan frowned. Whatever she wanted would take time... that was something else he didn't have. What a hopeless existence his life was.

I'm not sure I can do much there either. My days are numbered. Did you read my message?

There was a pause. He imagined that Sandy had scrolled back to read the beginning of their online chat.

What? Why? Are you being threatened by someone? Can't you go to the police?

The police? That's funny. I'm not sure even they could help with the jam I'm in right now. I might as well tell you. I was out of money in Seattle so I borrowed from a guy who said he could help me. I was on a bad roll with my trades. I didn't realize at the time the guy was the mob. They want their money back and I don't have it. They threatened me. I got scared and left—skipped town in the middle of the night—and came to New York. That was my second bad decision. They found me and the extortion is worse than ever. I'm not lying. I'm sitting here on a park bench. It's a beautiful day, I hear and see birds, beautiful robins... and they could shoot me dead in the next five minutes.

He wondered how she'd respond to *that*.

Ivan, how much do you owe them?

It was a pretty stupid question, Ivan thought, given that Sandy just said she needed money, too.

Ten thousand.

Why did she need to know that? What was she up to? She obviously wanted him to do something that she couldn't from behind bars. Did she think he was lying just to blow her off? It didn't make sense. But he reminded himself that *she* had initiated this contact, not him.

If I transfer ten thousand dollars to you, completely on trust, will you help me? I will definitely help you, and not just with the mob. If you're losing money day-trading, you're not doing it right. If you join me, and I show you the secret, you'll have more money than you ever dreamed. I will hire my P.I. who will prove my innocence and free me from this place. We could get together, Ivan; start the life of my dreams. Just you and me, how does that sound? By the way, I have some interesting ways to show my gratitude, which will have no limits if you agree.

It was the first smile that appeared on Ivan's face in a very long time. Did Sandy really have ten grand that she would transfer to him? Was she the last-minute miracle he'd been dreaming of?
Wait a minute. He read her words again, reminding himself that when something sounded too good to be true…

Sandy, I appreciate the offer. But I wasn't born yesterday. I see two big problems here. First, I got this way because of day-trading. Thanks for offering to make me rich, but you're kidding yourself if you think you will make any money at it. I'm sure you have some off-the-wall technique that you truly believe in, just like we all do. But me screwing around with your trading ideas is time I could better spend trying to save my own life.

Her response came quickly.

No, Ivan, you're wrong. I am not kidding myself. I know what I'm doing and I'm betting a life of freedom from jail on it. Think about what you just wrote. You've been sitting there writing me, repeating that you've run out of time. Then you say you could better spend time trying to save your own life. You either have the time or you don't and, if you do, it doesn't sound like you have the first clue what comes next. So, what is your decision, Ivan? Figure it out by yourself, or give me an account number. It'll take me fifteen minutes to deposit the money.

He looked up, left and right. There were two elderly men playing chess off in the corner of the park, a man and a woman untangling their dog leashes and several mothers, chatting, pushing their strollers. The air was clear and, even in the city that never sleeps; there was a sense of peace... and no sign of Hairy Hands. But that could change in an instant. Ivan was about to risk his life on an Internet chat. Was he really speaking with Sandy Allen? Whoever it was made a good point.

What other choice did he have?

Hey, what the hell. If you're willing to bail me out, what do I have to lose? Nothing ventured, nothing gained, I guess.

Thank you, Ivan, thank you so much. But let me just say one more thing first. I'm totally at your mercy here. You'll have complete control of the money I send you, and there is much more to come. If you betray me, I will hunt you down. You will wish it was just the mob after you.

Ivan thought before he replied. She was right. He had total advantage over her. If it became necessary, he would use that to the fullest. Her warning didn't impress him. He was sick and tired of being threatened.

That's some tough talk there, lady, but guess what, you're in there and I'm out here. So your gun is loaded with blanks and I know it. Besides, the mob represents death. Nothing you threaten me with is worse than that!

He deleted it before hitting *send*. He needed her money. Let her think he was intimidated. Now, that was as far ahead as he needed to think. Who knew where this would lead? Instead he wrote:

Sandy, don't worry. The beauty of this is that we need each other. Hurting you would only hurt me, too.

He paused.

And I'm looking forward to that gratitude expression thing you mentioned, once you're out.

Chapter 30

Ivan moved fast. He had to capture Sandy's life-saving money before she changed her mind.

Her ability to trade, or at least to direct him, was clearly most important to her, so he opened a new online brokerage account right away. He sent her all the login information she would need. He prayed she wasn't kidding, that when she transferred the cash for trading, she'd also send him the ten thousand he needed to give to the mob.

She didn't let him down. He checked and, sure enough, she had deposited thirty thousand into their new joint account.

Holy shit Sandy, I don't believe it. You actually did it. You just saved my life. These guys have been following me for days. Now I can get them off my back.

He closed his eyes took several deep breaths. One at a time. Nice and slow. In the space of a few hours he was suddenly at peace. His problems had just disappeared.

But it didn't take long for Ivan's thoughts to stray. He looked again at the online account on his phone screen. There they were—thirty thousand beautiful dollars, ten of which were for his needs. All those zeroes… His chest felt warm and the palms of his hands were moist. He was back in business. It seemed like such a long time since he felt this way.

A long time… a *very* long time. It would be a shame to just let all that cash go, to let this wonderful feeling slip through his fingers. The mob didn't need to know he gotten *all* the money he still owed them so soon. But he couldn't let the funds sit in the account either because Sandy would see they were still there. He was supposed to be in a life or death hurry. He wrote.

I will transfer the money to them right now.

Instead, he moved ten thousand into his old personal trading account. She would see the money going out of her account, but wouldn't be able to tell where it went. The more he thought, an idea—a good one—started to take shape. There was that old saying, "it takes money to make money." Whatever Sandy's "technique" was, if it did work, he could make additional cash for himself and not have to share it with her. He would invest the ten grand, without her knowing, and line his own pockets. He could stall the mob for just a little while longer.

Opportunity knocked.

If he was right that she was kidding herself about the amount of money she could make, he would recognize that quickly and just trade her ten thousand the way he knew best using his own personal style.

She didn't need to know what he was doing and neither did the mob. Who could blame him? This was ten grand he was talking about!

OK, Ivan, read everything I'm about to write carefully and, after you're done, delete it all. From now on my name is Tradur Gurl and you come up with a name for yourself. Don't use my real name again and I won't use yours. In any messages we send, never mention where you are geographically, not even a street. OK? And DEFINITELY don't say I'm in prison.

Ivan said that sounded a bit paranoid, but he agreed.

We're going to run pump and dumps.

He mouthed the words while he was reading. He'd heard about this type of scam, but never met anyone who actually did it. He also knew there was a good chance the Fed's would catch them. This was high risk stuff. Now he understood why she needed him. He could do the trading and, if they got nailed, she wouldn't care. She was already *in* jail.

Tradur Gurl, I think maybe you've taken too many shots to the head in there. The regulators have, like, super computers on their side doing all kinds of surveillance. We'll get caught! Are you sure you know what you're doing?

It didn't take her long to reply.

Yea, I'm twenty thousand sure. The Feds catch the rookies who buy too fast. I'm a pro. Besides, this might all be new to you, but pump and dumps are as old as dirt. I think the first one was around 1700. The directors of the South Sea Company said things were great when they weren't at all. They drove the stock price from around one hundred to over one thousand pounds and then sold all their shares. When the truth finally came out, the price dropped to around two hundred. Nice trade.

The Feds have <u>tried</u> to shut pump and dumpers down, you're right, by using high tech stuff, but computers are our best friend because they connect us to the greedy public. Here's how it works. We only deal in "penny" stocks, the juniors that don't trade much. We find a good one and buy up all the shares we can. But we do it slowly so no one notices. Once we own a lot of the freely trading stock, we start the "pump." The public thinks they can get "valuable" information from the chat rooms. Ha! Yeah, valuable to us. We plant the story of a "rumored" large discovery of gold, oil or whatever. It doesn't matter as long as it looks like it's worth buckets of money. We say shit like "The company isn't prepared to discuss this yet. I have spoken directly with someone in the know. Does a ten-bagger sound good? They are still waiting for the final test results to come in, but if you wait until then..." There are so many people on the net who watch these things, many know it's probably a scam, but then they start asking themselves, what if it isn't? The buy orders start coming in, but since we've bought all the supply, it doesn't take long for the stock to run. That action gets the attention of the technical analysts who say the stock has "broken out" of its normal pattern. More orders drive the price higher, faster.

We watch the trading carefully, and when the buying starts to slow, we dump. We sell every, last share as fast as we can. That's when the Fed's wake up, but by then it's too late. They call the company and demand they issue an immediate press release saying there's no news to explain what happened to the stock. That's when everyone figures out they've been conned. They all try to sell at the same time, but the stock craters. It's funny to watch the free fall. But we don't care. We're out and have made a nice pass.

Ivan started to smile. It sounded like she really did know how to do this.

OK Tradur Gurl, you win. What do you want me to do?

Start buying shares of the stock symbol XZQX but, like I said, just a little at a time. It doesn't matter what the company name is or what they do, just do it. Once we have our position, I will script you on the rumor you're going to spread. This is a good one. If we get a triple and, looking at the numbers, I think we will, that's thirty yards for each of us. You pay me back and I am that much farther down the freedom highway. And understand, man, this is just our <u>first</u> trade!

He laughed again. All of a sudden, it was raining money! Now he knew how he could use his secret stash. When he bought the shares of XZQX for Sandy, he would also buy some for himself, but she would never know because his purchases would be from his private account. If the stock did triple, Sandy's trade would make a sixty thousand dollar profit for them to share. He'd get twenty thousand from her after paying back her loan. He'd also make another twenty thousand in profit for himself using the money that was supposed to go to the mob.

Forty thousand dollars in one trade. Whew!

Chapter 31

The SEC computers noticed.

A report alerting possible stock-market trading irregularities arrived in minutes to William Casey, head of SEC enforcement for the greater New York area.

Of course, the computer usually sent some version of cautioning several times a day. The machine's complex series of algorithms that hunted for suspicious activity were the most sophisticated in the world. William knew that, while there was always potentially something behind one of its alerts, most often it was explainable.

Just the same, you could never ignore it. He sat, reading the report, which was the only paper on his clean mahogany desk. William believed in order and that was his rule—one at a time—deal with the issue, delegate or discard. Then, on to the next.

His dress matched his view of life. Everything was neatly trimmed and orderly including his moustache (his one expression of liberalism.) His freshly-pressed white shirt with yellow collar, and red, black and white stripes hung smartly down his neat frame. His dark blue suit, 42 regular, straight off the rack, was the same size he'd worn since graduating from Columbia Law School, over 25 years ago.

Years of trying to outsmart criminals, whose primary weapons were their minds and computers, had taken its toll, though. When he looked in the mirror, there was no hiding that a frosting adorned his formerly rich brown hair. Wrinkles appeared on his face when he smiled.

He looked up at this week's analyst, sitting at the workstation in the far corner of his office. Every intern got the opportunity to shadow the boss for a several days in the morning. It was a glorious opportunity to learn by watching what he did, the types of issues he regularly faced and the decision-making process he used.

"Tina, HAL is crying wolf again. Go through the report and make sure nothing is there."

She nodded. William knew that she was probably curious to know why he referred to the surveillance computers, a series of thick black panels, safely stacked somewhere deep in the earth, as HAL. But the movie 2001: A Space Odyssey, in which the evil computer HAL became famous, had premiered many years before she was born. Let her figure it out.

She worked quickly and efficiently. Casey liked that.

"Mr. Casey, this morning, HAL—as you call the computers," she looked at him with a glancing smile—"reported over 25 potential problems. I've gone through them and all but five look easily explainable."

He tried to show interest. The interns were an eager bunch and needed encouragement.

"But one situation seems, maybe, somewhat peculiar."

He could hear her hedging. None of the interns wanted to take ownership that they had found something "big" only to suffer embarrassment later when the boss revealed that what they'd missed was patently obvious.

"Maybe, somewhat peculiar... OK Tina, continue."

She looked up quickly, adjusted her glasses, and kept reading.

"So, there's this one stock, symbol XZQX. Over the past two weeks, there was a large increase in small transactions. The average daily trade count was more than two standard deviations higher than the mean, which is, as you know, statistically significant. By itself, this increase in the *number* of transactions isn't necessarily a concern. There could be all kinds of reasons for transaction increases; corporate announcements, analyst reports or material changes to the industry outlook."

William almost stopped her, saying he didn't require a lesson. But she was trying to advertise what she knew. Fair enough.

"Normally, the increase in transactions almost always happens along with a big rise in total share volume. There has been some increase for sure, but most of the trades were for small amounts—not that you could buy a lot of this stock anyway. The available freely trading shares are quite small compared to the total outstanding."

Now she looked up, hopeful.

"Also, with the increase in total transactions, the price usually rises or falls a lot too. It doesn't make sense. The XZQX price hasn't moved."

Casey knew that whenever the number of trades moved without the other two in sync, something was potentially up. That's why HAL reported it.

"Tina, have you considered that someone might have initiated a "quiet" buying program so other investors wouldn't notice? If they did, they'd sense something was up and start buying too, dramatically increasing the share price and thus, the original buyer's cost. The buying strategy is perfectly legal. Large institutional investors do it all the time."

He wondered if she would step up to the plate, declaring that the computers were on to something and, at the same time, risk exposing herself as a rookie. It was an important rite of passage for the younger staff.

"Yes, Mr. Casey, I thought about that. But couldn't this also be a pump and dump scheme? All the usual clues are present. It looks like someone picked this particular stock and has skillfully manipulated the trading. The operator hopes no one, including us will notice them buying up all the free shares."

He was pleased that she did.

"…and then the pump and the dump action goes down. All the operator's profits come at the expense of their victims who blame their losses on tough markets. They usually have no idea what really happened to them."

He had to hand it to her. It was a solid conclusion supported by a series of facts, logically applied.

"Well done, Tina, good work. Now, you run with it. Find out which brokerage firm has the account or accounts that are doing the trades in XZQX. Get one of the senior guys to help you if you don't know how. See if they'll give you any information. They probably won't. Go through as many public chat rooms as you can for any conversation about this stock. If you have actually discovered a buy program in advance of a pump and dump, we want to catch the "pumpers" as soon as we can. Maybe we'll get lucky and identify a computer and its location. We don't have many other options at this stage."

He thought Tina was having a hard time containing her smile as she rushed out the door.

Chapter 32

If anyone happened to notice, or the police asked for a description, the witnesses might remember a lone man wearing reflector sunglasses and a grey hoodie pulled up.

Odd for a warm day.

At the combination coffee house/computer rental store, patrons wearing bright, light summer attire sipped lattes at curb-side tables. In Brooklyn, they dreamed of this kind of weather.

Ivan walked quickly past them and headed towards the back of the store. There was a row of prefabricated fake pine desks, far enough apart so the person sitting next to you couldn't easily "peek" at your screen. A steel cable running through a hole in the corner of the desk secured the computer and monitor. Hours of grimy fingers had left their residue on the keyboards and displays. It was late Sunday afternoon—his second to last "appointment." He and Charlie had been at it all weekend "spreading the love" as Sandy called it.

He selected a workstation as far into the corner as possible, did not remove his hood or his glasses, but hunched down low behind his monitor. His hand shook as he put his pre-paid cash card into the slot.

Hey there, fellow traders, it's Why Me Coyote. I'm hearing very strong rumors that XZQX has developed a new cancer drug and will announce a Phase III trial soon. The stock should rocket!

He'd asked Charlie to do the same thing across town. It was necessary to bring him in on the pump stage because the two of them could cover far more ground faster. More importantly, Ivan gave Charlie the task of visiting the public computer rooms nearer to his apartment.

There was one small problem, though. Charlie asked too many questions.

"Ivan, I don't know anything about all this trading stuff, but one thing doesn't make any sense to me. Like, if we found a really good stock, why wouldn't we want to keep it to ourselves?"

His doubts forced Ivan to come up with a quick answer.

"Yeah, I guess for a newbie, it might not make sense, but think of it this way. A company's share price won't rise unless more people want to buy the stock than sell it. We *wouldn't* want to tell anybody what we are doing until after we finished buying. But once we do, it's in our best interest to spread the good news. If you ever watch those TV shows that interview professional money managers, they'll always tell you whether they own one of the stocks they're talking about. They won't come out and say it, but the implication is clear. If they own it, and they're the pros at this, then you should own it, too. And when people then go to buy the shares, it helps the price go up. It's done all the time."

Charlie had never seen one of those shows.

"Yes, Ivan, but we're doing more than telling people we own the stock. We're telling them about rumors of good things that might happen."

"Charlie, it's an unwritten rule that once a day-trader identifies a *positive investment situation* and buys his position, it's fair to share the opportunity with others. It's just the way things are done. It's almost like a brotherhood."

Ivan had to suppress his smile. "Brotherhood." Good one.

Charlie had looked up, eyes wide. But Ivan could tell. It didn't sound right, even to a neophyte.

"But why then are we going all over town typing our message on a bunch of different computers?"

"Charlie, look. You understand now that it's in our best interest to share our story as far and wide as possible, right? It's totally within the rules. Different computers link to different sites. The more computers we use, the better."

Ivan hoped that Charlie didn't know much about technology and was relieved that the last comment seemed to satisfy him. His instincts were disturbingly relevant.

In the current shop, Ivan felt that everyone was watching him, but glancing to either side, he saw that he was alone. He wanted done with his business and gone before anyone else came in. But these older computers were so slow.

The potential market for this drug is into the billions, that's right b—

His caught his breath. An elderly woman sat down at the station right beside his. She wore a high-collar dress that reminded him of a table cloth and her grey hair was permed. He watched out of the corner of his eye. She seemed preoccupied with where to put her oversized purse. Finally, placing it safely between her feet, she tightened her lips and started pushing the keys with her index finger.

Ivan tried not to make any sudden movements while he finished his message. Maybe she wouldn't notice him.

She made a noise of some kind, rose and was standing right next to him.

"Hello there, young man. It is so beautiful out, don't you agree? We should all be sunning ourselves. But these computers, I suppose there's no escaping them these days, is there? Just my luck, it is *my* turn to host the girls for bridge. One of them told me about this *fabulous* recipe for scones. She said 'Oh, just search for it on the Internet,' as if everyone knows how to do that. She took one of those <u>Computers for Seniors</u> courses and now she's an unbearable show off."

She stopped talking when she realized that he hadn't acknowledged her.

"Oh, but look at me nattering away. You look busy at something there. Delores—she's the one that is such a smarty at these machines—says you make friends on computers. Well, I don't know about that. I'm just trying to find a silly scone recipe. I will say though, it is actually somewhat exciting. I am *surfing the Net* for the first time. Why do they call it that anyway? Delores told me this would be easy. But I keep pushing the ON button and nothing is happening. Could you help me? I have no idea what is wrong."

Ivan could see from where he was that she hadn't put her pre-paid time card into the slot. It would be the easiest of things to correct, but it would also mean his leaving a greater impression than he wanted. He decided to create a diversion. Let her find her knight in shining armor somewhere else. He leaned over, pretending to examine her workstation.

"Lady, I see it from here. You have a problem with your power bar. That will affect everything. I can't fix it. The person before you was having problems, too. They charge a pretty penny to use these things. They should at least *work*. You need to go see management."

Finding her purse, the woman stood up and stammered, "You're darned right. And I pre-paid for thirty minutes! Thank you so much."

He waited for her to be out of sight, finished sending his last message and slipped quietly out the side door.

He wished he could see the look on the woman's face when the manager showed her what she was doing wrong.

At the final Internet café, Ivan started to perspire. The hood itched and he just wanted to get back to the safety of Charlie's basement. But this time, he was the one that needed help. The memory stick that contained all the necessary information wouldn't load. A kid two machines down in a black t-shirt and backwards baseball cap looked like he was playing some sort of game. Ivan saw his curious look as he asked him for help. What kind of dude wears a hoodie in the middle of the summer and sunglasses indoors—some kind of freak, maybe? Ivan waited while the kid leaned over to read the error message.

"Oh that," he laughed. "That happens all the time. These machines are old and get a ton of use, right? The USB port is probably defective or dirty. Just plug it into another slot. Should work."

Ivan did as instructed. The computer instantly recognized the memory stick and the files stored on it.

"Oh yeah, there you go. What a loser I am. Thanks, man."

The kid nodded his head, put his ear buds back in and walked back towards his machine.

"No worries, dude. Chill."

Ivan waited until the kid focused on his game again. He found the file he was looking for containing links to Twitter, Facebook and Pinterest and several other notable day-trading sites. The computer crawled. He pushed the button and held his breath.

Finally. *Message sent.*

He was surprised this time by the figure standing next to him, a different one than the kid who helped him. This one seemed a bit older, wore a t-shirt with a message Ivan didn't understand, peach fuzz, traces of acne. It was the boy who sold him his time card.

"Hey, dude, I just thought I'd let you know, like, there were some guys in here yesterday asking if I'd seen anybody that looked like you. They had your picture. I told 'em no, and that was the truth, but one of them, a big sucker, huge hands, he says to me that he'll come back and hurt me if I lied to him."

Ivan's excitement about his sent message instantly disappeared.

"Like, this guy—he was scary, right? I don't want no trouble in here. I'm just trying to get through school. So, dude, why don't you go use some computers across town, OK? Don't come back here again."

Ivan muttered something like "Uh, yeah, don't know what you're talking about. Gotta run," and was on the street in seconds.

Chapter 33

Inside the SEC offices, there was a room with white walls and brighter than comfortable lighting. It had no windows, a table in the back corner with a coffee maker on it and a mini-fridge full of water bottles below it. There were no distracting pictures on the wall and in front of each of the twelve seats around the rectangular table were a fresh yellow paper pad and a new, sharpened no. 2 pencil. A 70" digital TV hung on one wall. The technology, including a computer, printer and digital scanner sat below it on a credenza.

They called it the war room. After William Casey delegated the XZQX file to the intern, it hadn't taken long before his team summoned him into the room. As he walked in, one of his senior associates, agent Sardonsky started speaking before his boss sat down.

"Someone was very busy this weekend spreading the 'good news' about an imminent announcement by XZQX of the start of Phase III trials of a new drug that *cures* cancer. This is the same stock the computers highlighted for unusual buying patterns over the last couple of weeks."

When Sardonsky first joined the team, some of the other staffers joked that it was true; managers hired in their own image. He was neat, well-trimmed and always *freshly pressed*. The agent didn't sport a matching moustache—yet. Although a couple inches taller than Casey, when neither the boss nor Sardonsky could hear, they referred to him as mini-me.

The agent opened up a text file on the large screen. William quickly read the now all-too-familiar language.

This could be the grand slam. The mother load. The big kahuna.

Tina sat in the background in a chair next to the coffee machine. Her eyes were wide. William, at the head of the table, started flipping through the computer printout sheets.

"Were you able to trace the IP address of the computer that sent the pump messages?"

"You mean computers," Sardonsky said. "We found the exact same text sent from over fifteen different rent-by-the-hour machines in Internet cafés all over Manhattan. We are dealing with at least two 'authors' because the same message was sent twice, within five minutes of each other, from computers located across town. That's physically impossible."

William looked up, paused and nodded his head. If there had been any question that a pump and dump swindle was under way, there wasn't now.

"What did the computer rental store managers say?"

"The usual. Most of them said they sell the time cards up front and then their 'clients' go into the back and pick any machine they want. They can't—and don't want—to know what goes on behind them."

"We'll see about that once we start shutting them all down."

Sardonsky looked at his boss, but didn't speak. William knew what he wanted to say, that they had tried that many times before and the courts didn't support them. Someone using your equipment to commit a crime didn't make you an accomplice unless the Feds could prove that you knew about it and did nothing to stop it.

"A few of them mentioned a guy in a grey hoodie and reflector sunglasses, but there were no other distinguishing features. No one had any more information—they said—because they got busy running the restaurant side."

William wiped his hand down his face.

"No one wants to get involved. It's the same old story. What did company XZQX say?"

"We asked them if there was any truth to the rumor of a pending big announcement and they were 'shocked and alarmed.' The story was a complete fabrication, or so they said. They assured us that they manage all sensitive corporate information at the top. Then they started coming after me, saying 'this is a crime that could hurt my company's reputation and harm shareholders. How are you going to fix it?'"

"Yeah, right," William said. "How is it these things always end up being our fault?"

He looked at the ceiling.

"Maybe we just get the exchange to issue a 'cease trading' order tomorrow morning and shut the stock down. If this is a scam, and someone is itching to dump all their shares, that would tie their hands."

"We talked about that. The exchange rules say we'd have to disclose why. Potential stock manipulation wouldn't help matters. We might hurt the *dumper*, but we'd also cost all other shareholders some serious money. The fact is we don't have enough proof. We have suspicions, but that's all. Whoever it is needs to dump the stock, and then we'll have enough to show that a crime has been committed. If we get a warrant, you know, there's more we can do."

Sardonsky waited, but they had been through this before too. Judges did not support arresting someone *before* they committed a crime. There were no other questions to ask.

"So, we're dealing with pros. We watch them get away with the first one and we just hope they come back for more. Then we've got a better chance."

The agent nodded his head in agreement.

Chapter 34

*C*oyote, what's the status?

Hi there, Tradur Gurl, the status is awesome! Buying the stock was easy, just like you said, if you take your time, and show a little patience. The pump went smooth as silk. Charlie and I worked all weekend and must have hit every Internet Café known to man on Manhattan Island. I dumped all the stock this afternoon. That was a little trickier. There was another seller in there so I used caution.

Ivan knew that if she ever got hold of the online trading data, she would notice that someone dumped a lot of stock right in front of their trade. She must never learn that he was the seller. He unloaded the stock he'd bought for himself first. Just in case she ever did look more closely at the trade, better to plant the seed of the mysterious "other seller" now.

You were bang on. It was a triple! The stock hit records for volume and price today! 'Awesome' is the only word to describe it.

Coyote, careful about your language here. The Internet isn't secure.

Tradur Gurl, relax. I didn't mention the stock symbol. We're good.

Make sure you deposit the money in my account ASAP after settlement. We split the profits fifty/fifty.

Ivan laughed aloud. With him putting his trade in front of theirs he was actually capturing almost two-thirds of the juice.

Yeah, TG, that's more than fair.

Ivan was a bit surprised that it didn't take Sandy long to line up their next trade. She, apparently, *was* good at this.

OK, Coyote. I found another junior drug development company. This one is trying to develop a treatment for osteoarthritis by harvesting the roots of dead rainforest trees. What a joke. But after we're done with them the world will know they've achieved their greatest dreams. Management owns the majority of the shares; there aren't many left for the public to buy, which is perfect. Even better, the company's stock has "popped" and then come back to earth twice in the last four years as news "leaked" of the long-awaited discovery that never materialized. That might mean that someone already gamed the stock, but it doesn't matter. It's ripe for another session.

Ivan, again, buy the stock slowly—even as few as one hundred shares a day if you have to. This is a smaller company than the last one.

Ivan assured her he had everything under control. On the first day, the stock traded ten thousand shares. Their joint account showed he'd bought two thousand. Sandy commended him saying it wasn't easy to soak up twenty percent of a day's volume and not affect the share price, which he hadn't.

What Sandy couldn't see was that with each day's purchase into her account, Ivan was making an equivalent purchase into his own ledger. Since she hadn't said anything after their first trade—that someone might be front running her—he knew he could repeat. At one point Charlie asked why they were making two purchases, one into one account and one into some other account that Ivan had access to.

"Charlie, when you're trading these small stocks, you don't want to show your hand. It's much better to make two buys of two thousand shares than one buy of four thousand shares. When people see the bigger trade, they might think a size buyer is coming in and raise their sell price."

Charlie shook his head. "Wow, I sure have a lot to learn."

Ivan nodded—no lie there.

Ivan kept buying the shares—some every day—and then suddenly on a Friday afternoon, Sandy texted him to stop. It was time for the pump phase.

"OK, Charlie," Ivan said, "let's go share our good fortune with the day-trading community."

Charlie looked at him for several seconds.

"Oh, right, that again."

This time the trade was less profitable than the last—only a double. Ivan was ecstatic. In three weeks he'd gone from nearly dead to rich. He could pay off the mob, and soon give both Betty and Charlie their money back. And they were just getting started! This was cause for celebration if there ever was one.

After he relayed the profit numbers of the rainforest trade to Sandy, she texted,

I'll start working on the next one. It'll maybe take me a week or so.

Yeah, Charlie and I may have recovered by then.

Meaning?

My brother-in-law and I are going to celebrate our success tonight downtown at the Stone Tavern. I don't know if you've heard of it, but it's where the Wall Street traders hang out. We're traders now too. We belong there.

I've heard of it. Wish I could join you. But don't go yet. Until the trade settles—three days—we don't have our money. We have to make sure no one files a complaint or asks for a review. And don't get stupid and shoot your mouth off. A real trader's greatest skill is listening. No one else needs to know about our business—unless, of course you want to join me in here.

LOL, Sandy, I'm not that stupid. Not to worry. This isn't my first rodeo.

Ivan was slightly annoyed when Sandy reminded him her name was Tradur Gurl.

Chapter 35

HAL spewed its analysis. Two big trades in XZQX went across the tape. The circle was complete. Statistically, recent trading activity was highly unusual.

William Casey didn't bother to look at the report. He was waiting to see what his wingers had turned up. The game was on. Sardonsky took the lead.

"While all the pumping was done using various PCs all over town, the actual trading was done on just one. We spoke with the Internet and email provider for the IP address of that computer. We told them we're in the process of getting a warrant to investigate a potential felony using their service as a platform. I said the search is very thorough and often turns up other crimes they didn't even realize were going on. I reminded them that they could be charged as an accessory if they couldn't show that they had taken reasonable steps to prevent such activity. But then I said speed was of the essence in this case and the warrant could take several days. Any help they could provide *now* would certainly count in their favor, should we decide to consider their weak compliance procedures as part of the investigation."

William listened. "And...?"

"We've got the last several days of emails between someone named *Why Me Coyote* and *Tradur Gurl*—obviously fake names, although the girl's real name—if it is a girl—looks like it might be 'Sandy'. *Coyote* accidentally used it in a chat. They went all through the steps of how they completed a pump and dump trade. The *Gurl*, who is using a pre-paid cell phone out of Seattle, Washington, by the way, is the leader. Earlier this morning, after the dump was completed, *Coyote* was bragging about how easy it was. We're not sure, but this might not have been their first such pump and dump scheme."

"Does any of this connect to XZQX?"

"No, at least, not yet. They were smart enough never to mention the name of the stock they were working."

William folded his hands together. They would need more, but it was a start.

"Oh, and wait. There is one other thing. Apparently *Coyote* was bragging that he and his helper were going to celebrate their success and get royally drunk at the Stone Tavern. It's a bar near Wall Street. Many traders go there after work. *Gurl* made him agree to wait until this coming Friday night just to make sure the trade settled without any restrictions. We don't know their names or faces, but if we could get someone in that bar, things could change quickly in our favor."

For the first time, William smiled. Yes, the tag likely would go well. That was a famous bar. He'd put more than one of its clients behind *bars*.

They'd been talking about ways to encourage Wall Street professionals to help clean up their own business, even down to specific individuals. This was a perfect opportunity and he knew just the right candidate.

"Contact the Exchange and make very sure that there are no settlement restrictions on that trade whatsoever. We want those two to make it to the bar."

Chapter 36

Blackie noticed his phone bank light up, but ignored it.

"Fucking idiots, leave me alone," he said aloud.

He sat in his usual pose, leaning all the way back in the armless reclining office chair straining against the size of the man. He quietly surveyed his three Bloomberg screens like a cat eyeing its prey. The trader was thirty-four years old, but he looked like a man in his fifties. His face carried extra weight and his teeth bore witness to his never-ending coffee habit. Red veins in his eyes bulged after years of peering into computer terminals. The stitching of his white shirt pulled against his soft belly. When he did make it to the gym, the routine was the same: push-ups, pull-ups and anything else that would enhance his already menacing biceps. New York was a big city, but in the bars that the traders frequented, they knew he was a tough kid that grew up on the street—best left undisturbed.

The phone kept ringing, but then stopped... finally.

Divine intervention shaped Blackie's "career." With only a high-school diploma, he started as a message runner down the streets of New York. At every higher level of responsibility, his bosses were overwhelmed with his drive and dedication. Once he found a spot on the trading desk, it didn't take long for him to work his way up the ladder to captain his small ship—his trading desk—in a sea populated by the world's largest brokerage firms. He'd been head trader at Bryson Securities for over ten years and ran his area with an iron fist.

The phone rang again and this time he grabbed his headset. Someone was about to pay.

"WHAT THE F..?"

He stopped mid-sentence when he recognized the caller's number and changed his greeting.

"Trading."

A short pause.

"Morning, Blackie. I was starting to wonder where you were. There are some, ah, people here in my office that want to meet with you."

It was Bryson himself, the Chairman.

"Yeah, well, they'll have to wait. The market is opening in twenty minutes and I'm just lining up my first trades."

The market opened at nine-thirty a.m. The hour before that was Blackie's sacred time. He needed to decide. Would fear or greed run the show for the first few minutes after the market opened? Was Greece going bankrupt or had BP found more oil in the North Sea? More important, how could he make money off the news? The first few minutes of trading often determined his success or failure for the remainder of the day.

"I know what time it is, Blackie. This is important. Boardroom in five."

Blackie clicked the release button and threw his headset at his Bloomberg screens. He cursed with every step as he walked towards the meeting.

When he entered the boardroom, his rumbled white shirt, tousled hair and paper coffee cup seemed at odds with the twenty-foot long mahogany table surrounded by executive black leather office chairs and the row of fine china cups stacked neatly by the coffee machine.

William Casey was standing next to Bryson, waiting for him. The Chairman made quick introductions as he moved towards the door.

"I can't stay; I've got something else up town. Blackie you can run with this. I have promised your full cooperation."

Blackie took a gulp of coffee and wiped his mouth with the back of his other hand.

"Blackie, it's been awhile. You look well. Chairman Bryson tells me business is good and, more importantly, you have become a key member of his management team. Congratulations."

Blackie looked at his watch and nodded his head towards the senior SEC officer.

"Casey."

"Right then, you remember me. We certainly haven't forgotten you."

Blackie just stared at him.

"Look Blackie, we are sorry to pull you away, but we've got a situation and we're here to ask for your assistance. You were instrumental a few years ago helping us nail Alexei Petrov and Sandy Allen for their insider trading scheme. I think you've probably noticed that the frequency of that type of crime has dramatically declined, and that is largely thanks to people like yourself, professionals who understand the ins and outs of the business and are willing to help."

He wanted to tell Casey to go blow smoke up someone else's ass, but he knew what would happen. He didn't remember being "willing to help" last time. His boss had threatened him with his job. And now… "Full cooperation?" Fuck.

"But criminals never rest and we're on to our next mission. I'm sure you're familiar with so-called pump and dump schemes. They are growing like mushrooms."

Blackie looked at Casey when he heard the word "we're" and then noticed a woman in the corner of the room, dressed in a black business suit with wide lapels. She had short black hair and dark eyebrows and she was as tall as Blackie, who was short for a man. She wore an American flag on her lapel. Casey hadn't introduced her. She was staring at him.

"Everybody knows about 'em, but they're always done on little junior companies. I don't trade that shit." He nodded his head at the door. "So, sorry, I can't help. Gotta go."

Bryson had been gone long enough that he wouldn't see Blackie leave. He threw his paper cup towards the trash can. It ricocheted off the top, sprayed the last bit of coffee on the wall and came to rest on the floor. As he started to move towards the door, he saw Casey put up his hand.

"Hang on, Blackie, I'm not done."

Blackie paused, wiping his hand across his face, looking at his watch.

"As I said," Casey continued, "we are concerned about the increasing frequency of pump and dump manoeuvres, and are taking a more aggressive enforcement approach. Our current focus is a series of recent trades that we're almost certain are a pump and dump scheme, right here in the Greater Metropolitan Area. We have plenty of evidence that demonstrates all three phases: the clandestine stock collection, the pump and then the dump. Now we're trying to catch the operators—faces and names. Agent Margaret Stark is spearheading our effort. I'm going to let her pick up the lead from here."

The woman walked deliberately over to the table. She held out her hand towards Blackie, who just stared at it, then directly at the woman.

"Look, lady, I'm real happy for you that you're off to catch bad guys. But…"

"I am Agent Stark to you."

Blackie looked at his watch again. A skirt certainly didn't intimidate him.

"OK, *Agent Stark*, maybe you're new to my world, so I'll explain how it works. My opening trades are shot now, anyway. You're chasing a small cap crime and you're speaking to a professional *large block* trader. Here's a tip. You're wasting my time. Waste yours if you want, but not mine. The market is open and you're costing me money."

Casey spoke up.

"Easy there, Blackie. We understand the difference between your job and this crime. We aren't asking you to *trade* anything. We want to hire you to perform undercover surveillance to help us identify the culprits. We have firm evidence that they are going to a local bar this Friday night to celebrate. Pump and dump operators sometimes like to brag. They call it taking a victory lap in car racing. We'll tell you the stock in question. You go the bar and mingle. Since you speak the language of a trader, you'll easily fit in with that crowd and, we believe, would have a far better chance of identifying the culprits. That's all you have to do. Go in there, listen more than talk and point the finger. Then we'll step in."

Blackie cracked his knuckles and smiled.

"You want me to be a spy?"

It was Agent Stark's turn again.

"The actual term is 'confidential informant.' But yes."

Blackie stood, still smiling and shaking his head.

"Thanks for the offer, Casey, Stark. No."

As Blackie started to move towards the door, Casey put his hand on Blackie's forearm.

"Blackie, that's not very helpful. I think it's time you took a seat. You are not excused. I'm not going to tell you again."

Blackie pulled away from the agent's hand. He was about to explode. Not *excused?* Who the fuck did they think they were dealing with? He folded his arms and stood in the same place.

Casey continued, a bit louder this time.

"Suit yourself. We suspected performing your civic duty might not inspire you. As I recall, you weren't actually that thrilled about helping us last time. So we'll try another way. We're prepared to offer you a deal. Help us now and we won't prosecute you."

Blackie jerked his head.

"Prosecute me... for what?"

"That case about the big insider trading bust I was just praising you for isn't closed yet. There are still a few loose ends. Like, for example, you were an accessory to the crime. You've never been brought up on charges."

Blackie replayed the last sentence in his mind.

"What? What a load of crap. I had no idea what they were doing. All I did was the trades I was *asked* to do."

"You're right, Blackie, all you did was complete the trades. Tell me again, what's your job here?"

"You know what it is."

"Right, you're the head trader. As head trader, would you say that you are responsible for all trading that happens on your desk?"

Blackie's eyes narrowed.

"Yeah... So what?"

"Well, the crime that resulted in the deportation of our Russian friend and the banning of Sandy Allen from ever working in the securities industry again could not have been committed without both a series of buy trades that Sandy completed on *your* desk—right under your nose—and a big sell trade, which you did *yourself*. So tell me, Blackie, if you aren't responsible for those trades, who is?"

"You got to be fuckin'... that was years ago. You caught your bad guys. Case closed."

He watched Casey lean forward, placing both hands on the desk.

"Oh no, Blackie, you're wrong. Sometimes it takes many years to clean these things up. We just haven't gotten to you yet."

He smiled.

"But now we have. There is enough evidence that you aided and abetted perpetrators of a serious crime that we'd have no problem getting a warrant. With that warrant, Blackie, we'd subpoena your trading records for a long way back—maybe to the day you started work. And we'd review *every single trade* you've ever done. Tell me, is that something you'd like us to do?"

Blackie looked at the ceiling.

"Yeah, maybe you *better* think about that. You have until the market closes this afternoon to say 'yes' to our request. Then you and Agent Stark will only have two days to prepare. The party is going down Friday night."

Casey got up and motioned towards the door.

"For your sake, it's a gathering you won't want to miss. Remember what your boss said? I think it was FULL cooperation. We're really looking forward to it."

Chapter 37

"So, what do I gotta do?"

Blackie called Agent Stark from his Bryson Securities trading desk. She picked it up immediately.

"Blackie, you're making a very wise choice, but this isn't something to discuss over the telephone. We need to meet someplace."

The Hotel Wall Street was just a few blocks from Bryson Securities. A seven-story building with red brick and concrete façade, it stood amidst towering glass office buildings on all sides. It had a red awning and a large flag announcing its entrance between two waist-high pillars topped with a bronze bull figurine on one side and a bear on the other. The bull's nose shined after years of people rubbing it for good luck.

Stepping into the small bar just beside the lobby, Blackie saw the only patron was a woman in jeans and a Stones Tongue t-shirt, listening to music on her ear buds. Blackie looked at his watch and wondered if he'd heard wrong. Was he in the right place?

The woman got up and walked towards a booth in the back of the room. It was Agent Stark. Blackie shook his head and followed. Some stupid game, playing Dick Tracy.

"Nice outfit."

Stark thought it was a compliment.

"I can't say this shirt is mine, but it seems to work. Now look Blackie, before we begin I'd like a fresh start. Our first meeting with William Casey didn't go that well. I don't want to fight with you. It's inefficient and leads to poor outcomes. So, how about we start over?"

Blackie looked at her and sighed.

"Agent, the *only* reason I'm sitting here is because your boss threatened me. You got that?"

It was as if she didn't hear him.

"So, I thought maybe if we got to know each other a bit better, it wouldn't be a bad idea. Tell me a bit about yourself. Why did you decide to become a trader?"

Blackie shook his head.

"OK, not a problem. I'll go first. I grew up as an army brat. I can't remember all the different military bases we lived on. But my father was a no-nonsense kind of guy. Whatever you did had to be the best or don't bother doing it. He was decorated for his service in the Vietnam War. That's how I decided I wanted to be a cop. Remember, whatever I did always had to be the best. I graduated first in my class in the John Jay College of Criminal Justice in New York City and then went on to get my Master's degree from the University of Albany, SUNY."

"So you like to shoot guns, just like dad. Good for you."

"I suppose someone could conclude that, but no, not at all. With my two degrees, I got many offers to bypass the tradition of "walking the beat." That's where they use the guns. I decided if I was going to be a cop, I had to experience it first-hand. But everyone laughed at me. I'm just a little defenseless flower in the sea of bad guys, right? I proved them all wrong. Throughout school, I took Taekwondo lessons. I'll show you my black belt someday. The entire time I walked the beat, after over 100 arrests, I never fired my service revolver—not once."

She smiled.

"I did break a few arms though… but come on Blackie. I've been doing all the talking. Give it up."

Blackie wasn't sure what he thought working with this woman was going to be like, but it was anything other than this. He kept reminding himself of Casey's threats or he would have walked away by now.

Maybe he could shock her with his story and get her on with whatever the hell it was they were supposed to be doing.

"OK Stark, here's my story. I never knew my mother. Dad said, soon after I was born, she decided the whole thing was too hard. She left in the middle of the night. He did the best he could, but there never was enough of anything—money, food, clothes, you name it. The first time I was going to school, we broke into a Goodwill bin because my dad said it was important to make a good impression. The biggest day of his life was when I graduated from high school. He never got that far. In the summers, he'd bring me to his work with him. Taught me all there was to cleaning floors. I remember, he took an old sweeper and cut it down for me. He never complained, but I could tell. It bothered him a lot that this was the best life he could give his son. Eventually the bottle ate his liver. I showed up at his work, explained what happened and the manager hired me on the spot. I was on my own. I took over his broom."

Blackie waited for her reaction. There was none. She was nodding her head.

"Like I thought, we have a lot in common."

He sat up straighter and tried to form words.

"It's not as crazy as it sounds Blackie. We've both had to overcome huge obstacles to get where we are. You dealt with your upbringing and I, being a woman in a hugely male-dominated profession, had to overcome things you wouldn't dream of. But we both did it Blackie. We're survivors. You know what that does to a person? They have no patience for bullshit. Do your job or get out. I know. I've heard that's how you run your desk. *Everybody* thinks you're the biggest bully on the planet, but I get you... and I'm like you."

She reached down and opened up her file.

"We're going to work just fine together."

Blackie had listened to every word. For one of the few times in his life, he could think of nothing to say. He wasn't sure he'd ever met someone like this before.

"OK then, enough chat. From now on, secrecy is critical. You are who you are in real life, but I will never appear as me. We will use this encrypted phone for all communication between us." She handed Blackie a nondescript flip phone. "You'll use more sophisticated electronics if the situation demands it."

Blackie was coming back to his senses.

"Thanks for the phone, but you still haven't told me what I'm supposed to do."

Agent Stark waved away the waitress.

"As we mentioned in our meeting, we've identified what we're almost certain is a recent pump and dump trade. Our Intel says the alleged perpetrators are going to the Stone Tavern tomorrow night to celebrate their big win. In our experience, some operators like to appear in bars where the real traders go. They have too many drinks and brag about how they beat the system, why they're better traders than the Wall Street big shots, that sort of thing. They're often loud and obnoxious. They won't openly admit to how they did it, but a keen eye can see the opportunity and ask a few questions. Your job is to identify them and try to engage them in a conversation, one trader to another."

"So I go to the bar and get drunk? Nice gig. When do I get paid?"

The agent stared at him.

"Blackie, since we're going to work together, why don't you drop the sarcasm. You may think this is a laughing matter, but we don't."

He shrugged his shoulders, but he was losing patience. Nothing about her plan made any sense to him.

"OK, you want serious? What exactly is it you think I'm going to do, walk up to some guy and say 'hey, nice trade, was it a dump?'"

Stark leaned forward over the small booth table, her face a foot away from his.

"Come on, Blackie, don't sell yourself short. You're one of them. You engage anyone in whatever conversation you like. It's what you do. You have to go in and evaluate the scene. Is the bragging man experienced or a rookie? What approach should you take to engage him? Who should you chose to be? Are you one pro sharing your technique with another? Or are you a frustrated day-trader yourself, fascinated about the man's recent success, eager for just the slightest tip the master might provide? We know the people will show up and that there has been a crime. All we want is you to help us connect the dots."

He looked at her, but didn't speak.

"Blackie, think like you're on your desk, the market is open and a trader at another firm asks you, just before the market closes, to warehouse a big position for him overnight. He says it's a good stock; he's just over his capital limit and has to pare down before he goes home. Says he'll buy it back from you at the same price next morning. You both know you'd get fired if you got caught. Do you believe him? Does what he is saying make sense? Your profession—you guys refer to it as liar's poker, don't you?"

Blackie knew that Stark read his silence as uncertainty. In fact, it was discomfort.

"You appear to know more than most people about the realities of a trading desk."

She sat back up. "Blackie, I do my homework. I know a lot, about your business and now, more about you. Thank you. There were many candidates for this job and I, not Casey, chose you. I did that because I believe that with your help, we'll have the greatest chance of success."

Next to the row of booths on the wall were several round tables on the floor. The hostess had just sat someone at the one right next to them. Blackie looked at his watch. It was almost lunch time.

Agent Stark said, "We'd better get going. We're done here, right?"

Blackie opened his hands. "Like, do I have any questions? Uh… yeah, I do. Like when do I start?"

She got up. "You've already started, Blackie. Now go back and live your life, but keep that phone charged and on you at all times. I will call tomorrow with more details."

Blackie shook his head and waved his hand. He still was sure this was a complete boondoggle. However, Agent Stark didn't seem like a person who wasted time. He liked that.

"I'll leave first. You wait five minutes and then go."

The next day, the vibrating in his pocket startled Blackie for a minute. He almost fell off his rolling chair as he twisted around, fumbling to locate the source. Finally, with the small FBI flip phone hidden by his large grip, he rose quickly from the trading desk.

"I'm going to the can. Watch my GM position. If the stock starts to drift, dump the whole thing."

He walked off the floor, remembering Stark's instructions to find a "secure" place. The bathroom certainly wasn't protected. He walked towards the boardroom, leaning his head towards the door while a concerned secretary watched his every move. Hearing no noise, he turned the handle.

"Blackie, don't go in there. There's a meeting scheduled to start in an hour."

Blackie looked back, smiled and ignored her.

"Bla—!"

He locked the door behind him and pressed the call back number.

"Blackie," Stark said, "good. We are live! They are definitely going to the bar tonight. The message didn't say what time, so get your ass down to Stone Tavern right after the market closes and keep your ears open. Get a table for four and sip—I mean sip—soda water so you don't have to pee. I don't want you to miss anything."

Blackie had thought more about the operation and still wasn't comfortable.

"Yeah, fine, I'll show up. I still ain't sure this will work."

There was a short silence on the other end of the line.

"Don't worry. I'll work with you. That'll improve our chances. I'll dress undercover and will arrive after you. You might not recognize me at first, but just play along. Understood?"

The line went dead. Blackie held the phone away from his face.

What the hell did *that* mean?

Chapter 38

A small boat gently rocking. Wooden, not aluminum, to eliminate reflection. Far enough from shore to avoid suspicion. Just another local, fishing for dinner.

Using his telephoto lens, Silas held the camera steady and waited for the wave to align him. Rock, click, rock, click.

He had been sure Sandy was dreaming in Technicolor, but he couldn't deny his own eyes. There they were, on their porch decorated with rainbow-colored conch shells. Coconut-laden palms swayed to the music of the sea. Steps to the beach and robin's-egg blue water. The house looked like five or six bedrooms for the two of them. Alabaster white. Not another house within earshot. The pictures on file were of them fully dressed, but here they wore swimsuits. The facial match software would provide greater certainty.

He knew it wasn't necessary.

Michael Franklin and Angela Messina were alive and well, sporting some lovely tans. He'd been watching them for several days. They were waited on hand and foot for meals, massages and anything else they might want. A security guard seemingly watched everything, arms crossed, frowning. Money bought their freedom.

That was, of course, their Achilles heel. It seemed like *everyone* on this island was on the take. There was always someone with deeper pockets.

It had been relatively easy for Silas to find the real estate agent that helped the young newlyweds (or so they called themselves) find their dream rental. He knew they were likely to use an agent because then, only one person would see their faces rather than many if they searched home after home. It took a few tries, but he finally found someone whose facial expression completely changed when he showed her the pictures and heard the details. He stayed with the story he'd used at the rental car agency, but added that his efforts had gotten him closer. He knew the woman was in Belize somewhere. But this time he also said that while he had no way of knowing the size of the inheritance, he suspected it was upwards of one hundred million. He was certain that the couple would happily demonstrate their gratitude if the agent could help find them. He'd personally see to it that she received a large cash compensation for her troubles. However, in the meantime, ten thousand cash from him was to show that he was serious.

There was a risk, he knew, in using this approach because the agent could reason that if the couple needed money, how could they afford the eight thousand per month rental? But one hundred million was impressive and the words "large cash compensation" would resonate in her ears.

Bribing the staff was also easy. He found out what the couple was paying them and gave each of them six months' income up front. They bought the same story, especially the part about the huge gratitude payment that would for sure come their way. The guard had already let him on the property after the couple were asleep one night to take pictures using his infrared equipment. The more pictures he took from different times and angles, the better validity of the photo evidence. It also gave him peace of mind that the staff wouldn't blow his cover. These pictures he had now taken from the water were just the icing on the cake.

He had the fugitives. Now for the last part of the assignment. How much money did Sandy actually have?

And what would she pay to get out of jail?

Sandy, it's Silas. We need to talk.

Sandy sat with her phone in her hands in her lap. She hadn't wanted to pester him, constantly asking how the search was going. By reputation alone, he was as good as there was. But she didn't like the tone of his message.

Oh no, Silas, that doesn't sound promising. You're not giving up, are you?

No, Sandy, not at all. The news I have could help us both quite a bit.

She held her breath.

I found them.

This time Sandy didn't even try to hold back her scream. She typed as fast as her shaking hands could, tears streaming down her face.

Oh my God! You did it! Oh Jesus, Silas, you fucking did it. I knew it. I TOLD you… Where are they?

His response seemed to take forever. Was it not time for texting the equivalent of a high five? Why did they *need to talk?*

I warned you earlier that the cost of this search could spiral and I was right. You remember that original estimate of fifty thousand? Well, throw that out the window. I've spent thirty thousand in bribes alone. I'm a reasonable person, but I'm running a business here. I've gone back and tallied my cash outlays—and my time. I haven't looked at another case since I took yours on.

Silas cut the crap. Why are you doing this to me? You have both hands around my throat and now you're going to choke me for more money. Do you have one fucking shred of honor or decency?

LOL, Sandy. I left those at the door when I put on my P.I. badge. But enough of this chitchat. I'm a busy guy and I'd like to complete my assignment with you. I've got a package of photos that will prove beyond doubt that Michael Franklin and Angela Messina are alive and well. As part of my service—at no extra charge—I will testify under oath, if you want, that I took these photos and I will confirm both the place and dates. I told you at the beginning of this adventure it could cost you one hundred thousand, and so it will. I should be charging you more. If you want to purchase my little package, that's the price.

Sandy closed her eyes and shuddered. She had repeatedly gone through her budget. Everything was going to plan. The guard had been a bit more expensive, but that was OK. Then she lost half her money through the Bitcoin theft. And now this. The trading with Ivan was helping but she still didn't have enough.

Silas. You know I don't have that much money. Why are you doing this to me? This is a life and death situation. If I don't get out of here, I will die. Either another inmate will kill me or I'll do it myself. Please, Silas. I'm begging you.

Silas smiled as he read her message. Sandy Allen had all kinds of arrows in her quiver. But she had overestimated her ability to pull at his heart strings.

Sandy, remember who you're talking to. I don't know anything about how much money you have, or more importantly, your ability to get more. So let's turn off the drama. This is a business deal, plain and simple. I've got a special package for you that let me remind you, you hired me to find. I've upheld my end of the deal—pretty nicely I'd say. Now it's up to you. Either pay up or the memory card goes into the shredder. It's up to you.

You're scum, Silas, pure, heartless scum.

No, no, Sandy. No need to thank me. It's all part of the service.

Chapter 39

The place was filling up fast.

Stone Street Tavern was a popular watering hole for Wall Street traders, especially Friday afternoon after the market closed. Inside, rows of dark wood stalls, each with a single round-glass candle, contrasted a series of fold-up tables on the street. Tourists, wannabes and the curious liked to be part of the action. They gathered early at the outside tables, soaking up the ambience of the huge towers around them, slurping martinis and raw oysters and taking selfies against the colored signs outside of the bar.

The professionals preferred inside, staying as far away from the noise as possible. They were here to bring their heart-rates down. They hunched over their tables, drinks held between their hands, speaking in abbreviated sentences and hushed tones. Competitors filled their part of the room and, like all good traders, they tended to listen rather than speak. When they did, it was with surgical precision. No one bragged about their wins or moaned about their losses. No one talked loudly about the markets or his or her recent trades. Squandering intelligence of any kind was unthinkable. Information was power.

Blackie was early enough to get his table for four inside and had to stare down more than one idiot that wanted to join him. As Agent Stark had demanded, he sat sipping his club soda. This was familiar ground. Some of his competitors acknowledged him with a slight nod. Blackie knew they'd find it odd he was sitting alone. Not their concern.

Blackie noticed the two men come in that surely weren't Wall Street traders. They weren't in suits and they looked all around seemingly spellbound by the room full of professionals. The mood of the inside contrasted with the outside; the music, the clinking glasses and laughter. One of the two men seemed to want to sit in the open-air, but the other pulled him into the traders' area yelling, "A round for the house." Some of the outside tourists who heard him rushed the bar.

Every trader looked on in disgust. Blackie knew they found the dolt annoying, disturbing and just plain ignorant. He had violated their solitude.

And Blackie knew he had found his marks.

He watched one of them try to find a seat and waved his hand over the table.

"Sit here for a while if ya want. I'm waiting for someone."

All according to plan. Blackie had to hand it to Agent Stark. She knew they were coming and he made the contact. His instructions now were clear. Start to fish. See what he could learn before she arrived.

He had just started, learning that their names were Ivan and Charlie, when a woman entered and walked toward the traders' area. Eyes diverted and conversations stopped. Wall Street was used to beautiful, confident women, but somehow this one was different. Dressed in a red suit with a front-split skirt and a cream blouse that flowed over her lapels, she stopped and looked around, surveying the room as if it was her territory. Her lips lightly pressed together as her eyes slowly cast left and right. Then, she raised her chin and walked towards her target. The click of her heels echoed.

For a moment, Blackie was just another one of the males who gaped. Then he realized who it was. As she approached the table, her step quickened and she smiled.

"Oh, Blackie, *there* you are! Sorry I'm late. F-me and getting a cab in this city."

She leaned over and brushed both of his cheeks with hers in the finest French fashion.

"Who are your friends?"

Blackie had to stop himself from staring. This was police work?

"I'm Maggie… Maggie Stark." Her high cheekbones augmented her faint smile.

Ivan stood to introduce himself and when she offered her hand for a shake, he took it and kissed it.

"Well, Maggie, you're in luck. I just bought a round for the house. What'll you have?"

He bared his lips and whistled between his teeth, waving at the waitress who, Blackie judged by the look on her face, restrained from giving him the finger.

"A round for the house? Hey, big spender. What'd you do, win the lottery?"

Her elbows and wrists formed an upside down V on the table. She rested her chin on the top of her fists.

The drinks arrived and Margaret continued to focus her attention on Ivan. Charlie just listened and smiled as Ivan bragged about his Wall Street dealing expertise and his latest killer trade. Blackie tried his best to look interested.

As Ivan talked, Maggie developed a pained look.

"Shit, Ivan, it's like a rock concert in here. I can't hear a word you're saying. Grab your drink and let's head over to the corner there. It isn't much of a seat, but at least I will hear you!"

That left Charlie and Blackie alone. Neither had said more than two words. The waitress that Ivan had whistled for arrived, asking if they wanted another. Blackie asked whether the guy was still buying.

"Absolutely," she said, narrowing her eyes towards Ivan.

Charlie never had more than one drink. Betty would get that frown of hers. But this was Wall Street and he was now a big-time trader. And she wasn't there.

Charlie was surprised that Blackie started asking *him* questions.

"So, you guys are day-traders, huh? You're going to think this is weird. I'm a full-time professional Wall Street trader, but I wouldn't trade from home. First off, you're using your own money not the company's. The business supplies me with enough technology on my desk to launch a rocket. Is there, like, some computer program you just load? I only trade what people tell me to and you guys have to find your own stories. And every stock I deal in is big and liquid. The stuff you work in could kill you if you're not careful. So, hats off, my friend, I gotta hand it to you."

Charlie smiled. The alcohol was making his face warm. This Blackie guy, *a professional Wall Street trader,* was complimenting *him.*

"Oh well, Ivan is the expert. He's teaching me. He used to trade when he lived in Seattle; at least I think he did. Then he moved here, closer to his sister, my wife. We are operating out of my home except when we go out and tell everyone what we've bought using public computers. It's very exciting. We'd been working on this big trade for a while and then, a few days ago, we sold for a big profit. Don't ask me how Ivan picked the stock to buy—*that's* something I have to learn, for sure. I think he has somebody helping him because he's always sending or answering emails. But it doesn't matter. We did two trades; one was for a lot of money. Ivan was so happy he said we had to come here to celebrate!"

Blackie smiled and shook his head.

"Listen, I don't want to pry, but would you tell me the name of the stock you guys made your big win on? I'd appreciate it, man. Maybe there's some meat still left on the bone."

Charlie rubbed his chin.

"Yes, of course! Ivan, my partner, has told me several times that once we buy a stock, we should tell everyone. Now, mind you, we already sold this one—soon after we bought it, when I think about it. We don't own it anymore so I guess it can't hurt to share the information. I don't even know the name of the company, but the trading symbol is XZQX. Please be careful, though. I don't want you to lose any money on my account."

Charlie was flattered that Blackie had pulled out his day timer and was scribbling notes. His eyes didn't move from Charlie's as he listened to his story of his former work, how he'd quit—"just like that"—walked right out after sixteen years. Fortunately, he and his brother-in-law had been friends for a long time and he was now showing him the ropes.

Blackie thought he already had all the information he needed. Margaret had told him to leave as soon as he did.

"Hey Charlie, I gotta go, but thank you *very* much. Here's my card. Please, let's stay in touch."

"That's great, Blackie. I don't have a card yet. Maybe I'll see you in here again sometime."

Hairy Hand's associate sat unseen in the opposite, dark corner. Their team had been following Ivan all over town including this little stop-off at the bar, where he was spending money—money that he owed the Seattle mob—like a drunken sailor. His boss, who was already under the gun to collect in full and return home, would fume.

Now there was an additional concern. Some great-looking broad had randomly chosen Ivan to sit at a private table so he could stare at her tits. There was no such thing as coincidence. She was a hooker. That meant more of the mob's money headed down the toilet.

He left the bar to bring his boss up to date.

Chapter 40

There was no time to waste.

Silas had found them. Sandy didn't want to spend one second longer than she had to in this shit-hole.

Once she was sitting in front of the warden and presented her evidence, he would understand that an injustice had, in fact, been done and that the real master-mind of the Ponzi scheme and, don't forget, a murderer, were both still at large.

All thanks to her. They could immediately begin discussing her release.

Officer Hicks, who had taken her meeting request to the warden, now approached.

"Inmate Allen, bad news. The warden will not meet with you."

She feigned a look of surprise.

"What!? But—"

The guard held up his hand.

"Don't start with me. I told him your whole sorry story—at some risk to my reputation I might add. I said you had pictures. He listened to me for a minute and said he'd seen and heard it all before and he wasn't in the mood. So, the answer is no. This whole fiasco is now over."

Sandy shook her head, but she'd been prepared for this.

"Officer Hicks, no, it isn't over. I would appreciate it if you would please pass on a message. I know my rights. Since the day I walked in here I have never, not once, asked for an audience with the warden. It is not an unreasonable request on my part. Ask him if the name Victoria Parsonage rings a bell with him. You may have heard of her. She is a highly aggressive and vocal human rights—especially prisoner rights—activist. Wherever she goes, the reporters follow, because she is loud and commands attention. In law enforcement circles, she is a serious pain in the ass. Well, she's a friend of mine, a good friend. This is one of the things I used our cell phone for that I didn't tell you about. I have relayed my story and she offered to help me in any way I need. If your boss wants to disregard my evidence after he hears it, fine. To violate my civil rights by denying me my chance to present it at all is a different matter altogether.

"Ask him if he wants to come to work past a media truck with reporters sticking microphones in his face."

She doubted, and hoped to hell, that neither the warden nor the guard would try to contact her powerful lawyer "friend" because the woman wouldn't know Sandy Allen if she tripped over her.

The guard looked at her.

"Yeah, OK, I'll give him your message, but let me ask you something. Are you sure you want to threaten the most powerful guy in this joint? He could make your life, miserable as it is now, a hell of a lot worse."

Sandy shrugged her shoulders.

"What have I got to lose?"

Chapter 41

Ivan was sure he'd get lucky.

After all, she let him keep buying her drinks. But without warning, the woman he was hoping his money would impress said she had an early appointment. On a Saturday? But she was gone, with the promise that if he came back next week at the same time, they might get to know each other better.

He finished his drink, looking for more eye candy. Then he strolled back and found Charlie alone, too. He didn't know when the other guy had left, but there were three empty glasses on the table. Then he noticed his partner's head bobbing like a fishing lure. They needed to go now or he'd have to carry him around the dirty, dark streets of New York. Not a chance. He might as well wear a "please mug me" sign on his back. Besides, he couldn't deny his own snake-like pattern as he moved across the room.

"C'mon, Chuckles, time to blow."

He pulled Charlie up and they both almost went down, his partner in crime smiling like the village idiot. However, it wasn't far from the table to the door, the curb and a cab. How he'd get Charlie from his own front door to his bed was another matter. Tonight, maybe, was a couch night. He didn't want to face his sister holding her semi-comatose husband.

The cool air opened his eyes a bit as they slowly moved around the corner down the street from the bar's entrance. Ivan leaned Charlie up against a wall while he whistled for a cab. His brother-in-law tried to imitate, but made a *pfffttt* sound, sending drool down his chin. At first Ivan was worried about the scene they caused, but then realized there was no one around. This was New York! But it was quiet.

"Hello, Ivan."

It was the man who always dressed in black. Ivan slid Charlie down to a sitting position on the pavement and motioned Hairy Hands to the side so Charlie couldn't hear.

"Wait here, Charlie. I'll be right back."

Tradur Gurl

The mobster put his face close to Ivan's. He wasn't smiling.

"Where ya been, Ivan? We been trying to get in touch, but ya don't never seem to go home no more. We checked ya clothes—ain't been touched in over two weeks. Ya still owe us ten thousand in interest expense and lookin' at the celebration ya had dere tonight—buyin' drinks for the house and all—ya must have come into some money. That's good... very good, because my people won't wait no longa. Ya will pay us tomorrow when the bank opens."

If Hairy Hand's face was any closer, they would touch. His whispers were deafening.

Ivan pulled his face back, but didn't lose eye contact. In the morning he would reflect on what he was about to say. Maybe it was the booze talking, he couldn't be sure.

He did know that he'd had enough.

"I have your five thousand—not ten thousand. I borrowed twenty-five thousand from you and I paid it back. You say I owe you ten thousand in interest? That's like a forty percent rate, which is ridiculous. I won't pay it. I will transfer five thousand only into your account as soon as I can."

One of the man's large, hairy hands grabbed Ivan's shirt beneath his throat.

"No, Ivan, ya ain't calling the shots here. Ya never have and sure as shit ain't now. We won't wait no more. Ya will pay us ten thou tomorrow. Meet me at the bank at eleven. Don't make me wait or I might lose my temper. Ya don't want that to happen."

Ivan shook his head

"Look, dirt bag, I'm tired of you trying to push me around and I'm not going to take it anymore. I will pay you *five thousand* and you're lucky to get it. Yeah, sure, I'll meet you at the bank. I'll give you the receipt for the deposit into your account and then you just head on back to Seattle and leave me the fuck alone, understood? If you keep bothering me, my next call is to the cops."

Hairy Hands pushed him away. Ivan's back hit the wall with a thud.

Hairy Hands didn't like Ivan's choice of words… at all. The little cockroach had both offended and threatened him.

And, for the first time, he'd mentioned the police.

He turned and walked away.

A black SUV with shaded windows waited.

After Agent Stark walked by Blackie with the unspoken reminder to leave the bar when he had learned all he could, he excused himself to the bathroom. As instructed, he waited ten minutes in one of the stalls and then went out the side exit. He walked one block down the street until he saw the SUV. When he was five feet away, the door opened. Stark motioned him inside.

She was on her phone. When the door closed, the driver, whom Blackie assumed was also a cop, merged back into the traffic. She flipped the handheld closed saying "roger that," and faced him.

"What did you get?"

He stared at her, shrugged and then looked around the car. "This confidential informant gig is all right! Are we headed to another bar?"

Her look made it clear they weren't.

"OK, fine. Sulk. The dope's name is Charlie. He doesn't know shit about what he's doing. He said they're using his computer at home to trade, using that online service called Trade Away. Their big score was XZQX. He said it loud and clear. Said Ivan, the guy shooting his mouth off, was real happy because they made a lot of coin. When he gave me the stock symbol, he warned me, saying he had no idea how Ivan picked it or even what the company did. He said he'd seen Ivan sending and receiving email messages from someone, and that person must have been helping him. But he never asked him about it. Thought that was just something he'd have to learn."

"So, Ivan has a secret contact. We located the computer they used to do the trades. It looks like Charlie resides in a modest bungalow in Yonkers and our friend Ivan appears to live there, too. That begs a question. If he has a home, why isn't he using it? If Ivan is using Charlie as a front, who is his mystery contact?"

"Wait a minute, Agent. I got something else. Just as I was leaving, Charlie asks me if there isn't a better way to tell everyone they'd bought stock than travelling all over town using public computers."

Stark smiled as she opened her phone and started talking to an immediate connection.

"We've got enough to get warrants now. We won't go for a full-blown house search yet, but get to the email provider first thing. I want to see *every* message sent or received by that computer. Monitor all signals of any kind coming and going from that house. There's a third suspect and we've got to find out who it is. Go back to Trade Away and find out the banking facility that links to the brokerage account. Their XZQX trade just settled. Did he leave the money in the account or transfer it to the bank? We want to track the movement of every penny into or out of that account."

She clicked the phone closed and turned to him, frowning.

"And Blackie…" Her frown turned to a smile. "Not bad, not bad at all. Maybe you should have been a cop."

Blackie could see that the car had pulled up outside his building.

"Yeah, no thanks there. I don't like the hours."

Chapter 42

The morning sun peered through the gap between the living room drapes and the window frame, highlighting airborne dust. Ivan, dressed in wrinkled, dirty clothes, slept in Charlie's easy chair. The beam moved from his feet, to his chest and then to his eyes.

He woke with a start, realized where he was, and searched the room. Charlie was curled up on the couch, snoring.

Ivan sat up and scratched the back of his head, turning his face away from the light. Images and memories from last night rushed in. His head throbbed, but he knew he didn't have time for a hangover. In spite of the booze, he had been awake most of the night. He now understood that the mob was never going to leave him alone and that the chance for a final payment did not exist. He'd give them money today and that was all … until they created a reason for one more payment, and one more after that. There was no end to this nightmare.

That is, if they could find him. He'd been careless coming to New York. This time, he'd make sure to lose them. Today was the day. Thanks to Sandy and her trading method, he had money and the means to make lots more. He could set up shop anywhere in the world. Christ, she was doing it from behind bars! Where would he go? Switzerland? The Caymans? It didn't matter. He was tired of running. This was his last trip.

His sister wouldn't like him pulling up stakes, saying (again) he should find a woman and settle down. But that was always Betty's point of view. He wasn't convinced Charlie would make it day-trading, but Sandy would have to become his mentor now to finish her plan. She would fume that Ivan had bailed, but he had to think of his own future before hers. Besides, she was living a fantasy. No amount of money was ever going to spring her from the pen. She was behind bars where she belonged and, mad as she might be, she couldn't touch him.

Hairy Hands said to meet him at the bank by eleven. That was good. He had something he had to do first.
Then he would go.

Chapter 43

Liquid burned Charlie's throat, ready to erupt.

He woke himself with a snore that got caught and for a moment he couldn't breathe. The smell. Beer and cigarettes. It was his clothes. Images. He and Ivan at the bar. "A round for the house!" Ivan talking with the beautiful woman. He met the trader, a real trader. What was his name? Celebrating. He tried to rub the sleep from his eyes and then he felt the pounding. His head.

He was on the couch—dirt smears on his pants. How had he gotten home? Where was Ivan? The bile tried to force its way up again.

He grabbed the table in front and pulled himself to sitting. The window. Bright. He turned his face away. A piece of paper on the table with a hand-written message.

Charlie
I've got an early appointment at the bank and then I'm heading over to my apartment to pick up a few things. The market is closed today—Saturday—so why don't you research something and see if you find our next winner.
Ivan

He went down to his basement trading station. He wasn't ready to face Betty. She would lecture him for hours and he was in no shape for it.

Besides, it was darker down there.

Sandy was *this* close. Silas had the package of photos that would set her free, but the bastard was taking full advantage of her. She was furiously doing the math on the phone's calculator. He was charging her one hundred thousand. The guard, depending on when they let her out, might cost forty thousand, not the sixty if the search took a year. That was good but someone had stolen half of her two hundred thousand Bitcoin stash. She had made around forty thousand dollars—so far—in their two pump and dump trades.

She had just enough, but she was running it close to the wire. Once she got out, she couldn't survive on *no* money.

More disturbing, the guard said some of the other inmates had been commenting on their "arrangement," wondering when they'd get their turn to use the phone. Either he was trying to extract even more from her or he was telling the truth. She could lose her contact with the outside at any second.

There was time for only one more trade and it had to be big… and fast.

All or none.

She hoped Ivan was ready.

The cooler air in the basement made Charlie feel better. He wasn't sure why he came down other than to avoid Betty, nor did he have any idea how to "research the next stock," as Ivan had suggested. But if he sat down at the computer, something might come to him. He was going to have to learn how to do this on his own at some point anyway.

As the machine started up, he noticed the blinking "message received" light in the corner of the screen. When he clicked on the icon, it took him to the mail account. There were four messages sent to Ivan in the space of five minutes.

He wasn't sure what to do. Someone was trying to reach Ivan in a hurry. He knew enough about the Internet rules to know you weren't supposed to read someone else's mail. On the other hand, Ivan always talked to someone about their trades. Maybe it was he or she trying to reach him with another trading idea. Judging by the frequency of messages, the author appeared excited. Charlie saw an opportunity. He could get the company name from the sender and start searching for information. Ivan would praise his initiative. Besides, they were partners. Ivan trusted him.

He opened the first message…

Coyote! It's Tradur Gurl. We must start buying the next trade ASAP.

Coyote? Who was Coyote? Tradur Gurl? Is this who Ivan had been speaking with all this time?
…And then the second.

Coyote! Urgent! Where are you? RESPOND!

He was going to hit the reply icon, but stopped. It was one thing to read someone's mail, but a different matter to respond to something not even sent to you. That was serious intrusion, but unless someone was making a big mistake, this did appear important.
He wished Ivan was here.

Hello. This is Charlie Gray speaking. Did you mean to send your message to this address?

Across the country, Sandy looked at her phone like it was infected. Charlie Gray? What the…

Charlie Gray? Are you the guy who's been helping Coyote? Where is he? Why are you on his email?

Charlie's face started to burn.

I'm sorry. I didn't mean to intrude. I thought maybe I could help.

You'll help by getting Coyote. Right away!

I'm not sure who Coyote is.

Holy shit, Charlie. It, he, is Ivan! What the hell is going on over there?

It *was* the person that Ivan had been dealing with.

Oh dear. Ivan's gone out. He left a note this morning that he had an appointment. He told me to start working on the next company.

What! That's crap. Tell him I want to talk to him, right now.

Yes, absolutely, Tradur Gurl. But he isn't here.

Charlie, I KNOW that!

Yeah, right, of course you do. I'll tell him as soon as he comes back.

After Charlie closed the email application, he wondered why Ivan and whoever Tradur Gurl was were using fake names. Was that part of how you did day-trading? And this Tradur Gurl wasn't very nice at all. She sort of reminded Charlie of Mr. Abernathy.
Better Ivan should deal with her.

Chapter 44

A guard yelled into Sandy's cell saying she had a visitor. She knew it had to be Silas and, once again, he'd come through just for her. Her meeting with the warden was in an hour. When she reached the visitation room, she smiled at the familiar figure.

"Nice to see you, Sandy. You look good in orange."

Looking through the plate-glass window, one of six in a row, she spoke through the monitored handset. It was nice to see a friendly face. Her private eye hadn't aged much. Even though retired, it was easy to see he'd committed to maintaining his cop body. He could have passed for one of the guards. But the gold chain around his wrist gave it away. His private eye business was doing very well.

"Here are your pictures."

She'd always admired that about Silas, even when he was trying to get her in bed. No bullshit, get to the point. She'd told him she had little time and he listened. He must have taken the red-eye back from wherever he was. Other than trying to take her last penny, he had some admirable qualities.

As he started to slide the envelope under the glass, a guard stepped forward, grabbed it and inspected the contents. Pictures, that was all. He turned the envelope upside down to see if there were any trace items and, satisfied that it was just an envelope, gave it all back.

"Look, Sandy, just look. They are as clear as day."

As Silas had promised, it was Michael Franklin and Angela Messina. There they were. Smiling. They wore swimsuits and stood on a beach amidst a series of palm trees. She could see the coconuts. The picture had a date in the corner. One week ago.

She would never forget what they looked like.

"Silas, these are fantastic! It proves what I've been saying all along! Where were these taken?"

He seemed to be slow in responding, but then it came to her. She hadn't paid him yet.

"Oh Silas, are you kidding? The warden is going to want to know. It'll blow my credibility if I don't."

He looked straight at her and shook his head.

"A deal is a deal, Sandy. As soon as I see my final payment, you'll get their address. Make something up. He won't know any better."

Sandy stuffed the pictures back in the envelope. Glaring.

"You're one mean motherfucker, you know that? You always have been."

Silas smiled and shrugged his shoulders.

The warden knew this meeting was a waste of time.

He had seen it how often? Prisoners came up with "secret" information, providing new, unknown evidence that exonerated them and fingered a new suspect. It was a typical, last-ditch, desperate effort. Even though the woman said she had pictures, every proposal he'd ever seen was fiction and not worth the time of day.

But this inmate had managed to hit his one sensitive spot. It was coming up to annual review time by the state board. The first rule, unwritten but not to be violated, was avoiding media of any kind. Raises were hard to come by anyway and the board wouldn't hesitate to seize the opportunity to deny him one. Sandy's threat—relayed by the guard—to go to the press if she didn't get a hearing had struck a chord. Still, though, it maddened him. He didn't like inmates telling him what to do.

Sandy had been in a room like this before.

She supposed they were all the same: bare white walls and a cold, tile floor. In the middle sat a rectangular table surrounded by four metal-framed chairs with yellowed vinyl seats. On one side of the room was a mirror, which she knew was two-way so that witnesses could record answers given during interrogations. She doubted there were observers behind the glass today. She thought the warden might not want anyone to witness what she had to say.

He arrived with Officer Hicks and another guard. The extra muscle, she imagined, was to ensure order. No doubt that many prisoners would give everything to put both their hands around the warden's throat. Since they were all in the same room, they had cuffed her hands and ankles. Why? Was the man afraid? Unlike the two beefy guards standing on either side behind him, he was compact with short brown hair. Even though his suit was cheap, it was clean and pressed. He wore a starched white shirt and unremarkable brown tie.

She imagined him as a middle-grade office clerk rather than an enforcer assigned to watch over hundreds of killers and thieves.

He let Sandy sit for ten minutes while he reviewed her file. Then he slapped it closed on the table.

"All right, Inmate Allen, you've already wasted far more of my time than you're worth. What is it? Spit it out."

Sandy didn't hesitate. She was not intimidated by this man or any other.

"Warden, thanks for meeting me."

He didn't return her smile.

"OK, look. I'm not saying I'm innocent. Someone tricked me into a situation that I couldn't regret more and it is *appropriate* that I have spent some time in jail. That's in the past now and things have changed. I have solved the crime that the police couldn't and for that alone I should go free. They convicted me for running a Ponzi scheme when, in fact, the person that masterminded it roams free on a beach resort. He has with him, his *partner in crime*, a woman that you all suspect committed murder. I hand them both to you today on a platter."

The warden couldn't listen to any more.

"Jesus Christ, Allen! Is that why you dragged us in here? We're done with your pleading and explaining and the rest of your bullshit story. Need I remind you that you went to trial and were *convicted?* That's how things work in this society and it's also where your story ends."

Sandy's eyes did not waver from his.

"Warden, you're wrong. That's not where my *story*, as you call it, ends. There are two people out there living in the world who have beaten the system, or so they think. I have *found* them! I know where they are. I have pictures to prove what I'm saying is true."

She had given the envelope to Officer Hicks, who handed them to the warden.

"Interesting. How did you come across these incriminating photographs while you have been behind bars? I don't recall issuing any weekend passes."

Sandy caught herself from glancing at Officer Hicks.

"I have, uh, friends on the outside that took them for me."

"A friend, yes, maybe we'll dig into that a bit later. Let's say your *friend,* in fact took these. Where are these people if not at the bottom of Puget Sound? If you want me to help, I have to know this."

She hesitated just for a moment, long enough for the warden to notice and look at her.

"Mexico."

The warden looked back down at the pictures.

"Yes, of course, Mexico. Good guess. There are lots of coconut trees in Mexico."

He picked the pictures up, stacked them neatly and put them back in the envelope.

"I have to say, Allen, this is some of the finest photo retouch work I've seen. Your friend is very talented. A trained eye, of course, sees a few rough spots, particularly around the hair. That's always one of the toughest areas. But I have to hand it to you. This was a very good attempt."

"Warden, please listen. This isn't an *attempt.* These are real people—Michael Franklin and Angela Messina in the flesh, alive and well. I hired a private investigator and he took the pictures himself! The dates are on the pictures. He will testify."

The warden smiled.

"A private investigator. You are a resourceful girl. Everyone knows these people will say anything you want once you pay them. Those dates are easy to put anywhere."

Sandy started to protest again, but stopped as the warden picked up the envelope.

"You've obviously got your hopes up about this and you're wasting precious taxpayer money. So I'm going to save everyone the trouble."

He tore the envelope including the pictures into four pieces and tossed them back on the table.

"Guards, escort the prisoner back to her cell."

Chapter 45

A loud knock on the front door.

"Ah, *there* he is," Betty said. "It's about bloody time! Where on earth has he been?"

She was finishing the dishes. Ivan hadn't come home for three nights now and she was getting concerned. Besides, she'd been waiting to talk to both him and Charlie about their recent night on the town. She had told Charlie a dozen times their behaviour was deplorable.

Charlie was relieved, too, because Tradur Gurl hadn't stopped sending emails and now Ivan could deal with her. Every message said they *must* be "loading up" in a company today. She kept asking how many shares they had bought and Charlie kept not responding, which seemed to make her more frantic. The answer was zero because Charlie had never bought a single share of anything. Her language wasn't getting any more pleasant.

He wondered why Ivan knocked. He must not have taken his key.

As he stepped towards the front hall, thinking about what Betty just said, it dawned on him where Ivan might have been for three days, and he smiled. His mind flashed back to images of the bar and the woman. Could Ivan have just enjoyed a little romantic holiday? He would love to hear him explain that to Betty.

Charlie lost his smile when he saw the two men standing on his front step in khaki slacks, sport coats and ties. They were better dressed than the usual door-to-door solicitors were, but it didn't matter. He'd had plenty of experience chasing these people away. Before either one had a chance to speak, he started to close the door saying, "No thanks, not interested."

He and Betty had been talking about getting a peep hole installed.

One of the men, the bigger one, stuck his large black shoe in the doorway as he pulled out a gold badge encased in a small leather wallet.

"I am Detective McNish from New York City Homicide. We're here to see Elizabeth Diversky. Is she at home?"

The name Elizabeth didn't immediately register with Charlie. Betty never used it, nor had she called herself Diversky since they were married. He was about to force the door closed when he heard his wife's voice over his shoulder.

"Yes, that's me," she said. "What is it? Is something wrong?"

"I wonder if we might step inside, madam."

They sat in the living room. Betty offered them tea or water. They declined. She said to please call her Betty.

The older of the two men continued.

"There's no easy way to say this, Ms. Di… uh, Betty, so I'll just get to the point. I'm sorry to have to inform you that your brother Ivan is dead."

Charlie would remember Betty's composure. He didn't recollect her exact words, something like "oh my goodness," but it was the lack of histrionics that surprised him. No one knew how anyone would react at a time like this, he supposed, but it was as if her always-pragmatic approach towards everything had taken control in the absence of any rational explanation for what the officer had just said.

Ivan was dead?

"A body was found yesterday in an apartment above a convenience store on Main Street by the landlord who'd heard noises in the middle of the night. Ivan was his tenant."

Betty and Charlie looked at each other, confused.

"Officer, I think there's been some mistake. That's not a very good part of town. I'm quite certain that my brother doesn't live above a convenience store. Regardless, he's been staying with us to help my husband get his new business started."

"There was mail addressed to him there. His driver's license had that address on it. I agree it's not the Trump Tower, but that's where he lived."

Betty didn't respond. The officer continued.

"The SEC requires finger prints from all registrants and Ivan's were on file. We took prints off the corpse and they matched. He had your and your husband's address on his cell phone. So that's why we're here."

He'd been reading from his note pad. He finished and flipped it closed.

Betty and Charlie just stared at each other. What was happening didn't seem real. It was like something you'd see on TV.

"But Betty, there's more. Ivan didn't suffer an accident or take his own life. We're treating this as a murder investigation. He suffered a single shot to the head at close range. That is a clear indication of a mob-style execution. Can you think of anyone Ivan might have known or been doing business with that would want to cause him harm?"

Betty's body seemed to shake. She put her hands to her mouth. Murder? The mob?

"Oh no, officers. You're making a terrible mistake, coming here like this, saying these things."

The officer seemed not to listen.

"I know this is a bad time, Betty, but I need to ask you more questions, the sooner the better. As time moves on, our chances of solving the crime decrease rapidly. It appears your brother worked in the stock market. Can you tell me about that?"

Betty spoke into her lap. She seemed afraid to look anyone in the eye…

"Yes, he did his stock trading thing at home."

"Right. We saw some of his statements. Tell me. How did you think Ivan was doing in his day-trading business? Was he having any money troubles?"

Betty looked up and smiled.

"Oh my goodness, no. His business was doing well! He kept showing up in fancy new cars. It was so good; my husband Charlie quit his job to join him."

The officer looked at Charlie while tapping the pencil eraser on his note pad. Sometimes people didn't tell the truth, even to their loved ones.

"Well, Betty, that apartment he had over the convenience store would seem to argue otherwise. We've gone through the statements I mentioned and your brother appeared to have made a profit—a small one at that—only twice in the last few years. You mentioned that he was driving fancy cars. We didn't find any vehicle ownership records. Please, think harder. Anything you could give us, even the smallest bit of information, could be valuable. Like, for example, why did he leave Seattle and come east?"

Betty spoke to the ceiling.

"He said he wanted to move closer to me... and that he had started up his new business... Oh, wait. He did tell me once that he didn't leave his last company on the best of terms. He said he was going to hire a lawyer to get some money back that they took from him. But that was several months ago. I can't imagine..."

"Through the SEC records, we discovered that he was terminated from Fifty States Investments. We spoke with senior management who told us they could have classified it for cause, but, as is sometimes done in the industry, they prefer to avoid the cost and time of litigation. So, your brother received a severance package and signed a release, exonerating the company from any further liability."

Charlie was frowning as something disturbing formed in his mind. Why did Ivan leave Seattle? Was he running from the mob? That might explain why he wanted to live in their basement until he "got himself grounded." If he'd received severance money, what happened to it? He seemed so successful, but then why did he live above a convenience store? What about all the new cars? Was that just a façade? Few profits in years?

Everywhere he looked was a pile of lies. It was as if he was back at the insurance company. He remembered rejecting an insurance claim once from someone saying her relative had tricked her out of her life savings. He closed his eyes.

After a few more questions, it was clear that neither of the Grays was aware of Ivan's other life. Detective McNish didn't want to wear Betty down any further because he knew she would need to come downtown to identify the body. It was clear to him what had happened. Ivan borrowed from someone he shouldn't have. The wad of bills found stuffed in his mouth was a clear message of what happened if you tried to play piggy with the mob's money. He paid the ultimate price.

The detective decided not to mention the evidence of torture.

When Charlie entered the cold room, behind Betty and the officers, the first thing he noticed was the smell of formaldehyde. He put his hand over his nose, but he still had to breathe. He squinted against the fluorescent lighting that dominated the ceiling. They walked over to the wall of sliding aluminum trays containing toe-tagged bodies covered in white sheets. A man in a lab coat pulled Ivan's sheet down, just far enough to identify the face, but not reveal the wound.

Betty broke down. Seeing his wife in tears brought Charlie to the same. It took them time to collect themselves. Detective McNish helped them into his car and no one spoke on the ride home.

It was about an hour after dinner time, but neither was hungry so they went straight to bed. Betty kept muttering under her breath, "But I don't understand. This makes no sense. It's not real." But there was no denying who they identified in the morgue.

She curled up into a fetal position right next to Charlie and sobbed herself to sleep.

Lying on his back, looking at the ceiling, Charlie felt guilty that he wasn't as devastated by the loss, but his head was full of other, terrible thoughts. It sounded like Ivan's murder directly related to his stock trading. What had he done that brought his killers to such a horrible act? The detective kept asking about Ivan's money situation. Did Ivan owe the mob some? Could the murderers figure out that Ivan had a partner?

He'd have to tell the Tradur Gurl person. Charlie hadn't touched Ivan's inbox after the last time, but he saw it now had over thirty messages, all marked urgent. He imagined she would be very mad. Would she be so furious that she wouldn't agree to mentor him in his new career? Charlie had little hope without her help.

He was running out of choices. It didn't feel very good.

Chapter 46

Sandy screamed into her forearm.

No! Not now!

That greedy bastard got himself *killed*. Damn it!

She'd fronted him cash to make the mob go away. And then they did two profitable trades. There was cash all over the place. He should have been happy. But no, he decides to play—everyone—just to line his pockets. That must have been what happened.

She thought someone had been front-running their last series of trades. It must have been him. She never did trust the bugger.

She reread Charlie's last message. A stupid babbling idiot was her lifeline to freedom. She had to compose herself. This would make things harder. Hell, this entire scheme was almost impossible.

She paused and closed her eyes. Traces of a smile crept into the corners of her mouth. She reminded herself that in times like this, when the shit really hit the fan, she was at her best.

OK, Charlie. That is disturbing news. Just awful. Who would have known that Ivan was associating with such terrible people? I hope the police catch whoever did this and fast. But Charlie, life goes on, right? It's just you and me now. I know Coyote—shit, I guess it doesn't matter, call him Ivan—has been training you so we could expand our trading business. Now you'll just have to hit the ground running.

His reaction hadn't occurred to her.

Tradur Gurl, my wife, Ivan's sister, has been upstairs crying her eyes out all night. The man isn't buried yet and all you want to talk about is the next trade? That's pretty cold, don't you think?

She wanted to reach through the phone and choke some sense into him, but the wheels were in motion and there was no time to train someone else. They were at the absolute crucial part of her plan and all the elements had to work. She'd have to get him onside and now.

She paused for longer than necessary. She wanted him to believe that his comment had struck a deep chord with her.

Yes, Charlie, you're right. I must seem heartless and I apologize. I guess I'm acting this way because, as terrible as it sounds, I am not surprised by what happened. You and I have never spoken, but I see that Ivan hasn't been honest. Ivan and I, we've known—or we knew—each other for a long time as day-traders. I think he told you how tough this game is. He had to borrow money from some bad people and look where it got him. The real tragedy is that he and I have figured out a new trading strategy that really works. We were well on the way to getting him and me out of a deep financial hole.

She paused again, for effect.

You notice I said him and ME. I have big money problems too. I'm not as desperate as he was, but I might as well be. I'm getting regular threats to pay my loan back, too.

It was a complete fabrication, but she needed to plant a sense of her desperation—meaning they were short on time—into his mind.

She feared revealing the truth about her prison background would scare him away.

Charlie, with your brother-in-law gone, I REALLY need your help. You're my savior. If there is any good news, Ivan and I were THAT close. With just one more trade—what he and I were working on—these evil people get their money back and exit my life forever. I know it is a terrible time for you and your wife and I hate to ask—but they've given me an ultimatum. They sent me a message this morning. **Did you hear the news about Ivan? You're next.** *Please, Charlie, execute the trades I need or, well, I don't want to think about it.*

She paused again.

You'll have more to worry about than just Ivan's death.

She kept her fingers crossed. There were so many blatantly obvious questions he could ask, any one of which could create more delays.

Tradur Gurl, I'm worried. If it was the mob, will they find out I was his helper and come after Betty and me, too?

Do you owe them any money?

Oh, good heavens, no!

Then don't worry, there's no risk to you or your wife. I give you my word. They were after Ivan and now me. Besides, if they know you're going to help me, it's in their best interest to leave us both alone. All they want is their money, Charlie. I swear on your brother-in-law's grave.

She thought it was good to add that last part in case Charlie was religious.

Then it came to her. She knew where his pressure points were. Ivan had mentioned that his brother-in-law had quit his job to become a day-trader. He'd taken out a big personal loan secured by his house. Ivan was supposed to teach him and now he was up shit's creek.

He wouldn't be able to say no to anything Sandy asked.

Charlie, I just thought of something. Ivan told me that you had quit your job, one that you held for years, to become a day-trader. He was going to teach you, right? How was that going? Are you all ready to go out on your own? If not, well, you've got bills to pay, right? I guess maybe you need me as much as I need you.

Now the pause came from his side, but she was sure it wasn't orchestrated like hers. She pumped her fist. She'd nailed it—and him.

Well, OK, I guess. Tell me what to do.

OMG, Charlie, thank you so much. First things first. Please go into the program that Ivan set up for doing our trading under the "Why Me Coyote" account and tell me what it says under "total assets."

Charlie followed the keystrokes she gave him and, apparently easily found what she was looking for. But he said something was wrong. He'd have to double-check.

Uh, Tradur Gurl, it says the total assets are zero.

WHAT? There should be something like forty thousand in there. Are you sure?

I've had quite a bit of experience going through financial statements in my old position in the insurance industry. The account did have a balance of almost forty thousand two nights ago, but I see there was a transfer out yesterday of the entire amount.

Sandy ground her teeth. The mob must've gotten the passwords from Ivan. She shuddered thinking how. She'd have to transfer some more of her own money over so Charlie could buy the required stock. She closed her eyes. That would bring her personal balance to negative if she factored in the full cost of the guard and Silas' bill.

She really did have just one more trade.

Chapter 47

Was Charlie's ignorance a blessing or a curse?

A bit of both, Sandy thought. While the man didn't have a clue how to trade, that also meant he wouldn't know the difference between legal and illegal—if she positioned things well to him. Based on Ivan's description, he seemed like a willing pupil, following instructions to the letter, going to numerous public computer sites to help spread the pump, and never raising any concerns. Her risk now was that she had to bring him closer to the truth than Ivan appeared to. That was an added complication.

There were no other options. The clock was ticking and there were shares to buy. Sandy started giving Charlie a crash course on how to trade.

Charlie, to create a large stock position without affecting the market price you need to monitor the ladder of bids and offers, never buying more than twenty percent of the indicated stock for sale, and then recalculating each minute if necessary.

God, the guy was slow responding. She imagined him moving his lips as he read.

Tradur Gurl, you're going too fast. I've read your instructions three times, and I don't understand anything you just wrote. I know this is important, so why are you hurrying me? I'm going to make a big mistake and mess everything up.

Sandy had anticipated this. Ivan had also told her about Charlie the person and his background. He was mister steady Eddie, the turtle against the hare.

Not any more, my friend.

Charlie, by the way your new name is Linus, you know Charlie Brown's best friend from the cartoon? There are times when you just have to put your fears behind you and step up to the plate! Give yourself more credit and stop second guessing. You—and I—will get it done.

I don't know, Sandy. I was getting more confident, but now that Ivan is gone—heck, I've never met you or even know where you live. How am I supposed to explain this to Betty?

If what Ivan told her was true, the last thing Charlie wanted to do right now was come clean with his wife. He didn't realize the size of the powder keg he was sitting on. It was time to raise the ante.

Tell me, Linus, how much did you bring to the table? I'm sure Ivan said you'd need enough to stay in the game, to suffer the odd loss, which by the way happens to all of us. Money is your life blood in this profession. Run out and you die.

Ivan told me the regulators required twenty-five thousand in capital and I gave him another fifty thousand to invest with.

Sandy was stunned. Ivan was more ruthless than she thought. He had defrauded his own sister's husband.

He said that? OMG, Linus, Ivan is a lying skunk! You don't need anywhere near that much money to trade at home. The twenty-five thousand is just a minimum balance you must keep in your account if you trade, like, five times a day.

What? I watched him transfer twenty-five thousand. He said it was to the regulators. If it didn't go to them, where did that money go?

Sandy thought she knew exactly where it went.

Linus, it's becoming obvious to me that you have overlooked something—something big. When I asked you to call up the balance of the trading account, and you said it was zero—that there had been a large transfer—you didn't seem too concerned.

Oblivious was a better description, she thought.

No, I guess not. I was surprised because you seemed to think there was money in that account when there wasn't. I guess Ivan must have moved the funds somewhere else. I'm sure the police will sort that out.

Now it was important that Charlie fully understood that he was in deep trouble and only Sandy could save his bacon.

Linus, Ivan didn't transfer the twenty-five thousand to the regulators; he sent it to the mob to pay back money he owed them. There's nothing for the police to sort out. It's gone.

But Tradur Gurl, that was a lot of money!

Linus, speaking of a lot of money there's another fifty thousand not spoken for. How important was that to you?

Well, what do you think? It was VERY important. I had to borrow it all. I gave the company my personal guarantee.

Sandy shook her head as she wrote. If she didn't have so much riding on this, she could imagine herself almost starting to feel sorry for Charlie.

Did you carefully read the contract you signed?

Yes, well, no. Ivan was in a big hurry.

Security for a 'personal guarantee' means every asset you own or ever will own. Is your house in your name or your wife's?

There was now a long pause. Bingo.

Uh, well, my wife did inherit the house from her mother, but at the time we put the title in both our names. We went to see one of those financial planner guys and he said it would be best.

Sandy went in for the kill.

OK Linus, I think I got the picture. You have put your fifty percent ownership of the house up as security. Think about what happens if the company that loaned you the money ever has to collect on that security.

His responses were coming faster now.

Well, I guess they'd force us to sell the house, but that isn't going to happen. Look Tradur Gurl, you're bringing up a good point. With everything that has been going on, I haven't checked on my own account. Do you know what Ivan called it and what the password is?

Again, she waited longer than necessary to maximize his fear.

Linus, I just checked and can only find one brokerage account.

But then where did Ivan put all my money, the other fifty thousand?

Like I said Linus, I'm pretty sure he paid the first twenty-five thousand directly to the mob. He was telling me he was desperate before you came on the scene. That loan you took must have saved his ass. For the rest, I now think he had an account that he kept secret from both of us. I was almost certain when I reviewed the trades that someone knew our plans and was front-running us. Now I'm sure it must have been Ivan.

Deliver the final blow.

Charlie, it doesn't matter. Ivan could have had ten accounts and the mob, through their horrible interrogation methods, could easily get account numbers and passwords—all the information they would need.

Sandy wished she could see his face.

It's gone, Charlie. All of your money is gone.

The basement door opened.
"Charlie dear, is everything all right? I thought I heard a scream."

Chapter 48

*S*howtime, Linus.
You have Monday to watch how the stock trades and then Tuesday morning we go live.

Charlie shuddered as he read her last message. He wasn't ready, but she didn't seem to care. It was Sunday. He'd almost begged her to wait a few more days, but she was in a real hurry now, like she had some sort of deadline. One minute she'd say, *Oh don't worry, Linus, I'm sure you'll get it*, and the next minute she'd fire back with profanity and exclamation marks.

If it was so darn urgent, why didn't she just trade it herself?

But he knew he couldn't go there. He feared the worst if he made her too mad. Would she "fire" him and go find someone else to trade with? For all he knew, she was on the verge of doing that anyway. But she kept reminding him that ALL of his money was gone, stolen by the mob, thanks to Ivan. When he'd suggested bringing in the police, she almost made Charlie cry. It sounded like Ivan was doing something ILLEGAL, she said, since the mob was involved. Charlie could do what he wanted, but in her experience, these types of things often got very messy and the cops, in their eagerness to catch a bad guy, sometimes roped in innocent people. She'd seen it with her own eyes. If Ivan was doing something illegal, Charlie was an *accomplice* whether he knew it or not.

Financial ruin—and jail—awaited him.

What would happen to Betty?

The stock is ZQXR and it trades on the NASDAQ exchange. The average monthly volume is twenty thousand shares and I think we could buy ten thousand shares in total without upsetting the market.

For now, pick up the stock at three dollars or below - the lower the better. Put in your bids at the open each day for five hundred shares. If you get hit, go another five hundred and see what happens. If someone steps in front of you, you'll have to use your judgement. Look at the lineup of the bid/offers and the volume. Keep an eye on what the overall market is doing because all boats rise when the tide is coming in. No matter what, never trade more than twenty percent of the day's volume.

You got all that, Linus?

He closed his eyes. *Lineup of the bid/offers? Get hit? Steps in front of you?*

She wanted him to *use his judgement?*

It was like he was watching a movie where he knew an actor was going to die before they did. He was that character. And he was trapped. There was no way to avoid his fate.

What a mess he'd made of his life. He felt like he hadn't slept since he heard about Ivan. What happened was horrible, even if he had lied to them. Betty had been so silent. Usually she'd hum a tune while she'd been working in the kitchen, but now the entire house was just quiet.

He thought it was sad that the last time he saw Ivan was in a bar. He hardly remembered it, but still... He got to sit and talk to a real Wall Street trader that complimented him on his recent success. And there was that beautiful woman. He smiled a bit thinking back to when he'd answered his front door thinking it was Ivan, wondering how his brother-in-law would explain *her* to Betty.

He snapped his head up. The Wall Street trader! He searched frantically in his desk drawer for his card.

"Trading."

"Oh yes, hello. May I speak with Mr. Black, please? Jonathan Black."

Blackie's index finger was poised above the disconnect button. The markets opened in an hour and he had no time for this. But he paused. Outside annoyances like telemarketers couldn't see the trading phone numbers and this call came in on his primary line. The only way the caller could have that number is if he had given it to him.

"Yeah, that's me."

Blackie slipped the cell phone Agent Stark had given him into his pocket. The receptionist watched him commandeer the boardroom again and just frowned.

"Yeah, so it was that Charlie Gray guy from the bar. Said he had to talk to me. That it was urgent. I'm wondering where Ivan is in all this and whether he knew his winger was calling me, but I didn't say anything. He said he did not want to say any more over the phone, but wondered if we could meet again. Right away, like this morning if possible."

Chapter 49

"Wear a wire! Me?"

Agent Stark had just been reading the emails between Linus and Tradur Gurl.

"Yes, Blackie, Charlie wants to see you urgently. Tradur Gurl is in a big hurry to start up her next swindle and it's stressing him out. It's a perfect opportunity for him to tell us all he knows. You'll wear a wire and we'll monitor from inside the truck. But make him wait until tonight. There will be more people around and less chance someone will notice you. Meet him in the Stone Tavern again, but grab a table in the back, like where Ivan and I sat. It's quieter. We'll hear everything."

"This is stupid. I told you the guy doesn't know shit about what he's doing."

"That's why he called you."

She could hear his irritation rising.

"Yeah, Agent, but you're missing something. Why does the dope want to talk to me? He's got Ivan who, if I show up, will wonder what's going on. I don't like it."

The press had certainly picked up that there'd been a murder in town. Nowadays, in a city the size of New York, that was news that fell off the front pages relatively quickly. Importantly, Margaret was able to delay the release of the *name* of the victim, pending notification of next of kin. She knew, however, that Blackie would find out soon enough and better he heard it from her. Working with him was tricky at best but she believed she had established a sense of trust. She didn't want to lose that. She needed his cooperation.

She wondered how he'd react. They said it took nerves of steel to trade on Wall Street.

"Blackie, Ivan is dead. They found him, murdered, a few days ago. It was a mob hit. We're thinking he must've been into them for a loan and they came to collect. He may have even skipped town from Seattle to try to hide from the payment. Not a smart plan. That would explain why he was keen to live in Charlie's basement. They must've found his apartment. There was evidence of torture. They probably did that to get his passwords. They also cleaned out his brokerage account. The homicide guys are looking into it, but these types of killings are most often almost unsolvable."

Blackie was quiet for some time. "That explains it, then."

Nothing. Nerves of steel?

"Uh, yeah, it does. It also makes you the star of this play now. Charlie needs you because Tradur Gurl has given him a stock to buy, pump and then dump. He knows he's in way over his head. He's resisting, but she's putting the screws to him so he can't say no. We've been reading the emails. She's in a big hurry. She keeps reminding him that his own money is gone, thanks to Ivan. Unless he wants to lose his house too, he *must* do what she says. We're still not sure why she doesn't just do the trades herself, but we'll find that out too soon enough. We've been waiting for them to fire up their next fraud. This time we have a warrant. We'll record the whole con and then shut this operation down for good."

"But I'm the one wearing a wire?"

"You have to, Blackie. At first, you play hard to get and he will beg you. Eventually, you give in, but say there's no way you will trade in his personal account on your company computer. They'd fire you. Remember, you don't know these are illegal trades. It's critical that you get yourself on his home computer because it's a treasure chest. We also want to make sure there are plenty of emails going back and forth between Tradur Gurl and Charlie for the next few days. We've been able to determine that the phone she is using is one of those pay-as-you-go jobs—not much use in catching a criminal—but while she is using the phone, we're going to track her location via satellite. We may not know who she is, but when we find out *where,* we'll be that much closer to nailing her."

She'd had this conversation before. Most people were not thrilled.

"Nice plan there, Agent Stark, but I have this allergy to getting killed. Wearing a wire when the mob is involved isn't exactly a life-prolonging move. I think I've fulfilled my side of the arrangement here. This time I mean it. I'm going to pass."

Margaret didn't want to lose either her temper or momentum.

"Well, I guess we could call William Casey back to re-read you the riot act that got you signed up in the first place. But I prefer a softer approach. First, don't worry about the mob. They got what they came for and are long gone, especially with homicide guys everywhere. Second, wouldn't you describe yourself as an honest guy in a forest full of thieves? Help us take one down and you'll do something good for yourself and your industry."

Blackie did not respond.

"Listen, Blackie, I'm the good girl here. In exchange for you fulfilling your civic duty, I'll make sure the books are closed forever on the old insider trading case. Casey can never threaten you with that again. I'll make sure of it."

Blackie probably recognized the old bait-and-switch approach. *I'm your friend and then there's the mean dog Casey in the corner over there. Help me and I'll find a leash.*

But he still didn't respond.

"I might even buy you a beer after we're done."

Finally he said, "Stark, if I get killed doing this, it will seriously piss me off."

Chapter 50

Inside the black SUV, the technicians were putting the final touches on Blackie's electronic vest. Margaret Stark gave him some last-minute coaching.

"Now it's obvious that you say nothing about being involved with the cops. We're sure Charlie doesn't realize he is an accessory to a crime. If he did, that would send him over the edge. He's already spooked enough about his brother-in-law getting iced *and* maybe losing his house. If we lose him, we lose Tradur Gurl. She, now, is the prize."

Blackie just nodded his head.

Charlie had found the table in the back of the bar where Ivan and Margaret had sat. When they got their beers, it didn't take long for him to get to the point. As coached by Margaret, Blackie was careful to look surprised by Charlie's news.

"Wow, Charlie. Ivan's dead? The mob?"

"I know, Mr. Black, I know. It all seems scary. I was emailing Tradur Gurl. She's the woman who has been helping Ivan all along. This thing with Ivan and the mob has been going on for some time, it seems. She told me Ivan mentioned it to her when they first started working together, but it's obvious he didn't tell her the whole story. She said she never mentioned it to me because she knew we were related and it wasn't any of her business what Ivan did and didn't want to tell me. But here's the thing. He crossed them—didn't pay them back—and you don't fool with people like that. It cost him his life."

Blackie had to hold back his smile. Here was cowboy Charlie strutting down the street, explaining life with the big boys. He remembered though, there were people waiting in the SUV.

"That is terrible, Charlie. Poor Ivan. Why don't you call me Blackie? Everyone else does. I'm wondering, though. You keep talking about this Trader Gurl person. Have you met her? Do you know anything about her?"

Charlie shrugged his shoulders.

"I'm sorry, no. I think her real name is Sandy. Tradur Gurl is just the name she uses for trading. My trading name is Linus." He smiled. "I think she and Ivan became partners a while ago. Watching Ivan, it seemed like Tradur Gurl picked out the companies, and then it was Ivan's job to buy the stock. Once he finished, Ivan and I would go visit public computers and share the good news that we thought was coming. I guess that is some sort of practice amongst day-traders—sort of a share-the-wealth kind of thing."

Blackie hoped the truck had its ears on. Charlie had just described the classic pump and dump.

"But Linus,"—Blackie winked and Charlie smiled again—"you must know *something* about this Tradur Gurl person. Like why wasn't she just doing the trades herself? She sounds pretty experienced."

Charlie shook his head.

"Sorry, Blackie, all I know is that she and Ivan used to email each other three or four times a day. I think that was when he was in the process of buying shares. Therefore, she'll expect to hear from me starting tomorrow morning. She said she wanted *progress reports* as I buy the stock."

Bingo, Blackie thought, Margaret gets her email traffic.

"But Blackie look. Tradur Gurl says she's going to use her own money to pay for the stock I'm supposed to buy and she promised that all profits would go to me until I pay off my loan. That's wonderful but then she tried to explain to me how to buy the stock and, I'll tell you, it's not that easy. You have to buy just a little bit at a time so no one notices that you're doing it. I don't think I can. I have everything on the line. If I mess up, I may lose my house *and* her money too. I need your help Blackie, please. There's just too much at risk for me."

As instructed by Margaret, Blackie made him sweat.

"Charlie, if I agree to do this, I can't trade personal stock from my computer at work. They'd fire me on the spot. I'd have to work at your house."

Blackie thought Charlie might cry.

"Oh my God, Blackie, thank you. You could save my life!"

Blackie waited while Charlie calmed down and collected his thoughts. They agreed when he would arrive.

"Oh, one thing, though. I didn't tell Tradur Gurl that I was coming to you for help, so it might be better that we don't tell her. I'm not sure she'd approve."

"Yeah, I agree," Blackie said. "That's a good idea."

Chapter 51

The next morning, when Blackie sat down in front of Charlie's computer, he said, "You know, Charlie, since you want me to buy this stock for you, and you don't want Tradur Gurl to know, it's like I've become Ivan. It might make sense for me to just go through the emails she and Ivan exchanged so I don't do something out of character. It's just a precaution. Why don't you go grab a coffee? It won't take me long."

Before Charlie had even closed the door to the basement, Blackie had pulled out the memory stick and put it in the USB port. After a series of keystrokes, given to him by Margaret, the small light on the white piece of plastic blinked like a Christmas tree. It had finished copying all email messages and was back in Blackie's pocket before the door opened again. When Charlie walked in, he had something in his hand.

"Blackie, I thought this might come in handy, too. It's Ivan's cell phone."

The market had opened and it was time to start buying stock.

"OK, Charlie, I'm just looking at ZQXR. I think you said Tradur Gurl thought it would take about six trading days to buy ten thousand shares, but looking at the float and the average daily volume over the past six months, I don't think it will take that long."

Charlie made a crooked mouth.

"Sorry, Blackie... float?"

"Oh, right. How do I explain 'float'? Every stock has a certain number of shares outstanding. If, for example, a company had, say, one million shares outstanding, then all one million shares could theoretically trade on any given day. But the reality is, especially for these junior companies when they go public, that guys like the president own a chunk of stock that they are never going to sell. Let's just say that senior management own three hundred thousand shares. The 'float,' or the number of shares that are available for trading, would be, in this case, seven hundred thousand shares. It's important to know that number, especially if you want to buy a lot of stock but not disturb the market."

Charlie beamed.

"Thank you, Blackie. I think I understood that."

"Since Tradur Gurl wants to buy ten thousand shares in total, looking at the numbers, I'll finish by Thursday. Sound good?"

"Very good. That will be faster than she thought. She'll like that."

Blackie bought the last of the shares on Thursday afternoon, ten thousand in total at an average price of two dollars and seventy eight cents, well within Sandy's guidelines. Blackie knew he could have bought many more, but that was all she wanted. Charlie kept saying how thrilled Sandy would be.

At first she was. Charlie gave her the good news. She had expected a shit-show and, instead everything went smoothly. However, something nagged at her. A guy who supposedly wouldn't know a trade from his elbow purchased the entire position in half the time she thought it would take. The price paid was also well below what she expected. Charlie the rookie had demonstrated near perfect trading skill.

Something didn't make sense.

Chapter 52

Acting alone, the pump took Charlie longer, but the result was no less sweet. He completed posting Tradur Gurl's message about ZQXR one public computer and one Internet chat site at a time. The share price responded beautifully, fueled by her inflammatory rumors plus the lack of available supply to those who believed and wanted in on the action. The share price rose by three times.

Seconds after Charlie left each Internet café, a federal agent hiding in the corner out of sight commandeered the computer he had been using and copied the necessary evidence, in some cases having to show his badge to the startled teenager who'd been waiting for a machine.

The following Monday, at their usual time, Tradur Gurl coached Charlie on the last and most critical part of the operation, the dump. If done wrong, they would be left holding the well over-valued shares. Disaster waited in the wings.

Now, Linus, listen to me. This has been a fantastic trade. I'm so happy that my research helped me find such a fine young company that looks like it is going to succeed for years to come. However, one thing you learn in the day-trading game is that you never fall in love with a stock. Once you've made your money, it's time to move on to your next success. We've tripled our money here so it's time to get out. We don't want to get piggy; there's an old saying on the street that sometimes the bulls win and other times the bears, but the pigs always get slaughtered. We have a large holding. As you start to sell, watch the price. You want to unload your stock holdings as fast as possible, but you'll have to trade it in pieces so you don't upset the market. You have to monitor not only the bid prices, but also the number of shares wanted at each, and the line-up. For example, if there are five hundred shares wanted at over eight dollars, but the next bid on the screen is for only one hundred shares at one dollar lower, don't take out the entire five hundred at once. I think you get what I'm saying now.

Charlie still didn't get it at all, but he wasn't worried. Blackie was coming over soon.

Not to worry, Tradur Gurl, I have everything under control.

The following morning, when Charlie reported that he had sold the entire block without so much as causing a ripple to the share price, Sandy knew something was very wrong.

Wow, Linus that is some fine trading. I'm not sure I could have done any better myself. Where did you learn that? Maybe I should get some pointers from you.

She was curious how he would answer that one.

I don't know. Beginner's luck I guess.

No, Charlie, I want to know. Did you have to step in front of many offers or were you just taking out bids the whole time? What was the general market action?

There was a hesitation. Then Charlie texted, *the stock just had good floating.*

Tradur Gurl

Sandy stopped, horrified when the reality hit her. Count to ten. She had to retain her composure. She found a corner as far away as possible from other ears in the prison library and dialed Charlie's home phone number that Ivan had given her. There was far greater risk in speaking instead of using email, but she had no choice. It took Charlie four rings to answer the phone, but she thought he must be surprised. She'd never called him before

"Uh… hello?"

"Hi, Linus, it's Tradur Gurl."

"Who? *Oh*! Really? Where are you calling from? We've never spoken. So… hi, Tradur Gurl."

"Charlie, this isn't a social call and I don't have much time, but I need to ask you a question. I'm just reading what you wrote me and I'm concerned. I need to find out more about how you did our recent ZQXR trade."

She could hear him fidgeting with the phone. She couldn't see his face and neck, but she could imagine them turning a deep red.

"Um, well, I don't know what else to tell you, Tradur Gurl. We sold everything and got the price you wanted so that should make you happy, right?"

She didn't hesitate. She couldn't know when the guard would come back looking for the phone, but she could now hear it in Charlie's voice. He wasn't a very good liar.

"Charlie, if we are going to continue as partners, we need total honesty between us. Do you agree?"

"Uh, yes, I guess so, sure."

She could hear his voice starting to crack.

"You guess so, or are you sure?"

"No, I'm sure, of course I am."

"Then please just tell me the truth. I won't get mad, but it is very important that I know. You just said 'we' sold the stock. You didn't actually trade ZQXR, did you, not the buying or the selling?"

Charlie started to deny her accusation, about how hard he worked and studied to learn, but she stopped him.

"The truth, Charlie, I only want the truth."

"No, Tradur Gurl, I didn't, but you have to let me explain. All those things you were telling me. I was so confused. I…"

"Charlie, stop it. I don't want an explanation. Just tell me, if you didn't trade the stock, who did?"

"A Wall Street professional trader Ivan and I met in that bar when we went out. He's been very helpful."

Sandy closed her eyes.

"Did you tell this person about me at all?"

"Ah…no. Frankly, I don't even know that much about you, so how could I?"

She could hear he was still lying through his teeth.

"Does this trader have a name?"

"Yes, it's Jonathon Black. He works at Bryson Securities. Like I said, with Ivan gone, he's saved me. I have his card right hear. Do you want to call him?"

Sandy spit the name in a yelling whisper.

"BLACKIE?"

"Yes, that's him! Do you know him?"

Sandy's hands were shaking.

"Yeah, we used to work together."

Chapter 53

"So, I guess you won't need that anymore."

Officer Hicks was standing over Sandy, pointing at the phone.

"Now that the warden has popped your little dream balloon, then I guess we're all done with the daily hand-offs."

Her mind was racing, still thinking about Blackie's involvement. Like thunder in the distance, Blackie was Sandy's recurring nightmare that just wouldn't go away. The last time they crossed swords, he and the analyst David Heart tried to nail her as part of an insider trading ring. She'd just managed to stay out of jail by turning state's evidence against the Russian company CEO who committed the crime. So what that she went along for the ride and picked up some coin too? The Feds didn't see it that way and her freedom from jail came with a price; they barred her from ever working in the securities industry again.

She had moved to Seattle where no one would recognize her, started up the Ponzi scheme with Michael Franklin and, ultimately, ended up in jail.

And now Blackie was entering her life again. Coincidence?

There were no coincidences. She and Ivan had been doing the pump and dump trades. Somehow the Feds must have found out. Might have been the f—ing computers. But it didn't matter. Now she had to move and move fast. It wouldn't take them long to figure out the brains behind the scheme.

She had to run. She had to get out of jail.

But the phone still was her lifeline.

"Officer Hicks, it might look like my "little dream" as you call it is over, but it isn't. To be honest, I expected the warden's reaction, but his behavior does not, for a minute, compromise the truth. He has people readily available that he could have called on to confirm the authenticity of the photos. He chose not to. Why? If I'm innocent, why keep me in jail? There is a lot more going on here than you realize and, I'm sorry to say I can't disclose it to you yet."

The guard scratched his head.

"I swear to God, when I listen to you speak, I think you could have made a ton of money doing something honest. You make up some great stories. What a waste. But a deal's a deal. The game is over. Thanks for the phone. Except I guess I'll have to pay the monthly bill now."

"Officer Hicks, one more day. Just give me that, please. Then I won't bother you about it anymore."

He was shaking his head.

"Look. You've stuck with me this long. I just need the phone one more time tomorrow. It won't cost you anything. Humor me. I promise. This is it."

He scratched his chin.

"Well, if it'll mean the end of your whining and complaining… but one day, that's it. Then this soap opera is over."

If only he knew, she thought. He reached for the phone, but Sandy's fingers were faster than Officer Hicks. Before handing it back to him for the day, she sent Silas the email she'd been writing.

Silas. Urgent! You MUST sign onto your email tomorrow at our usual time. Please. I need you!

She handed the phone back to him as she forced a smile.
"See you tomorrow, Officer."

The next day, Sandy opened her phone to a message.

Sandy. What's wrong? You know, if you keep asking me for favors, I'm going to turn the meter back on.

Silas… easy, easy, easy. I don't have much time to explain. I took your photos to the warden. He laughed at me, ripped them up and threw them back in my face.

What? He can't do that. Those were legitimate evidence suitable for a court of law.

Well he did. Listen, Silas, I have another job and this, one way or the other, is the last request I will ever make of you.

Sandy, that doesn't sound very good. Look, I'm your friend and I'm on the outside. We can talk. Don't... do anything stupid.

Oh for Christ's sake, Silas, if I was going to kill myself I wouldn't have wasted all this time. I guess... I don't know... If I don't get out of here... but I'm not thinking that way. Look, if I remember correctly, one of your tools that you use to find people is to hack databases and servers. I think you're pretty good at it or at least you used to be.

The reply was fast.

No, you're a bit wrong. I'm not good at it. I'm the best there ever was. But it's not something I advertise on my website. It is kind of illegal.

Sandy raised her fist in the air.
It took almost the rest of her hour to explain her plan, but when she finished, she added,

Silas, don't forget, it has to happen tonight—overnight—or I'm screwed.

LOL, Sandy. Don't worry. I got your back. I will say, though, you make life interesting.

Chapter 54

Margaret Stark and her team were in the conference room, surrounded by boxes and reams of paper. The table was almost covered by reports, intermixed with used paper coffee cups and partially eaten donuts and bagels. William Casey walked in and sat down.

Margaret gave him her report.

"We have the full taped recording of Charlie explaining to Blackie how they did all their trades, apparently unaware that he did a great job describing a pump and dump scheme. We reviewed all the email messages between him and Tradur Gurl about each trade. We followed him on every pump walk and copied the information he downloaded onto the chatroom sites from the computers he used. *And the satellite team worked their magic.* Blackie got Charlie to keep sending Tradur Gurl stupid questions that she kept responding to. The phone she is using is, get this, transmitting from behind prison walls, at the Blaine Corrections Center for Women near Seattle, Washington. Our Tradur Gurl is either an inmate or a guard."

Her presentation was interrupted by a technician who walked into the room holding a sheet of paper.

"William, sorry to barge in, but we've got the text that we lifted off of Ivan's cell phone. Turns out the chat was through LinkedIn. We hadn't searched that site. Not the kind of place you'd expect to look."

William held up his hand, and took the papers. "Ah, here you go. Listen to this."

The room was quiet as he read.

Oh, hey there, Ivan. It's a voice from your past! Sandy Allen ... or, as you first met me, Jennifer Salem. I've been trying to reach out to you. Ivan, I'm sure you know my story and where I am now... in prison.

"And then Ivan replies…"

Hi there, Sandy. I borrowed some money from the mob— who want it back—and I don't have it. They've been making some pretty graphic threats and I don't think they're fooling around.

William looked around the room.

"Oh my God! Remember, in one of the emails, Ivan made a mistake and called her Sandy instead of Tradur Gurl. Well now we know. The name 'Sandy' is none other than Sandy Allen. There's someone we know. This woman just doesn't quit. She's serving consecutive life terms and is still up to her old tricks—*from inside prison!* Very impressive. Now it's all starting to make sense."

Margaret gave a mock high-five towards the technician and said, "I suppose the threat of more jail time isn't going to concern her too much."

William nodded in her direction.

"We might not be able to extend *her* stay behind bars, but maybe we can add to her list of acquaintances… on the inside. I hear Seattle is nice this time of year. Let's make sure we get all the legal paperwork lined up before we go. We don't want to lose her on a technicality. We'll need a warrant to search for the phone she's been using. Oh, and don't bother mentioning to the warden that we're coming. He's running a country club instead of a prison. If he is aware of that fact, that's a problem. If he isn't, that might be even worse. Either way, he has some explaining to do. We'd hate to ruin the surprise."

Chapter 55

"Hope you enjoyed your last time."

Officer Hicks had come to retrieve the phone with a big grin on his face. The whole phone thing had bothered him from day one because the thought that he, a guard, would get caught and become an inmate himself horrified him. However, he didn't. The sham finished and he pocketed a lot of money for his troubles.

As Sandy handed him the phone, she said, "Thank you, Officer Hicks. I don't need this anymore. Now I need you. And you're going to need a friend—which is me."

The officer scrunched his brow.

"Here we go. What the hell kind of nonsense are you spewing now?"

Sandy motioned to the chair opposite her.

"You're going to want to sit down for this."

He continued to stand.

"Fine, suit yourself. I said to you yesterday that there were things going on that I couldn't explain, but now I can. In fact I have to. You know me as Sandy Allen, the convict. What you don't know about me is, as part of my sentencing, I became an internal agent—a mole if you will—to form part of a nation-wide investigation into rule violations within federal prisons. They asked me and I agreed, but in exchange I negotiated a full pardon. They assigned me to investigate this prison and, wow. There are a number of troubling issues. For example, there's a warden that has no regard for the legal rights of the prisoners—as you witnessed in our recent meeting—and smuggling by guards is rampant—as you so accurately indicated to me about the availability of drugs, right out in the open in the prison yard."

Officer Hicks' squinted.

"Oh my God, now I have heard everything. This is the most ridiculous crap ever. Thanks for the bedtime story, Allen, but we're done here."

"And one guard in particular violated about every rule in this facility by providing a cell phone to one inmate *and* accepting substantial cash bribes."

Officer Hicks wiped his face with his hand.

"I believe the term is *busted*."

Hicks leaned forward and cracked his knuckles.

"OK, I've heard enough of your garbage. We had a deal that the phone was a secret between you and me. I don't like people that welsh on deals. You may not know who you're dealing with, but I could make your life miserable. Get it?"

"Oh yes I do, Officer, and that, of course, is another violation. But look. There is a potential silver lining to this story for you if you make the right choices."

Hicks folded his arms and grunted.

"For the internal investigations to succeed, and this one certainly has, even the warden doesn't—or I should say didn't—know about the program. He, after all, is responsible for everything that goes on in here and he will lose his job and face his own bank of charges in short order. Here's the issue. We have discovered that somehow the warden has learned of my special status. His hands are tied. If he starts making major changes around here, it's a tacit admission of guilt. If he does nothing, he's just digging a deeper hole for himself. He either knows about the violations around his prison or doesn't, but it doesn't matter. His goose is cooked regardless. So, what does he do? He tries to remove the threat. He has leaked information to our friends the drug dealers, that I'm a narc. Officer Hicks, my life is now in danger. I need to get out of here and you're going to help me."

"What a bunch of garbage! If you are who you say you are, why don't the Feds just come in and bail you out?"

"This investigation is nationwide and the key is that it is under cover. For them to rescue me would blow the entire thing open, ruin years of planning and throw away millions of dollars. No, I have to escape. It won't look good on the warden's record, but he's going down anyway. As for you, I will guarantee full recognition for your cooperation. And I will just forget the cell phone ever existed."

Officer Hicks held his index finger to his lips and stared at Sandy.

"Yeah, I understand this is tough for you to accept. Let me help set your mind at ease. Go into the prison files and look at my record. Normally you couldn't. It's restricted for obvious reasons. I thought you might need some convincing so I ordered them opened—that's what I was doing on my phone just now. I'll give you all the login information you'll need. You'll have to wait until tomorrow because the wheels of bureaucracy move slowly. But when you get in, look at my record. What you won't see is a list of convictions for any criminal offense. What you *will* see are two magic words."

"FULL PARDON."

The officer stood up, nodding his head. Sandy then lowered her voice to a whisper.

"When you're done, hurry back. We've got to get me out of here. I hear the hit on me is scheduled in three days."

She prayed Silas could do what he said he could.

Chapter 56

Officer Hicks saw Sandy's record and was convinced. She was not who she seemed to be and, given the warden's behavior, her life could well be in danger. He didn't want any harm that might come to her to be his responsibility. He needed to get her out of there ASAP.

Silas created the plan, sent it to Sandy who, in turn, gave Hicks his instructions.

It was Wednesday, September 15, 8:30 a.m. PST, morning exercise time. Most inmates were in the yard. Hicks escorted a lone figure down the cell block hallway toward the washroom. It was a woman, about five feet, eight inches tall with blonde hair cut short, even shorter than what was required for the inmates. She wore a cap with the logo *ACE Plumbing* on the front that matched the one on the breast pocket of her gray coveralls. The full body suit was several sizes too large, obscuring any notable shape beneath, and her dark, worn work boots scuffled as she made her way. She labored as she carried her red, oversized plumber's toolkit close to her.

Hicks didn't know, or need to, that the woman was a hooker whose professional name was Silver. Silas got to know her well, not through her line of work, but because she had been more than willing to exchange information for cash in several of his past assignments. He'd hand-picked her for this job because she had three critical qualities; she'd do just about anything for money, she'd been in jail many times and wasn't the least bit intimidated by the environment and, most important, she had a close-enough resemblance to prisoner No. 3856197.

For security purposes, upon entry into the prison, she walked through a metal detector while the guard articled each tool in her toolbox including a multi tip screwdriver, a hack saw and several files. A prisoner would pay well for one of these treasures, so the guard would recheck the list carefully on exit. Nothing like a spare plumber's large pipe wrench left behind as a gesture of compassion by a sympathetic trade's person. They had once found an inmate, apparently at the short end of a dispute with another inmate, suffocated by a toilet plunger.

In the entry guard's zeal to itemize every metal object in the large rectangular container, he didn't seem to notice or care about the extra hat.

The maintenance worker and Officer Hicks walked slowly through the paths lined by cold, black steel bars and gray concrete. Although the inmates roamed freely, no one seemed to pay much attention. A plumber was common in the prison world. The cons seemed to like to take out their frustrations on the waste removal amenities. By regulation, the plumber was a woman. She was, after all, going to work in a female bathroom facility.

When they reached the targeted room, Officer Hicks opened the door and yelled, "Everybody out! This can is closed for repair."

Satisfied that the room was empty, Hicks allowed the worker inside and stood guard with crossed arms, his back to the door, having placed a large yellow "Facility under repair" sign in front. Some inmates came by, grumbled, but moved on.

After about ten minutes, when he heard the sound of the toilet flushing—three times—he knew the job was finished.

A different woman wearing full coveralls bearing the name *ACE Plumbing* on the breast pocket, with matching cap, emerged from the bathroom carrying the same large red toolkit. She looked at Officer Hicks, but didn't say a word.

Hicks adjusted her hat.

He left the "Facility under repair" sign outside the door. He knew Silver was hiding in one of the stalls, door locked with an *out of service* warning on it, feet off the floor just in case someone came in.

As Hicks and Sandy approached the prison entrance, she hoped the entry guard couldn't hear her heart pounding. He looked up from his newspaper, somewhat surprised.

It was 8:50 a.m. PST.

"That didn't take long. What do you people charge for something like that, a hundred bucks?! Hell, that's double what a guard makes."

Sandy kept her eyes low, seemingly uninterested in idle chat. She opened her tool kit for inspection. She knew Silas had done an excellent job of including tools that could easily be used in an escape attempt… to keep the focus on the toolbox and not the person carrying it.

Officer Hicks spoke up.

"Will you hurry this up, Joe? It's time for my break."

"*Your* break? Cry me a river. I've been here all night. In ten minutes, it's *my* break. Come nine o'clock, I'm headed home to get some sleep."

Satisfied that the exact list of tools that entered the facility was now ready to exit, the entry guard signed off and buzzed open the three doors that led outside.

Sandy had to hide her exhilaration. It was a sunny September day, no wind, and a few white clouds. Although the prison surroundings were a sea of concrete and asphalt, it was the most beautiful scene she had ever witnessed. She wanted to hug the sky!

She walked towards the white panel van in the parking lot, seemingly towards her next job, as a plumber would. Inside the van, she crawled into the back and covered herself with a blanket.

At ten minutes after nine, after the shift change, Officer Hicks approached the entry guard, accompanied by the female worker from *ACE Plumbing*, preparing to exit.

Silver now wore only one pair of overalls. Officer Hicks had found her a set of tired, scruffy-looking work boots from the old chain gang days when they enlisted inmates to pick up highway litter, because Sandy had taken hers. The new guard, on the nine a.m. to five p.m. shift, looked up in surprise. He hadn't signed any plumbers in.

"Wait! What the hell?"

He quickly pulled up the record books from the previous shift.

"It says here you were signed out fifteen minutes ago. Where's your tool kit?"

Silver spoke up.

"I was in my truck getting directions to my next job when I realized I'd left my hat in here."

"Let me see your ID."

The guard looked from the picture to the plumber's face and back again.

Officer Hicks spoke up.

"It's OK. Joe signed her in. He was just finishing his shift when she came back for her hat. He must not have wanted to create another record. I will vouch. I saw her take her toolkit out."

The entry guard shook his head. For safety, he searched her.

Holding up the results of his search, he said, "Hey, wait a minute. What's this?"

Silver spoke sharply.

"Are you kidding? I got another job waiting. What does it *look* like? It's my cell phone. I brought it in with me and now I'm taking it out."

The guard handed it back to her.

She should *never* have been allowed to carry that into the prison. It was a clear violation.

"Joe is an idiot. He should follow the rules or find another job. That's what I say. Go ahead. Get out of here."

Chapter 57

William and Margaret's flight took about six hours. It left New York at 7:00 a.m. EST and arrived in Seattle at 10:00 a.m. PST. On landing, they would hurry into a waiting car and call the prison warden's office to arrange their un-announced emergency meeting. The ride from the airport to the prison took about 2 ½ hours. With luck, they'd be face-to-face with the warden by 1:00 p.m. William couldn't wait to hear the man explain himself.

Still on the plane, he looked at his watch. It wouldn't be much longer now.

It was Wednesday, September 15, 9:30 a.m. PST.

As they neared Seattle, William enjoyed the view of Mount Rainier. The plane was on time, and with the morning rush hour finished, they would make good time. Once in the car, he spoke directly to a surprised and harried prison administrator who confirmed the hastily arranged meeting at 1:00 p.m.

It was, of course, the FBI asking.

When they walked into the warden's office, he didn't rise to greet them. He apparently was none-too-pleased by the surprise visit. He kept his eyes on the piece of paper he was reading and motioned them to the two chairs in front of his desk. William introduced himself and Margaret, and they showed their badges.

"I know who you are. What I'd like to know is why you came all the way from New York to interrupt my day. I'm a very busy man."

William thought to himself that the warden would likely pay them greater respect soon.

"You're right, Warden, we're all busy. I will get to the point. We have a search warrant for one of your prisoners who has been running a pump and dump stock trading scheme from inside this facility. She's been using a cell phone to communicate with accomplices in the New York area. That's how we became involved.

However, as we continued our investigation, we discovered the identity and location of the perpetrator. She is a felon known to us from a previous case where she plea-bargained her way out of a conviction for insider trading."

The warden looked up and removed his glasses.

"What? A pump and dump scheme? Using a cell phone from inside *this* prison? That's impossible."

Casey took the warrant out of his jacket pocket and waved it at him. There was no denying the meaning of the piece of paper. When the warden spoke again, the agent noticed a softer tone. He imagined the man was starting to realize that the allegations, if proven correct, would wash out his career.

"Good God, why didn't you tell me? We watch inmate activity like a hawk here, but I guess, every now and then, something falls through the cracks. Let's haul this woman out and start with the interrogation."

He pushed the intercom button on his phone.

"Get me a guard in here now, on the double."

Turning back to Casey, he said, "Who is it?"

William opened up his satchel and gave a file folder to the warden. It contained all the necessary evidence to nail Sandy Allen. The warden read the file.

"Ah, Sandy Allen. I might have known something was up. She was in this office a few days ago saying she had new information and should be let go, the usual stuff. Let's see what she has to say for herself now."

A knock on the door interrupted him.

"Come!"

Officer Hicks stepped in.

"Warden. They said you sent for a guard, that it was urgent."

"Yes, Hicks, come in." He waved at his guests. "These people are from the NY FBI. They have a warrant to search and question inmate Sandy Allen for possible federal trading violations. They believe she has been using a *cell phone* inside my prison! Bring her here at once."

The warden turned his attention back to the file folder in front of him, but Casey didn't miss it. Officer Hicks' face paled and his knees almost buckled. He grabbed onto the back of a chair for support. The warden noticed he was still there.

"Hicks! I said NOW!"

It didn't take long. When Hicks returned with the news that he couldn't find Sandy Allen, the prison was locked down and all inmates were ordered to their cells. They searched the entire facility and found Sandy's orange jumpsuit stuffed behind the toilet. On questioning, Officer Hicks admitted to escorting a tradesperson, *one* plumber, in and out. He accused Joe of hallucinations caused by fatigue after a long shift or some other foreign substance.

They would never find the remnants of her beautiful blonde hair that took three flushes to clear.

Authorities have begun a massive search effort, coordinated across several law enforcement branches. Although the fugitive, Sandy Allen, serving consecutive life sentences for several counts of federal fraud and other related offences, is not thought to be armed, she is considered dangerous and would "take any means necessary" to avoid recapture. Local residents are encouraged to be vigilant. Checkpoints have been set up in the area surrounding the prison and authorities are searching cars and trucks. Nearby bus stations and the Seattle-Tacoma Airport are on high alert, as are Canadian immigration officials. Anyone who provides information leading to the apprehension of the escapee will receive a twenty-five thousand dollar reward. The Governor of the adjacent State of Oregon has warned residents to be on the lookout.

Sandy, sitting in her motel room, shut off the news alert after one official, speaking to six or seven hand-held microphones, said *"We have the capacity to catch anyone we truly want to if we allocate the necessary resources, which, of course, we are in the process of doing in this case."*

"No, you don't," she said, as she tossed the remote on the sofa. On the ride from the prison to the motel, Silver described the close-call with the cell phone. Since Sandy suspected that Blackie was now working for the New York Feds and they had somehow infiltrated her and Ivan's email messages, she knew she had to get the device away from Hicks. It was full of incriminating evidence and, thus, far too risky for him to keep it especially once he learned he'd been conned. She'd convinced him that, in the midst of the extensive investigation of all the prison violations that was to come, the phone had become a dangerous personal liability to him. He quickly understood and was happy to part with it. As only Silas knew how, he wiped the device clean of all messages and then boarded a Greyhound bus. Just as it was starting to pull out, he ran up to the driver to let him off. He couldn't believe it. He'd forgotten something important. He'd have to catch the next one.

He was only following Sandy's instructions, leaving the cell phone, wedged underneath the seat cushion where it wouldn't be spotted, power on and transmitting its wireless signal for any and all who might want to follow it, non-stop to Dallas Texas.

Silas arranged for Silver to drive the van from the prison entrance to the motel and to give Sandy a room key. She went through one of the back entrances, keeping her head down and her plumber's hat pulled low to thwart the security cameras.

He had equipped the room with everything she would need to complete the transition that Silver had started in the prison bathroom. Sandy had already lost several inches of her hair. Now it was time for the blonde to become a brunette with matching eyebrows and a beauty mark on her cheek. She ditched the plumber's coveralls for a smart business-casual outfit, black skirt and a yellow blouse. The shoes with half-heels were a definite step-up from plumber's boots and not a bad selection for a guy. She'd have to mention that to Silas. He even packed her a small lunch. He'd prepaid the room under the name of "John Smith" for two days, although she knew she wouldn't need that much time.

The room was a short walk to the Seattle offices of the FBI.

Tradur Gurl

She moved into the bathroom and began the final process. She had an important meeting coming up and wanted to look her best.

Chapter 58

The police were everywhere.

The prison escape dominated the newscasts. In spite of the official press release, some reporters referred to the fugitive as "armed," which was ridiculous, and "extremely dangerous." Sandy liked that one. Live interviews of possible eyewitnesses grew like mushrooms. Prison officials were not available for comment. The quickly assembled task force assured the public that she would be trying to get out of town and it was only a matter of time before they apprehended her. Authorities were combing the airport, bus and train stations and even taxis. They stopped and questioned bicycle riders, people rollerblading and skateboarders. CNN loved it. They had already named it the "Manhunt for a woman." A rumor surfaced that they'd tracked an important cell phone to somewhere in Texas, but a spokesperson would not confirm or deny.

Her transformation to a short-haired brunette was excellent, if she did say so herself. She was just another professional woman on her way to work. No one even looked her way. As she walked across the street towards the FBI building, a patrol car with siren blaring and lights flashing almost hit her.

Christ, they were supposed to find her, not run her over.

The man at the security desk looked up, grim faced. There was no smiling at the FBI.

"May I help you?"

Sandy grinned inside. No one came close to recognizing her.

"Good morning! I'm here to see Agent Mueller please."

The guard screwed up his face a bit.

"Ah, do you have an appointment? I don't see any meetings in his calendar."

Sandy looked shocked.

"Oh dear, I was sure it was today… but I could have messed things up. I am so sorry. I had to travel very far to get here. Could you ask him, please, if he could fit me in? I'm willing to wait."

The man nodded and picked up the phone.

"And who are you?"

Sandy did not hesitate.

"He knows me very well. Please just tell him that Angela Messina is here."

She was sure that would peak the agent's interest. Angela Messina was supposedly dead.

News of the escape had, of course, reached Agent Mueller, who had been the one to arrest and help convict Jennifer Salem AKA Sandy Allen of running the Ponzi scheme. He had just finished a call outlining her background and likely MO to one of the search teams. He had told them to not underestimate her, that she was intelligent and resourceful—*very* resourceful. He did not admit it to them that, during the Ponzi scheme investigation, if it wasn't for Michael Franklin's confession note, she might still be operating her swindle today. He implicated her as the perpetrator saying his involvement resulted from sophisticated deception. Then, apparently out of utter remorse, he and his true girlfriend took their own lives.

The agent was leaving for another briefing when the call from reception came in. It was likely a crank visit from someone who remembered the details of Sandy Allen's trial and conviction. However a good cop knew that the best leads sometimes came from the unlikeliest of sources. He told the security guard to put the woman into a nearby conference room. It was a small room with white walls, a metal table with formed black plastic seats. When he came in, he took a seat opposite the potential informant. Sandy noticed he did not offer to shake her hand, but just began to speak.

"Miss... Messina is it? I am Agent Mueller with the white-collar crime division. Your cryptic reference to this name leads me to believe that you might have information regarding Sandy Allen, the escaped convict. If so, you have made a wise choice to come see me today. We welcome any information you might provide."

They looked at each other. Sandy waited until the agent started to fidget at her silence.

"You don't recognize me, do you, Agent Mueller?"

On hearing her voice for the first time and looking into her eyes, the agent cocked his head. His face and neck reddened as he leaned forward, scrutinizing her facial features. He sat up straighter, throwing his pencil onto the yellow note pad he brought with him.

"Well, Sandy, this is quite a surprise. I must say you have an interesting way of trying to flee town. Do you have any idea of the resources that are trying to find you? I should handcuff you right now."

Sandy had surveyed the room before agent Mueller arrived. It didn't seem like one used for interrogation. It lacked the two-way mirror on one wall to protect the identity of witnesses, police psychologists and the like. This was important. Only the agent must hear what she had to say.

"Agent Mueller, don't get mad or excited. Just listen to me—please. Believe me, your search is not a waste and, in fact, is a necessary evil as you'll soon understand. If you handcuff me and throw me back into prison, you'll never hear my proposal. It's a good one, sir, perhaps life-changing for both of us."

Mueller made a noise as if he tasted bad food.

"I thought I'd seen it all. You have about sixty seconds to explain yourself."

Sandy could feel the hair on the back of her neck bristle, but she forced herself to smile.

"Sixty seconds to change a life, huh? Then I will get right to it. I am innocent. I was set up to take the fall for a crime I didn't commit and now I have proof. As I told you many times during the investigation, it wasn't Michael Franklin and me running a Ponzi scheme; it was he alone. He's a brilliant con who took full advantage of my *circumstances* when I left New York to move to Seattle. Once he tricked me into doing some of his dirty work for him, he threatened to expose me and, with my record, I would surely go to jail."

The agent smirked.

"Funny how that turned out, huh?"

Sandy continued.

"He knew no one would believe my side of the story. He's a ruthless bastard who is bitter towards anyone who is more successful than he is, including his own father who, by the way, Michael cheated out of his last penny even after he learned the old man had a terminal illness."

Agent Mueller yawned.

"During your interrogation of me, I gave you the video-tape that showed something was wrong. On the night that the seemingly despondent Michael Franklin was headed to take his own life, he gets a ride from Angela Messina and takes his laptop with him. Does that make sense to you? Who takes his computer with him to kill himself? It would make sense, however, if you were trying to leave incriminating evidence—about me—that would throw the investigators off his trail and onto mine. Another thing. You guys concluded that Michael could not have survived the swim from the boat to the shore in Puget Sound. You said that in spite of his background as an expert swimmer, captain of his team in college and so forth, that the cold water and strong currents would do him in. I say nonsense. He must have worn an ultra-thick wet suit with flippers, a mask and a snorkel and probably went during low tide. AND he obviously had Angela Messina waiting for him on the shore."

"Miss Allen, there's little point repeating evidence from your trial. Your attorney presented your arguments in a court of law and a jury of your peers convicted you. I hope for your sake you didn't go to all this trouble to rehash old news. A cynic would say you are just trying to talk your way to freedom."

She again forced a smile. She must appear confident and in total control.

"No, Agent Mueller, I wouldn't waste your time or mine. Of course, I want to get out. Who wouldn't? Being in prison is like watching a slow motion movie where the main character—you—is dying one day at a time. When I started forming this plan, I had only two things in mind: freedom and revenge. That bastard Michael Franklin and his squeeze set me up. They didn't care what happened to me. I could spoil in prison like old fruit covered in flies, as long as they made it to the beach. To think, at one point, I was starting to have feelings for the guy. Maybe it's a good thing I was locked up when my associate located them. Had it been me, I might have killed them and then I guess we'd be having a different kind of conversation.

"But never mind all that. At least give me the benefit of the doubt that, however unlikely, it is *possible* that Michael Franklin swam to safety."

"Sandy, I don't know where you're going with this, but fine. It is not impossible."

"You just said that *all* my evidence was presented in court. That isn't true, either. I have proof that Michael and his girlfriend who, I'll remind you is a central suspect in an unsolved murder case, are alive. I hired a private detective and he found them living in a luxurious beach house in the Caribbean."

"I noticed that brown envelope you're carrying. You got it through the front-door metal detector, so I'm guessing there's no bomb inside."

"Here are recent pictures. You have the technology to confirm these are genuine. I now have the two of them under constant surveillance. They're living a sweet little life, for now. They aren't aware that I, and now you, know their secret so there is little flight risk. My P.I. is standing by, waiting for my instructions."

Agent Mueller opened the envelope and looked at the pictures carefully.

The sixty-second time limit had expired.

"All right then, Sandy, let's just say for a moment that your *private investigator* has located these individuals. In the interest of your time and mine, we won't go into things like who this P.I. is, or how he found them or, for that matter, you him. I feel like I've known you for longer than I deserve and I'm sure this valuable bit of information—if it does exist—isn't free. What will this bombshell of evidence cost the US taxpayers?"

Sandy inhaled deeply. She leaned forward, her eyes locked on to Agent Mueller's. She spoke slowly and deliberately.

"Nothing. I… only… want… out. Not just from jail, but the whole thing. I feel like I've spent my whole life on the run. My mind is always racing... even when I'm asleep. What's my next scam? How do I beat the law? Who might come back and try to get even? I never relax, ever."

She closed her eyes and opened them. She could feel the emotion welling up inside her. She must... not... cry.

"Agent, I know that every word I've ever said to you, or any other law official, has been a lie. It's how I learned to survive. My parents, when they weren't at each other's throats, taught me well. The only way to get ahead, no, shit, to *survive,* is to lie, cheat and steal; stab the other guy in the back before he stabs you. I've done insider trading, Ponzi schemes, pump and dumps...whatever line of *work* I choose, it is must be illegal. I've been thinking about that, a lot. Why do I always have to break the law? Now I think I have the answer... because it's *reassuring.* It proves to me that I'm in total control. My whole life, all I've ever done is fear that someone or something would get the better of me."

She brought both hands up to wipe a trace of moisture from one eye.

"That is until now. I'm done, Agent. I'm tired of being on the run and sick to death of hurting innocent people. You have that witness protection program thing. Put me in it. I don't care where you place me or in what job. Sandy Allen, the queen of the scam, will vanish forever."

Agent Mueller rubbed his chin.

"You say that now, Sandy, but how will I know you won't get up to your old tricks again?"

Sandy threw both hands in the air.

"My God, you're the only people who will know who and where I am. I'll wear one of those tracer things if you want. You'll watch my every move."

Agent Mueller ran his hand through his hair.

"All right then, supposing we did make a deal? What assurance do you have that I won't double-cross *you* once you've told us where Messina and Franklin are?"

Sandy frowned and then slowly smiled.

"Come on, Agent Mueller. You said you knew me. Let's put it this way. I told you my P.I. is waiting for my instructions. You can lie to me and lock me up again, but, as I think I've demonstrated, you can't control me. Imagine an article in *The New York Times* about how a con behind bars was the one that actually solved the case."

Mueller sat up straighter.

"And you *know* I'm good on my word for that, Agent."

"Are you threatening me, Ms. Allen?"

She paused, closed her eyes and opened them.

"I guess it's the only chip I have left…, but don't look at it that way. My plan is nothing but a win for you. You get all the credit for finding the guy who *really* orchestrated the Ponzi scheme. Isn't faking your death to avoid prosecution some kind of crime alone? You also capture his girlfriend and convict her of murdering her husband for his life insurance. That's the best two-for-one deal in town. Besides, whether or not the *authorities* ever find the at-large prisoner Sandy Allen, my escape hangs over the warden's head, not yours. He should lose his job anyway. There's a lot of bad shit going down in that joint."

She paused, closed her eyes again and spoke softly.

"But Agent Mueller, the best part of the deal is… Sandy Allen disappears forever and always. I mean it. Don't you think the world would be a better place if she did?"

Chapter 59

It was ten a.m. Betty still hadn't come out of the bedroom. No morning coffee. No breakfast. Nothing. Charlie didn't know if she was still asleep or just lying there. She hadn't had a decent rest since they learned about Ivan's murder three weeks ago. She tossed and turned most of the night now. He couldn't imagine burdening her even more, but he needed to tell her the awful thing he had done.

It happened so fast. After Ivan disappeared, Tradur Gurl sent frantic emails to Charlie about stock ZQXR. Blackie bought and sold the shares, and Charlie posted the positive news all over town. All went as normal. For a while it seemed like a great trade. Then something changed. Charlie knew his lack of experience frustrated Tradur Gurl to no end, but what happened to Ivan wasn't his fault. She should have been pleased with his initiative to recognize his weakness and get help.

He emailed her several times after their last and only phone call, but she hadn't replied. He could tell what happened. His getting Blackie involved was the straw that broke the camel's back. He heard it in her voice. She had abandoned him and walked away, and no doubt found a new partner by now. He'd received no money from the last trade and, as she so explicitly pointed out, the accounts were empty.

His worst fear had come true. He was on his own. He didn't know how to find the next stock and, even if he did, how to buy the shares or write the good news story. Out of work and broke.

The first loan payment was due in a few days.

He needed to tell Betty, but she seemed so frail now, bags under her eyes, her skin milky white. He started to walk towards the bedroom, but stopped. No, he couldn't yet. Instead he went into the basement to sit in front of his computer. Maybe something would come to him.

As he started up the machine, a strange icon popped up in the lower right-hand corner. He didn't click on it right away. He knew it wasn't email, but he'd heard about those viruses that would mess up all your files. It read: *Windows task reminder. IMPORTANT.*

He'd never seen anything like this before. He worried it was a bad message, trying to get him to click on it. Ivan had taught him how Google could answer just about any question you ever had. He moved his mouse pointer away from the dangerous icon and opened up a new Google question bar.

Is a windows task reminder message a virus?

He was surprised when his computer quickly displayed the answer.

"Windows task reminder is part of the windows calendar program. It reminds the user of a scheduled task that has reached its due date."

Charlie had never used the calendar program, but decided that Google would have warned him if this was a threat. He backed out of the Google page and clicked on the icon.

Task reminder. Read letter from Ivan. Look under easy chair cushion.

Look under easy chair...? Charlie hurried upstairs and lifted the cushion. Sure enough, there was a slightly crumpled envelope with his name on it. He opened the letter inside.

Dear Betty and Charlie:

If you are reading this letter, it means something bad has likely happened to me. As you probably know by now, I got involved with some people I shouldn't have, didn't pay them the money I owed them fast enough, and now my life could be over.

Charlie looked up from the letter. Ivan had known all along.

Three things. The first is I apologize. I've lied to both of you since day one. I am not a successful stock trader and never have been. Those new cars I brought by your house were a total pretence to make you believe I was successful. My new company fired me in Seattle for breaking compliance rules. I knew better. The reason I came east was to try to escape the mob. I lost all the money I borrowed from them trading.

Second: Charlie, Tradur Gurl's "great" investing method is 100% illegal. You had no idea. I tricked you into it. Tradur Gurl is a convicted felon operating pump and dump schemes from inside prison. I wouldn't trust her at all. Faced with a choice of taking money for her own personal reasons, or you losing your house, she would choose herself every time. You need to stop any association with her and, taking this letter with you, immediately go to the authorities. I hope that they will cut you some slack.

Third, and this is what I'm most ashamed of, I have used both of you to cover my own ass. Betty lent me seventy thousand dollars of Mother's inheritance. I convinced her not to tell you, Charlie. In addition, I encouraged you, Charlie, to borrow another seventy-five thousand using your house as collateral. I lost all of Betty's money trading. Charlie, I gave that twenty-five thousand I supposedly transferred to the "authorities" directly to the mob to buy me some time. Like I said, if you are reading this letter, then the worst might have happened and I fear for the rest of your money

It occurred to me that there might be a way to make some small amends. I have a life insurance policy left over from when I worked at Fifty States that I decided to keep when I left. I guess I always did wonder if I would ever settle down, get married and have children. As a result, the beneficiary of the policy has always been my "estate." Thinking more about my situation, I imagined if something did happen to me, some or all of the money might eventually find its way to you. But I wanted to be sure. This morning on my way to the bank to meet the mob, I will stop off at the Marketable Insurance Company and name you two as sole beneficiaries. The policy is for two hundred and fifty thousand dollars. If something has happened to me, the insurance proceeds will pay back both of my debts to you and give you a good income until Charlie can find new work. Charlie, please do NOT try to earn a living trading stocks from home. The risks, as you can tell, are far too high. It might take some time for the insurance company to pay out the claim because I imagine the police would be involved, but eventually you'll be fine.

This is a terrible way to say goodbye. I'll leave you with one thought. You two are the richest people I know. You have your love and years of marriage and that is worth more than money ever could be.

Love, Ivan

Charlie stared at the letter for a few moments and slowly rose from his chair. He and Betty had a lot to discuss.

Epilogue

The New York Times

Missing couple found *alive* in Belize

One of the most bizarre criminal investigations ever came closer to a conclusion today with the capture of Michael Franklin and Angela Messina in the tiny nation of Belize. Authorities are working through extradition papers for their transportation to the United States where Franklin will face a list of charges including operating a massive Ponzi scheme, and Messina, first-degree murder.

An FBI spokesperson said the public will get more details as they become available.

Seattle News

Search for escaped convict scaled back

Local authorities announced today that they have scaled back the search for Sandy Allen, who escaped from the Blaine Corrections Center for Women nearly four weeks ago. Investigators said that the fugitive woman who carried a long list of crimes is almost certainly no longer in the United States. Agent Mueller from the Seattle area FBI said, "We believe she may have fled to Canada, but, frankly, by now she could be anywhere."

A source that demanded confidentiality disclosed that the warden of the prison facility and at least two guards have been placed on paid leave pending a full investigation of the escape. The source said the men could face criminal charges. The Governor of Washington has called for a full review of the prison's operations.

CPSIA information can be obtained at www.ICGtesting.com
Printed in the USA
LVOW10s0814110216

474490LV00009B/38/P